THE SISTERWITCHES

BOOK 1

KATIE CROSS

KCW

The Sisterwitches Book 1

YA Fantasy

Fiction

DEDICATION

In this (and following books), our heroine Sanna is grappling with adapting to losing her vision.

While I worked very closely with several of my readers that have had (and subsequently lost all or almost all of their sight), every witch has their own story. Sanna's experience and emotions are her own. Not every blind person will have a similar experience—which is the beauty of story!

My sensitivity readers and I decided together on phrases, terms, and struggles that Sanna would face in this new life of hers.

To that end, I want to dedicate this book to Jayde Abbott and Daniel Bair, who have opened my eyes to this new world they live in.

(That pun is for you, Jayde! ;)

All the research, books I read, people I spoke with, culminated in meeting the two of them and getting to know them over the last year. In Jayde I met a real-life Sanna, and knowing both of you is one of my greatest honors.

From the bottom of my heart, thank you both for all your

time, dedication, openness, education, and perseverance with me.

Author's Note

THE SISTERWITCHES is a series that fans have requested for *years*. I couldn't even tally up the emails and DM's and message requests that I've received asking for more Sanna and Isadora.

Honestly, I'm with you.

They are so fun.

Returning back to the world and time of the Dragonmasters has been thrilling and consuming. The magic, the world building, the time period. I'm ecstatic to sweep you back to Sanna and Isadora.

To that end, a little preface.

If you haven't read the DRAGONMASTER TRILOGY yet, then I highly recommend you do, or else a lot of this won't make much sense!

SISTERWITCHES Book 1 picks up right as FREEDOM, the final novel in the DRAGONMASTER TRILOGY ends. I mean *right* as it ends. Maybe an hour has passed in the timeline.

In order to refresh your memory of what happened then, I'm including two very brief prologues taken directly from

FREEDOM. One for Sanna and one for Isadora. That will help you remember where we left our favorite sisterwitches.

Or you can skip those and get right to the meat of the story in Chapter One.

You'll find more character's point-of-view covered in the SISTERWITCHES series, like Maximillion. On occasion, Charlie, too. Lovers of THE ADVOCATE will be very excited to dive further into the halls of Wildrose Manor and all that lurks therein.

Now, it's time to get you reading.

Warmly,

Katie

WILDROSE MANOR

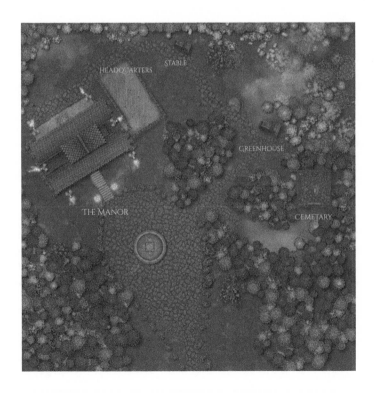

SANNA

Taken from the final chapter of FREEDOM.

Deasylva turned to Isadora. She inclined her head for a long pause, then straightened.

"Isadora, you have not only protected the witches of Alkarra but proven that witches can redeem themselves—or at least work out their problems. For your toil, I grant you continued growth in the Watcher magic, which originates in me and in goodness. You will advance in ability and strength, and as I see, will find ways to use it for good. Abuse it, and you shall enjoy my wrath."

Isadora breathed in sharply. "I would never dream of it."

Deasylva's lips twitched. "I trust you. Your power as a Watcher was so great because the magic responds to rising evil. You will feel a surge in your abilities again in the future, when need arises. For now, it will abate. Not all evil can be banished, and more is in store for Alkarra."

Deasylva turned back to Sanna. "Sanna, in giving the dragons the freedom they have always deserved, you have lost everything you held dear, except for your sisterwitch."

Sanna's troubled gaze met Deasylva's again. She still

couldn't reconcile the goddess with the writing that had appeared on the tree trunks.

"Luteis," she whispered. "And Daid and Anguis."

Deasylva's expression softened. "Unlike Isadora, you cannot continue in your magic. In recompense, I can grant something in restitution. While I cannot remake Dragonian magic—nor would I wish to—I will restore what is most important to you."

Sanna's heart skipped a beat. "Luteis?"

Deasylva's brow rose. "You do not choose your sight?"

"He will be my sight," she said softly.

"Then you shall remain blind, and your merging with Luteis will be restored, but without the power of the Dragonian magic. You will not be able to communicate through your thoughts with any dragon but him. You will remain protected from his heat and from falling while flying."

Sanna nodded.

Deasylva continued, "I go now to rest within my forest. I shall retire for many years according to the timing of witches, but I trust Letum Wood to your capable hands. When you go to Halla, one shall rise in your place, for my trees know those who belong to them. There is always one who responds to their cries."

Isadora put a firm arm around Sanna.

"Thank you, Deasylva," Sanna murmured, feeling a sense of loss and finality. There would be no interaction with the forest goddess again, and she was startled to realize she'd miss her.

Deasylva faded, her form dwindling into mist. The smell of honeysuckle and a faint breeze stirred up as she closed her eyes, and was gone.

Isadora let out a long exhale. "Well. One can't say that we don't keep things interesting around here."

Sanna studied her, trying to commit this last look at her

sister to memory so that she could never forget it. "When we go back, I will never see you again. I'll never *see* again."

"Not until we return to Daid in the halls of Halla," Isadora said, gripping both of Sanna's hands. "But I will be with you forever."

Sanna wrapped Isadora in her arms.

"Forever."

———

Sanna returned to darkness.

She stood there for a second, disoriented. Then she drew in a breath. Mentally settled in. Her sight was gone—she'd see no more. But she'd be fine. Isadora still held her hand. Luteis would be with her. The forest dragons still lived, and so would Letum Wood after proper care and attention.

Someone had to take care of all that strickenine moss and the trees that fell to Prana's salt water.

A rustle of leaves accompanied a breathless voice in her head. Sanna turned.

Little one, Luteis whispered, voice stark, *have you returned to me?*

With a cry, Sanna flung herself at his heat, her arms enveloping his snout. His heat didn't scorch her, settling to its usual pleasant warmth. The emptiness that had been haunting her faded as he joined in with her thoughts, where they both belonged. Tears tracked down her cheeks.

"Luteis," she whispered. "I'm so relieved you're back."

His tail wrapped around her ankle.

Deasylva tells me of your sacrifice. My love and relief is great. Only death shall part us now.

She stood there, touching him, until the ache in her chest began to fade. She pressed her forehead to his.

Let's go home again, she said, *and this time, let's stay. For decades. Maybe forever. Long ago, Isadora promised to teach me some spells that have practical purposes.*

Sounds like a worthy investment of time.

She grinned. "Maybe magic isn't so bad. Besides, we have our work cut out for us in Letum Wood."

I am inclined to agree.

"You're already mapping out a plan for cleaning up the fallen trees and strickenine moss, aren't you?" she asked, thinking about the complicated canopy that awaited them.

Patches of strickenine moss would still be everywhere. Fallen trees cluttered the forest floor that would need to be cleaned up. It was difficult to navigate some areas, and many trees weren't handling the close space well. They needed to be thinned out.

His wing twitched next to her.

False. I already have a plan and am looking forward to implementing it. The forest desperately needs us. We may have defeated our enemies, but we are not yet completely healed. It's time for us to focus on Letum Wood and allow Deasylva to rest. The mountain dragons ate enough of the beluas that we need not fear their numbers anymore, but it will take time for the forest to regrow.

It had all been so surreal. She still questioned whether she'd really lived through so much.

"Perhaps," she said. "But at least we have each other for the rest of our lives now."

That, he murmured, *is my ultimate plan.*

ISADORA

I sadora cleared her throat. If there was any time to tell
Max how she felt, it was now. But the words felt bigger
than her.

"Well," she said, "I suppose there's a few things we need to
discuss."

"Indeed."

Another pause. "Ah, I meant to thank you."

"For?"

"You were a perfect gentleman. You kept me safe and were
. . . my friend. I needed that. I-I needed someone on my side
after—"

She gestured to the burnt wood around them.

Max frowned and looked away. "What do you want,
then?"

"What do I want?"

"What will you do now? What is next for Isadora Sin
—Spence?"

She paused. The question had hovered on the edge of her
mind for days now, but she hadn't really acknowledged it. So

much lay behind it. Things she hadn't wanted to face yet. Like the fact that she felt desperately ill at the thought of not seeing him every day. Of not feeling his firm touch.

The fact that she bloody loved the man.

"The Head of Education reached out to me," she said. "They're thinking that a Watcher who can see personality traits in witches would be a good qualifier for admission. Identify quality students they can start preparing to serve in the Network, instead of the ramshackle way they find Council Members now. Charles wisely wants to start from the ground up in rebuilding the Network, emphasizing competent Council Members."

"Sounds perfectly boring."

"I know." She grinned. "Isn't it wonderful?"

He hesitated, brow furrowed, then nodded. "After all this war? Yes, it is."

"But that's not what you really asked me. You asked me what I wanted. I want a cottage in Letum Wood." She drew in a deep breath, then let her shoulders fall. "Close to Sanna and Mam. I want a job that makes a difference for the Network, and I want a house full of the teacups that Mam and I paint together. Then, maybe, it will feel like our lives haven't totally ended. As if . . . Daid could still be with us."

And I want you in all of it.

"What about you?" she asked instead. "What does the great Ambassador Maximillion Sinclair desire?"

A bird wheeling by interrupted the long silence.

Max's brow furrowed. "Peace."

"You have that now. The new plan is—"

"Are you going to leave?"

"Leave?"

"Are you . . . do you want something else?"

"What do you—"

"The good gods, Isadora!" he cried. "You *know* what I mean. Do you want to remain handfasted or not?" He paused, heartbeat visible in his throat. His voice became husky. "Because if you want to go, I won't stop Charles from granting the annulment. But if . . ."

The words trailed away, leaving Isadora stunned. She stared at him, hardly able to comprehend.

"But if?" she whispered.

His nostrils flared. He stepped closer to her, grabbing her arm in a surprisingly gentle grasp for all the passion in his face.

"But if you didn't want to go. If you wanted to stay. With me. Then . . . I believe we could build something together. Something . . . peaceful and real and . . . not empty and cold."

She inhaled, her nostrils thick with the heady scent of vetiver.

Max drew her so close she felt the soft caress of his breath on her face like a piece of velvet.

She swallowed hard. "In the South, when I asked you whether you were afraid of me after Carcere, you said yes, but not for the reason I thought. What was it, then?"

His expression softened. "I thought I had lost you," he whispered. "That I couldn't protect you, and it almost destroyed me. It was then that I realized the depth of my feelings, and that frightened me."

Her breath caught. "Do you really want more, Max? Can you handle me being near you every moment?"

His eyes darkened. His hands tightened around her waist.

"I crave it, Isadora. Like a dying man. I . . . I don't want you to go. Will you stay? Will you endure a man as insufferable, arrogant, and terrified as I am?"

Isadora pressed her palm against his pounding heart.

"Yes," she whispered. "I want you, Max. I believe I've loved you since we first met."

His lips claimed hers, his arms tightening around her. No magic had swept through her so thoroughly, with such ravenous power, as his touch.

Isadora slipped under his power willingly, overwhelmed with the knowledge that she'd never have to leave it again.

ONE

ISADORA

The creaking carriage raced down the lane.

Mud splashed over its rickety wheels, spraying in waves. Freezing rain pattered on top of the roof, sluicing down the black cover pinned as protection. A drip along the far seal meant it didn't do its job very well.

The *clop* of horses' feet, broken only by an occasional, low call from the driver rang through the icy night.

Isadora swallowed back rising nausea.

A dozen scattered memories replayed through her mind, over and over again. The husky sound of Maximillion's voice. The deep longing in his words when, only an hour ago, he asked her to remain his wife.

Will you stay? Will you endure a man as insufferable, arrogant, and terrified as I am?

Such passion she'd never seen in him before. A true dichotomy of a witch born of fire and . . . something else.

Tempest, probably.

Then, he asked the words he seemed most frightened of. *Come with me to Wildrose, Isadora?*

Wildrose.

Her lips soundlessly formed the name again. Wildrose. Wildrose. A place, surely. His home? Rumors swirled that he owned a lavish estate, but that it had been turned into a hospital for injured Guardians. That's all she'd ever known.

She'd never thought twice about it.

Now Wildrose would, in all legal, emotional, and physical ways, be *her* home as well. He could have transported them to Wildrose, but he calmly requested she endure a slushy ride from the neighboring village with the vague, *I want you to see it first from the road.*

Curiosity compelled her agreement. Now, she regretted the time it gave her to panic over their new state of marriage.

The good gods, she could hardly think it without wanting to laugh. Then weep. Could this be real?

Was she *truly* handfasted to Maximillion Sinclair?

Technically, they'd handfasted months ago, but that never felt tangible. As her love built for Max while in the Southern Network, she never dreamed he might return it. He hadn't given her a strong reason to assume otherwise. Their handfasting had been a ruse.

Smoke and mirrors.

Could such a beginning survive the challenges of daily life?

Her stomach churned as another conversation with Max resurfaced, more as a warning than a sweet reminder.

Your loyalty to your Network is appreciated, but you should know I'm not interested in love or happy endings. When this is over, we'll return to our lives as acquaintances. Our professional relationship can go back to the way it was, and you will be free to find a man who truly deserves you.

What had she agreed to?

Letum Wood flashed outside the carriage in tones of frozen umber and darkest pitch. Night draped the horizon and swept closer, like a blanket pulled over the world. With it came a sense of closure.

The finale of one part of her life—which she had mostly known and understood—and the opening of the next. Filled with the unknown.

And Max.

He cleared his throat, startling her back to the present. She didn't dare look at him. He'd see her spooked heart and instantly know her concerns. After their last conversation in the South, when she'd laid all bare and he hadn't reciprocated, she wasn't sure she could do that again.

Cripes, but she'd handfasted a witch she wasn't sure she trusted!

His broad shoulders swayed against hers as the carriage crossed a hole in the road, imparting a sense of stability in her sudden whirlpool of doubt.

Max sat next to her like a casual god. Black hair with a wayward curl that dropped to his forehead and a brooding sentiment that imparted handsomeness and austerity. His thick tresses had a habit of gleaming in untoward perfection. When mussed, it gave him an adorable, boyish look he loathed.

The thought made her lips twitch.

She wanted to hear his voice. In it, reassurances. A promise that they hadn't acted rashly and that love could be enough. Because love him, she did. She knew it. He knew it. The secret couldn't be gathered back together, like feathers in the wind.

A chest-tightening spiral threatened to take her breath away. Her eyes, glued to the bruised world washing by outside, began to widen. Truth dawned.

Max was taking her away.

They were *handfasted*.

Husband and wife and . . . all that meant.

Before the panic closed off her increasingly fast breaths, a warm touch landed on the back of her hand.

Startled, she gazed over.

Max studied her with his usual frown. The brooding intensity of his slightly different green eyes had taken on a hazel-like color in the dimness. Like her, he held the Watcher magic, which altered their eye color. Hers, more dramatically. His, far more subtle.

The edges of his lips tugged down chiseled cheeks.

"Are you all right, Isa?"

A shudder washed through her. The sound of her name on his lips would always affect her deeply.

"Yes."

His fingers squeezed hers. "It's going to be fine. We're almost to Wildrose."

She opened her mouth to reply, then stopped when a structure swathed in shadows came into view. Twinkling lights appeared between murky trees, illuminating an otherwise gloomy night. The warm weight of his hand on hers slowed her racing heart.

Wildrose rushed up all at once. Sparse trees gave way to an open field. Torch light flickered near the road ahead, signaling a long drive. The ribbon-like stone path cut a straight line across the property to end at . . .

. . . a most stunning manor.

"This is Wildrose." The pride in his voice carried a thousand stories. Tentatively, he added, "Your new home."

Max said he had a home, he didn't say he had an *estate*. Wildrose sprawled like an opulent mountain. Five stories, countless windows, a stone exterior rimmed with gargoyles and all manner of decorations. Two double doors sat atop a path of stairs leading straight from the circular end of the cobblestone drive and into the manor.

Not even the rain could truly dampen the majestic appearance. The glimmering glass panes, sparkling from the outside.

Stately porch, elegant columns. The hunched gargoyles on top spurted fire every few seconds.

Everything about Wildrose radiated sophistication and time. If Max were a house, Wildrose would be it.

The horses slowed at a command from the driver, then turned. Wildrose faded in the night as the carriage drew closer, turning at a right angle into the driveway.

Isadora leaned back. She could feel Max's intense scrutiny. Between layers of cool curiosity lay piles of desperation and hope. His voice sounded as if it had been scraped from the bottom of a barrel when he asked, "Well?"

"I have no words, Max."

At that, he frowned.

The carriage crunched over the gravel path. The horses trotted a bit faster, and the driver called to someone near the circle at the end. A young boy scampered out of sight. Max straightened ever-so-slightly to peer out the window. Scrutiny lined each wrinkle in his face.

Isadora closed her eyes, pulled in a breath. An hour into her new life, and already it overwhelmed her.

No, she wouldn't let it.

Agreeing to remain handfasted to Max could end up being a mistake. They might part years from now, bitter and angry. They could regret their decision in a week and implore the High Priest for the obliteration.

Or they might not.

The question of *what could we be together?* tangled in Isadora's mind, wrapped up in the tentacles of her brightest concern.

Is love enough?

As they turned around the circular drive and stopped next to Wildrose, she furtively hoped so.

Because Wildrose was one manor she wanted nothing to do with.

TWO

SANNA

What is the purpose of one's life if one has no higher calling?

Sanna scowled and rolled onto her side. Trust a dragon to be contemplative in the middle of the night. A rock jabbed into her ribcage. She wriggled away.

How does one find a higher calling? Luteis insisted.

"Argh! Go to sleep!"

A serpentine *hiss* followed. Fine. Let Luteis be annoyed. She didn't feel too happy with him either.

Silence followed, and it teemed with irritation.

Groaning, Sanna flopped onto her back. The air cooled around her, which could have been from the freezing rain, but also from fading sunshine. Night must be swooping in. She stayed dry under a gargantuan flake of bark the size of a house itself. Luteis' seething dragon heat kept the enclosed space toasty warm.

She stifled a yawn.

"What time is it?"

You're willing to speak when it serves your purposes, is that it?

She rolled her eyes, more metaphorically than physically. For being intelligent creatures, dragons had a hard time understanding body language.

"Luteis, you always choose to have philosophical discussions right before I fall asleep. Then it wakes me up, I don't get any rest, and we're both cranky."

Another mumble—this one she couldn't understand—issued through her mind. He shifted, the sound of clicking scales a soothing one. Outside, the rain continued to thrum. Soon, it would turn to snow. Rivulets splashed into puddles on the ground, releasing the scent of degrading leaves.

I don't know what time it is. It's past dark.

Right.

Dragons didn't regard hours.

After losing her sight setting the mountain, desert, forest, and sea dragons free from a goddess magic system that kept them slaves, the struggle to adjust to living without sight had been . . .

. . . interesting.

A week had passed in a frustrating eternity. Luteis hadn't left her side, but there was only so much a dragon could do. For example, he couldn't carry a pocket watch or read time. When in the depths of the forest and unable to feel the sun, watch the passage of shadows on the forest floor, or track the light in the sky, Sanna felt lost in her own day.

Eternal night, but not really. Other witches saw daylight. She didn't.

Sanna exhaled a long breath. Past dark, she could have assumed just by the change in temperature, but with sleet present, one never knew. She tried to summon enough exhaustion to put her into a quick sleep, but she hovered on the edge. In the space between *tired* and *sort of tired.*

Closer to bored.

The plunk of falling rain echoed along the forest floor.

The sound filled a world half-gone to shadow. A trickle of rain snaked down the trunk behind her, creeping onto the fabric at the back of her neck.

Your Mam is probably concerned for you in this weather. Your lacking scales and heat is a problem.

She fought back a smile. Mam and Luteis waged a hidden, secret war to be the one that worried over her the most.

"Mam knows I'm with you."

As if summoned, a flutter graced the gentle skin on top of her nose. She reached up with a scowl. Paper crinkled in her fingers.

As expected, he drawled.

Since Sanna couldn't see the words, and Luteis refused to learn *witch scratchings*, Mam had reluctantly agreed to use magic again and had developed a series of folds. If the paper resembled a heart, Mam wanted an update. If it was a rectangle, she needed Sanna to return. A square meant dinner was ready.

A square, then.

Sanna sighed. Mam couldn't help hovering a bit. She had no reason to fear with Luteis so close, but Mam didn't quite understand.

Another message followed. Sanna found it with the tips of her fingers and scowled as she felt the edges. A heart.

Dinner *and* an update.

A third.

A rectangle, too. Dinner, update, and a return. Clever, Mam. Sanna crumbled them, then pitched them over her shoulder. She clapped her hands together, ridding her palms of dirt. With one hand on the trunk behind her, she stood up.

"Luteis," she muttered. "One thing is blatantly obvious: it's time we find a place for us to live. A place that's *not* with Mam."

THREE

ISADORA

Darkness permeated the inside of Wildrose.

Isadora attempted to see through the windows as they stepped up the sprawling stairs and closer to the double front doors, but shadows lurked. Lights illuminated every floor of the exterior, including giant sprays of fire from the mouths of gargoyles perched at each corner of the top.

Why not a single candle inside?

Max held onto her fingers, his hand swamping hers, as they stepped onto the landing just outside the main doors.

Isadora half spun as the driver scurried toward stables, off to the right. The horses pranced happily closer to a building tucked into the end of a rocky path. The sizzle of slush plopping onto hot torches released black smoke.

A grassy lawn sprawled around Wildrose in undulating swells until it reached the far edge of Letum Wood, lined with shadows and giant trees that defied sense. The forest hemmed in on the property, stopping as if invisible glass walls held it back. A veritable do-not-cross line. It must be the only way to safely exist with such a magical forest. Firm, decisive boundaries and a prodigiously strong weed-eradicating potion.

Along the drive, rose bushes rambled the edge of the cobblestones, guiding witches closer to the manor.

Max stood rigid behind her, stress rolling off him in waves. She wanted to say something to ease him, but the words stuck in her mouth like glue. Wildrose was . . . so much. Next to Chatham Castle, perhaps the largest estate she'd seen. Questions riddled her mind.

Had he inherited it?

If so, from whom?

Did he have the currency to run and keep up with such a place?

How many witches did it require to maintain it?

Instead, she spun to face the double doors. Max dropped her fingers and extended an arm. She accepted without meeting his gaze, tucking her hand into his bent elbow. He pulled her close. The rise and fall of his ribcage, faster than she'd expected, pressed against the back of her wrist. The closeness gave a heady feeling. She wanted to fold herself into his arms, pull his jacket around her, and pretend all these reservations didn't exist.

"Faye has left," he said, as if that should answer all her questions instead of inspiring dozens more. "That's . . . that is . . . it's dark in here. I've been to the South and Faye has . . . well, more on that later."

With a clearing of his throat, he shoved the left door open.

It swung into a quiet, cool hall with a groan. Damp air permeated the foyer, which sprawled grandly overhead, stories above. A crystal chandelier nestled in the swampy darkness glimmered faintly.

Max closed the door behind him.

"I'll give you the full tour in the morning when there's

better light. It's not worth seeing it in the dark with candles. I would imagine you're tired."

A hint of question lingered in the words. Isadora only nodded. It wasn't much of a response, but also wasn't a lie. Her day hadn't been draining . . . up until now. Somehow, in the course of an hour or two, she'd experienced a full run of every emotion.

Max stalled them at the lip of a curving staircase that wound from this floor to the next, and the next. Miniature gargoyles, similar to the ones perched on top of the house, peered from the banister.

Creepy things.

Dizzy with questions and bubbling curiosity, Isadora tilted her head back. Four stories, hadn't there been? Or was it five?

"Are you hungry?"

Gentleness rang in his question, shocking her back to life for the second time. Memories of the frosty Maximillion, whom she knew quite well from their time in the South, followed. She turned to face him again, surprised to find an anchor in the depths of such a soul-searing gaze.

"Uh . . . yes."

He nodded down the hall to the left. "The kitchen is that way. I think Pearl mentioned sending food when I . . . well, more on that later, as well."

Hearing his voice in the echoing caverns of Wildrose lent some reassurance against the open maw. She didn't stand in a massive precipice ready to overpower her, though it felt that way. While they walked down the empty hallway, the ring of her shoes on the wooden floor the only sound, she asked, "Is anyone here?"

He opened his mouth, stopped, then closed it again. After a long deliberation, he slowly said, "Yes, and no."

Her brow lifted.

"There is no one on this floor or the ones above. At least, not tonight. Perhaps not for months, I'm not sure. Wildrose was built for, and dedicated to, service for other witches. Such extensive grounds were meant to help those that needed aid. There are always witches moving through these halls. Among . . . other purposes."

"I see."

The lassitude in his expression informed her that she did not see, but he remained quiet. The sense of swimming in deep waters overcame her. She wasn't quite sure which way was up.

"But not now," he said more robustly. "It's just you and me and whatever food Pearl has sent."

If he meant it to be a lighthearted comment, he gave no sign. The seriousness in his voice nearly made her laugh, which might convince him that she'd lost her mind. She certainly felt as if she had.

Handfasted to Maximillion Sinclair.

Living in an estate called Wildrose Manor.

Handfasted.

Despite their time together in the Southern Network, where they slept in the same room, pretended affection in front of others, and spent a decidedly large amount of time with each other, she'd always known it was a sham. The means to an end that could save tens of thousands of lives, if not more.

A week had passed between the fateful meeting of Networks and this night, when she finally spoke to him again. In those days, she'd constantly asked herself what would be next. She'd braced herself for the handfasting obliteration, all while dreading the thought.

Such a strange diversion from her expectation—namely, Max caring for her—meant that shock held her in its cold claws.

With a gentle tug, Max pulled her into a room with a close ambience. Windows, cluttered by green plants, reflected the low light from outside. Wash basins, hanging pots, towels draped off hooks in the wall. It held a cozy, well-used feel.

"This is the only kitchen. Some manors of this size have two, but there is only one here. Outside that door," he motioned to the western wall with a tilt of his head, "is a small patio where you will find a place to dump ashes from the hearth and basic composting. There's a well there, also."

"Convenient," she said, for lack of anything else.

Flames sprang to life on candles around the perimeter of the rectangular room. They bathed Max in a buttery light as he released her and crossed the kitchen.

"Ean is a young lad that helps me run this place. He'll take care of the soot and food for composting. It eventually goes to the greenhouse. He also keeps the firewood stocked."

Greenhouse?

Now that had an appealing sound.

Isadora slowed, drinking in the massive stone hearth—big enough that she could crouch in it—the copper pots and pans hanging from the ceiling, and the wooden island in the middle of the room. Cutting boards and sharp knives and a box cobbled together with hammer and nails lay across the top.

"Ah, here we are. Pearl delivers."

Max spelled a wooden box onto the kitchen island between them. A half loaf of bread, soft cheese, figs, dried currants, and a bottle of spiced cider inside a brown jug. How Pearl had managed to find such fare, Isadora couldn't imagine. Border closures imbued alarm everywhere and food had been flying off grocer and market shelves in outright panic.

The Advocacy, most likely, now that she thought about it.

Max produced two glasses filled with water and nudged one her way. She had a drink, then a deeper one. Until the cool liquid slipped down her throat, she didn't realize her thirst. Her stomach grumbled when she smelled the bread.

Max grabbed the loaf, hesitated, then tore a piece off the end. With a wry smile, he extended it to her. The sheer lack of formality released the building tension in her shoulders. She replied with a wan smile of her own.

"Thanks."

Max chewed through his first bite, reaching for the cheese. Relaxation slipped through the air as he spelled a butter knife into his hands. He glanced at her, back down again.

"You're stiff as a board tonight, Isadora."

She chuckled. "You, too."

He tilted his head in a sideways sort of assent, then broke another piece of bread apart. "Nervous, I suppose."

"For me to see Wildrose?"

"Yes."

His quiet admittance filled the empty air. Isadora paused, bread halfway to her mouth. What to say? So much existed between them. She popped the bread into her mouth and began to chew. Shivers raced up and down her back as Max studied her in smoky regard.

The food gathered itself together and hopped inside the box, which sprang into the air.

"Come," he said quietly. His hand found the small of her back. "Let's go upstairs and eat in the master suite. We can see all of this tomorrow."

———

She followed him into the hallway, bread in hand. The box floated behind her as they wound up a separate, smaller staircase at the end of the hall and up, up, up. They passed the second, third, and stepped onto the fourth floor. Down a long hall, they turned up one final staircase.

This was more narrow, twisted, and disappeared into the ceiling. He climbed it with only a little hesitation.

Borne by deepening interest, Isadora followed.

"The master suite is on the top floor, and it only spans half of the manor. It sits right in the middle. It's . . . ours, I suppose you could say."

A strange note in his voice must mean it startled him. Again, more questions rose. Like petals in a shimmering pond. They shed, collected, and waited patiently for the right moment to be found.

Max opened a wooden door with a carved, ornate handle. It swung open.

A master suite sprawled from side to side. It could easily hold four or five of her childhood attic back in Anguis, long destroyed by fire. A gigantic four-poster bed occupied most of the left side of the room. It stood between two wide, floor-to-ceiling windows that gleamed with shimmering raindrops. Ice and frost whorled around the edges in frangible designs. Partially opened drapes peeked onto the gnarled back of a gargoyle that grimaced onto the forest. The shooting flames had ceased.

To the right marched more windows. Heavy curtains, with thick fabrics and elegant ivy designs, cluttered each one. A divan with rolled arms and clawed feet canted at an angle near the hearth, between a leather sofa and a petite bookshelf. Snifters of ipsum sat on a table near a door that must lead to a washroom. Two giant armoires stood next to each other, both closed, wide enough to walk inside.

A second surge of rising panic quelled out of sheer awe.

"I suppose I've always thought of this room as Ranulf's," Max murmured in a musing, not-quite-there tone. He stood close; his heat radiated through her skin. He didn't touch her, but she wanted him to.

At the same time, the lack of physical contact gave relief.

Touching Max was like staring at the sun. Dazzling, yet one couldn't help but need it, crave it, cherish it. When it departed, the world became bleak, indeed.

"Ranulf?"

The rough top of the divan bumped under her hand as she ran her palm over it.

Another pause, this strained with uncertainty.

"Later?" she inquired.

His shoulders relaxed back.

"Later."

Bread in hand, Isadora strolled around the room. A break from the heady scent of vetiver would clear her mind, take her out of his charming power and into level-headed thinking.

Should that *ever* return.

The complimentary tastes of butter and yeast filled her mouth as she studied each part of the suite, munching bread as she strode. Max remained near the doorway, hands tucked into pockets, eyes glimmering in his undeviating stare on her.

Her circle complete, Isadora stopped in the middle and faced him. Words failed her. How could she explain how . . . gargantuan? Empty?

Lonely?

I want something manageable, she thought. *Small. Simple, like the home I grew up in. This is so much. This is you, not me. This is . . .*

"Lovely," she pronounced in a firm voice, with a fixed smile. "Wildrose Manor is lovely, Max. You have a brilliant home."

The words *our home* just wouldn't form.

Relief flooded his expression, then hardened into . . . something. Acceptance perhaps. Or the absence of vulner-ability.

"Thank you."

She lowered into a chair, brushed the crumbs from her

fingertips. Weariness swept over her. Today had been an unexpected culmination to all the days before, starting with their handfasting, then extending to their time in the Southern Network, and the negotiations between Networks that followed. The budding wars that had threatened to end could officially settle into the past.

In the quiet, the food box settled on a nearby table. Her appetite had fled, but she forced herself to finish the last bite of her dinner. At some point, the driver must have spelled her bag in from the stable. It perched on the other side of the room.

"I'm satisfied with this bread, thank you," she said.

"Then to bed." Max passed a hand over his eyes, stifling a yawn. "Tomorrow, after a good rest, we'll talk more."

All the slippery questions gratefully retired into the recesses of her mind. Though much lingered to say, she was glad to tuck it out of sight.

Tomorrow would be soon enough.

Four
Maximillion

The halls of Chatham Castle had never felt like an escape before. Today, he gratefully retreated to the chaos.

Leaving Isadora sleeping soundly in their bed, her wispy breaths gentle as a sigh, had been more arduous than expected. The urge to curl his body around hers, pull her close, and memorize the smell of her hair had required all his control not to satisfy. Isadora had no idea how much he longed to be at her side, tucked into Wildrose, with nowhere else to go.

Coward, he told himself with biting animosity.

The truth stung.

Though he had finally admitted a desire to keep her with him in maintenance of their handfasting, kissed her until every iota of his soul responded, he hadn't said half of what he felt. Nor the history of caring for her that he shored up in his most secret mind.

She had agreed to . . . be his . . . for all intents and purposes, without him telling her the full, terrifying truth.

That she was breath.

Soul.

The stirring power in his hollow, dormant heart. Isadora had been almost ever-present, with him as long as the magic.

She had no idea.

The words tangled in his throat when he thought them. He'd be a bumbling mess if he tried to speak them. Now, he had no idea what to do.

How did one build a life around—or with—another witch?

The question occupied half his attention, leading to poorly executed replies to letters, a judgmental look from his Assistant, Wally, for whom he couldn't answer a straight question, and too many dazed-out stares at the desk.

Charlie's bright smile and bouncing eyes greeted him when he returned from a meeting with the new Eastern Network Ambassador. The High Priest waited in Max's office. Halfway through the doorway, Max paused.

Charlie's grin widened.

"Max."

"Charlie," he drawled.

A stack of rolled parchments hovered about Max's desk, forming a floating hexagonal tower that could only be from Charlie. Not another political witch in all of Alkarra would use a spell to stack parchments into a design just for fun.

Charlie stood with his hands behind his back, brow high in expectation. The carroty red color of his hair gleamed like illuminated copper in the sunlight that slanted through the open windows. He wore a green velvet jacket today, and a freshly-pressed pinstripe vest of gold and black.

"Well?" Charlie drawled. "How is your bride?"

Max scowled. "None of your business."

Charlie laughed. "Based on the lack of fury behind your glare, she must have agreed to stay."

Max paused, then nodded once.

"If Isadora refused you outright, you'd be surly as a forest lion. In such an event, I would feel obligated to fend your most foul manners away from Council Members."

"You're lying."

"I am." Charlie chuckled again. "If Council Members can't handle your disposition, they have no business working for the Central Network. In the meantime, I'm hungry to know what she said."

"She agreed. She also wanted to remain handfasted."

Charlie's jaw dropped.

Max ignored him and plucked the top scroll off the pile. The rest of them clattered to the desktop in a neat rectangle.

When he realized Max had no intention of explaining further, the High Priest rallied himself with admirable aplomb. He cleared his throat, doing a terrible job of suppressing a smile.

"Well, Max. I'm happy to hear that, my friend."

"Thank you."

"Are congratulations in order for the happy couple? Or are we pretending that life shall continue on as before without any change?"

The tentative note of searching in Charlie's voice set Max's teeth on edge. Charlie wanted to know something else.

But what?

What could he possibly be thinking? Dodging would be the best policy for Max's scrambled state of mind.

He pretended to regard the top parchment, but saw only a blur of words. His brain resided firmly in the halls of Wildrose with Isadora. He'd turned her loose on the stately place without him. He should be concerned.

"You may congratulate us as you wish," he finally said.

"Then congratulations!"

"Thank you."

Charlie studied him, bright lashes tapered. "Well, you're

handfasted. You didn't even get a celebration. We should inform the Advocacy—"

"No."

"Max!" Charlie rolled his eyes. "Don't be a bore! You need to celebrate such a wonderful event. If not for yourself, for Isadora. Faye regrets that we can tell no one of our handfasting."

"We've been handfasted for months."

"All the more reason! Look what the two of you have accomplished in your time together. Saved the Network. Diverted wars. Managed to crack the secret of a magic that's been long hidden. As far as efficient couples go, I'd say you win the prize."

Max shot him another glare.

Charlie bit his bottom lip, then burst out laughing. "Fine, fine. You don't have to celebrate, but . . . what *are* you going to do? You've already handfasted, lived together. You have your job and Isadora has . . . given up everything to be with you. She has no career, no friends near Wildrose, and no idea how to *truly* live with you."

A cold sludge of pure panic settled in Max's stomach. Trust Charlie to put into precise words exactly what simmered beneath the surface of his foul mood. A spoken agreement to remain handfasted was one thing, but truly committing to it was another.

Max set aside the parchment. "I don't know what is next for both of us. Seems presumptuous to plan that myself. She was very tired yesterday. We have plans to speak at dinner tonight, after work."

"Now that you have a wife, you'll be eating more at home, I presume?"

"Yes."

"Are you afraid of the word *wife*, Max?"

"No."

"Are you sure? I haven't heard you say it yet." Merriment danced in Charlie's eyes, brightened by the challenge. "Say it, Max. Isadora is your wife."

"Isadora is my wife. Are you happy now?"

"Goodness, no. You sound like a forest lion. The poor woman will think you don't like her if you keep that up."

"Charlie—"

Charlie held up two hands. "Right, right. I'm done, Max. I won't tease anymore, though it isn't really teasing. You could use some softening. At any rate, I hope you figure out what's next. Isadora's giving up a lot for you. Just wanted to make sure you saw it."

In fact, he hadn't.

And Charlie knew it.

The smug sense of amusement spoke worlds. Still, Max couldn't fault him. Charlie had insight into emotional conundrums that he never seemed to possess.

"I suppose we'll figure that out tonight, after I give her a tour of Wildrose and explain that the Advocacy was in the basement, with headquarters."

Charlie's eyes bugged out. The question of *you haven't told her about Wildrose yet?* lingered. Isadora had been inside headquarters once or twice when she worked for the Advocacy, though Max had been very careful not to let her know much about it. She shouldn't know what lay beneath Wildrose.

Arguably, most Advocacy members didn't see outside of headquarters. Few had known of Wildrose's immediate connection to the society until all exploded when East Guards attacked Charlie and Faye outright. Max had been careful to hide Wildrose from Isadora. He didn't know why.

Didn't want to think about it, either.

Charlie wisely wrestled back his astonishment and channeled it into a nod.

"Very good. Well, you know where to find me, should you need anything. I'll be in my office, pretending to write official letters while secretly messaging Faye and deciding who to establish as Council Member. Now that we have a High Priestess, things will be smoother. Come by if you need anything!"

With a duck, a wave, and a flash of red, Charlie headed out the door. Max braced both hands on his desk, hung his head, and exhaled. The good gods help him.

What had he gotten into?

FIVE

SANNA

I cy raindrops lingered on leaf tops when Sanna strolled by the next morning, hand outstretched. Luteis kept a wing draped over her most of the night. She slept cozily tucked against his leg, warm and dry when she woke up despite the sleet.

They moved slowly through the forest, a bucket of cold water swaying with each step from her left hand. She kept a hand to the right to feel for branches, and Luteis at her other side. His leg brushed her shoulder every so often.

The crack of iced twigs, an occasional flutter of wings, moved around them. Sanna walked by three small trees standing right next to each other and paused.

Luteis waited.

"We're a minute or two away from Mam's house?"

Correct.

"Hmmm."

You remember those trees?

"Yes. One of them has a pocket of sap at this height, and there are three of them."

Her fingers probed. After the freezing rain, ice had

changed the edges of the sap pocket, but it remained familiar enough. She created a vague mental map from this spot. The triplet trees came ten paces before the rocks began. From there, the trail canted slightly to the left, then straight to Mam's.

Somewhat more confident, she began again, then stalled. Understanding her hesitation, Luteis said, *You're headed in the right direction.*

"Thanks."

With her winter boots on, she couldn't use her toes to feel. The rain froze the ground into thin plates of ice. She paused, stooped down. Her hands groped around for a moment before she felt the shockingly chill edge of a rock.

"Is this a stone on the path I made?"

Yes.

A rush of relief followed. She chuckled, giddy, and straightened.

"It works! Our trail of rocks is starting to be more familiar. As long as you get me started on the right path, I can find my way to Mam's."

A note of hesitation filled his voice.

Yes, it does work right here.

Right here rang through her mind. Well, Luteis wasn't wrong. She could turn slightly the wrong way and wander in the forest unless a noise drew her the right direction. She could so easily get lost.

Yet, Luteis never left her side.

Still . . .

She accepted it as a win that she could understand where she stood in the forest to *any* degree. Luteis had tamped down this specific trail from the stream to Mam's so Sanna could recognize where to fetch water. For the last three days, Sanna had painstakingly lined it with rocks on both sides, a little more than a hand span apart.

Awash with hope, she lifted the bucket and continued to walk.

I could always fly you to the stream, you know.

"I know."

Why don't you let me?

"I don't think I'm ready to fly yet, and it's beside the point."

What is the point?

Sanna fumbled with a response. How to explain the locked feeling in her chest? The sense of . . . nothing . . . ahead of her? He hadn't meant for it to, but Luteis' question last night plagued her.

What is the purpose of one's life if one has no higher calling?

She had the same question, only slightly different. *What happens when you've completed the purpose of your life so young?*

What if freeing the dragons was the biggest thing she'd ever do? Her life calling, as he'd named it. A sinking feeling always accompanied the question. She'd commanded an entire magic system and three dragon races. Explored the Western Network. Spoken to goddesses—though she hadn't even realized it. Nor had she paused to consider the deep ramifications of who she had been.

Sanna of the forest. Leader of dragons. Changer of worlds.

Now she exulted over fetching water from the stream. Life might have already reached its highest point, and she had nowhere to go but down.

"I don't know," she finally said, just to eliminate the annoyingly pessimistic thoughts. "It feels good to do something productive without Mam breathing down my neck."

Technically, I'm breathing down your neck.

Sanna snorted when a curling heat caressed her skin.

"True. It's a metaphor. It means she's been hovering really close."

I see.

His wings ruffled, as if he preened. The edge of her right leg caught a wet bush. The leaves shivered, sending cool droplets into the mud. She edged back to the left. Soft, loamy earth meant she was on the path.

"Do you see the house yet? I think we have a little longer to go. I didn't count."

Just ahead.

"Good."

Mam's voice crossed the distance. "This way, Sanna!"

"I know, Mam!"

Luteis's rolling chuckle slipped through her mind. She growled in his direction, but said nothing. Mam shouted loud enough for all the Dragonmasters to hear, even the ones that didn't live so close.

I was the High Dragonmaster! she wanted to shout back, but the words stuck in her throat. She didn't need sight to hear or understand the fear Mam lived with these days. That they *all* experienced.

"We really need to find a different place to live," she muttered.

You may take shelter under my wing for as long as you desire. I am warm in the winter. In the summer, you can sleep apart from me, as long as my tail can touch you. Again, I will attempt to convince you that a nomadic forest life is not a bad one.

"It's not the middle of winter yet, though. We haven't truly tested whether it would work."

I burn hot then as well. We can go wherever hunting and food takes us, as I used to. In that way, you need not leave the forest or rely on your Mam. Only me.

The thought sent a thrill through her. Adventure and dragons and freedom. It's what she used to have. Who she used to be.

Her head tilted to the side. "You really think we could live like that all winter?"

I don't see why not.

Sanna considered that as they crossed the last few steps. She walked more confidently now than last week, but it still took three times longer to do anything.

Why *not* roam with Luteis?

Wild.

Heathen.

Vagabond.

The words had a nice ring. They appealed more than she wanted to admit, but something tugged at her. Something wasn't right, she just . . . didn't know what it was. Running away from Mam's overabundance of caution and pecking certainly had her interest.

Your sister might not like it, Luteis continued. *I believe your Mam would be against such a thing.* His musing tone drew her from her reverie. *Are you willing to go against their wishes?*

"Is it their business?"

To her saucy attitude he replied, *is it not?*

"Sanna!" Mam called. "Over here. Are you all right? What's wrong?"

"Mam, I'm *fine.*"

"Well, good," Mam countered, equally hoity. "Forgive me for checking on you and being worried. I didn't hear from you last night!"

Her voice became a tad shrill. Sanna could picture Mam with her hands on her hips, graying blonde hair piled in a high bun. Her deep judgment and skepticism radiated from fathoms away.

"Sorry, Mam."

"Sleep outside again, did you? There are leaves and twigs in your hair."

Sanna would have glared at Luteis for not warning her,

but it wasn't his responsibility. Besides, he didn't care if she woke up with a mussed dress and muddy hair. His dragonian mind couldn't comprehend why twigs in the hair mattered.

Sanna either, for that matter.

"Yes, Mam. I slept outside with Luteis."

"Your attic room is always—"

"I know."

The awkward silence returned. The same one that had been swelling between them for days.

We're here to help you, Sanna, Mam said two days ago. *But . . . that might take different forms. We're all struggling with this for you. You might have to be extra patient while we figure out . . . things.*

A line of rocks met Sanna's feet. She reached down. They were slick from the falling moisture. Carefully, Sanna lowered the water bucket to the ground. When she reached out, the edge of the porch railing waited right where she thought it might.

She grinned.

Triumph!

Every day offered a different challenge so far. She had a good day three days ago. The rest had been mostly terrible. A small win early in the morning would turn the tide for now.

"I brought water."

"Thank you." The bucket scraped as Mam pulled it closer. "The trail seems to be working?"

"Thankfully, yes."

"I still don't like you on your hands and knees out there, but . . ."

She trailed away.

Sanna said nothing.

"Do you need more rocks on your line?"

"No, Mam."

"They may not be thick enough. What if you couldn't feel them? I—"

"Mam, it's fine."

"Well . . ." More burdensome silence. "Breakfast is inside."

A gut wrenching feeling stole through Sanna. She hated eating with other witches around, even Mam. She stuffed the embarrassment of them watching her aside. Well, she had to deal with it, or go hungry. The grumbles issuing from her stomach suggested that the former would happen first.

Minutes later, they sat at the table. Sighs and shuffles followed Mam around, along with unbroken spells of silence. Such a loud quiet. Letum Wood constantly had something to say. The noise made the hollow ache of missing the trees and their mossy, lovely trunks seem not so painful.

Sanna felt around the plate. Bread on the left. Fork on the right. A small crock of jam just above the side of the plate, like yesterday.

"Do you need me—"

"No," Sanna growled. "I can spread my own jam."

Mam silenced.

Sanna reached for the wooden spreading knife, a little thing, half the length of the two-pronged fork. With her left hand, she held the crock of jam, used her pinky to feel for the bread beneath her. Her right had dribbled jam out of the crock, onto the piece. Every day was a guess as to how much, like a surprise.

Engrossed in her task, Sanna startled when Mam broke the pervasive and eternal shroud of silence.

"I wanted to discuss something with you," Mam said.

"Is it my future?"

A pause. "Of a sort."

Sanna swallowed a rock in her throat, set the crock of jam aside.

"I'm listening."

"The other day, you mentioned being an emissary for dragons in the future. Do you remember that?"

Sanna almost scoffed. Remember? How could she have forgotten? Deasylva had given her the idea when Sanna last saw herself, her sister, and the forest goddess. The idea of being an emissary hummed underneath all this other . . . stuff. It gave a blossom of hope to her life.

"Yes, I remember."

"Were you serious?"

"Yes."

"What would you do as an emissary?"

"I don't know."

"Are you going to pursue it?"

"I don't know."

Mam chewed, swallowed. "Well, if not that, I was thinking maybe you could stay here. Help me and Elliot with things around the place? Things we could . . . you know . . . help you sort out? Jesse has been gone a lot but should be around more often. You like Jesse."

The prim, careful tone meant something, Sanna couldn't pinpoint *what* yet. Mam clearly had an agenda.

"You mean chores?" she asked. "You want me to help you do chores around the place?"

"Or . . . something."

"Like what?"

"I don't know. We'll find something for you."

"What about Luteis?"

Mam's tone was equally perplexed. "What about him?"

"What will he do?"

"Whatever dragons do."

"He stays with me," she said firmly.

Mam's exasperated breath followed. "Luteis isn't every-thing, Sanna. You must know that."

Sanna opened her mouth to counter, but stopped. A snort

of smoke issued outside. Clearly, the giant dragon took exception to what Mam said. A curling defensiveness rose like a prickling cactus.

"Well, he's my eyes."

"He's not. He's your dragon, *amo.*"

The gently-spoken words stood at odds with the fire they stirred. Sanna's hand tightened around her fork handle.

"Mam . . ."

A soothing hand settled over hers. Mam's palm was heavy and surprisingly comforting.

"Sanna, I'm not trying to pick a fight. Please understand. I just . . . you're facing a whole new world. A dangerous one. One that I think none of us are ready for. I don't know how to keep you safe in the forest and maybe being at home is best for you for a while. Jesse . . ."

She trailed away.

Then Sanna understood. She recoiled. "You want me to court Jesse?"

Mam's hand slipped away. The tinkle of fork against plate rang in the air. Mam must be fidgeting. "I won't lie," she said, drawling, "and say that the idea didn't cross my mind. But mostly I just think you need a friend. A witch friend, not a dragon friend."

"Mam!"

"He adores you, Sanna. And he understands your challenges. You could stay here, with us to help you, while you . . . adjust and court and . . ."

Horror rooted her into the chair. She gripped the sides, swallowing hard. Thank Drago she hadn't told Mam about Jesse's attempted kiss a year ago!

"Please tell me you haven't spoken with him?"

"No, not yet."

"Don't you dare, Mam!"

"Sanna! What is wrong with you?"

"I don't want to court Jesse. I don't want to handfast anyone. I'm . . . Luteis is enough for me. He'll take care of me."

Indeed, he drawled in her head.

She suppressed a smile.

Mam's voice did not smile. "Luteis is a dragon, Sanna. I appreciate your special connection, but it won't be enough. You two are different species. I understand his love for you, and that he'd give his life for you, but it's your depth of allegiance and loyalty to Luteis that has me worried. You cannot live for Luteis alone, Sanna. Neither of you are infallible . . ."

She trailed away. Something permeated Mam's tone beyond the cautious words, stilted manner.

"Life tends to happen to all of us," Mam continued with a voice that seemed to suggest she didn't speak about Sanna anymore. "And we adapt and grow from it. As you adapt to your . . . new struggles . . . you need to make certain that you aren't reliant on Luteis. That you can survive with others, too."

Bitterness infused Sanna's voice. "Forgive me, Mam, but I can't. I can't stand on my own in Letum Wood."

"Can't you?"

The inquiry stopped Sanna short. What was Mam trying to say? What didn't Sanna see or understand here—literally and figuratively?

Struck silent by the depth of the question, and all the fears it stirred up, Sanna said nothing. Her fingers rested on the tabletop. Appetite had long since fled, despite the tangy smell of jam in her nose and the gentle grit of breadcrumbs on her fingers.

Mam's hand slipped away.

"I also mention this because I wanted you to know that Elliot has . . . well . . ." She cleared her throat. Sanna stiffened.

Oh, no.

"That is," Mam continued, her voice pitched high. "Elliot has asked me to handfast him, and I've accepted. That will open up this house for you to use. Or you and Jesse to use, as it could be."

Shock rushed through Sanna like a cold wave, though the news was hardly surprising. Elliot had lost his wife, Babs, to a mountain dragon attack months ago. Mam had lost Daid before that. The grieving widow and widower, both attempting to live in Letum Wood and support their children, of whom Elliot still had several at home, would be wise to pool resources.

Still . . .

Daid stirred to life in her mind, a ghost she tried not to give too much thought to. She missed him. Yearned for his steady touch and reassurance more than ever. What would he think of her blindness? Would he coddle her, like Mam? Would there be fear in his voice when he spoke to her as well?

Sanna worked through her astonishment slowly. "Mam, I . . . ah . . . congratulations."

"It's not a funeral announcement, Sanna," Mam said with amusement. "It's a handfasting. We'll have a very simple ceremony here in the forest. It's more of an arrangement of convenience and companionship for both of us."

"When?"

"In two days."

"So soon?"

Her shoulders seemed to shrug. "What need is there to wait? It's winter. Besides, we're practically living together as it is, since I take care of his three younger children, plus the Parker children."

The breaking of the Dragonmaster families had been a harrowing affair. Finn and Adelina Parker had set out into the forest to try to recreate Anguis after it burned down, only to die. Trey Parker, Finn's eldest son, survived with his sister

Greata and younger brother Hans. They lived with Elliot and his four younger children in the large house next door.

"This does mean that you'll want to move in with us, I assume?" Mam asked.

Concerns burdened such a query. Sanna hid a recoil. By Drago, no! She didn't want to live in the same house as Elliot and Jesse and . . . no.

We need to get that house situation figured out fast, she said to Luteis. *And* not *this house either.*

Agreed.

With her most Isadora-like impression, she managed to not sound strangled. "Ah, no. Thank you, Mam. Luteis and I will figure something out."

"Sanna—"

Sanna held up a hand. "Mam, I know that you want me. I appreciate that. But I'm an adult now. I was the High Dragonmaster over three races of dragons. Isadora is handfasted and . . . with Max." She choked the last out, for it opened a whole *other* can of worms. "I don't think it's right for me to go live with my Mam and her new husband."

"I understand, but considering your lack of sight. Your . . . unfamiliarity in this world. Would that be safe?"

"I have—"

"Luteis, I know. But Sanna, Luteis isn't enough."

Rage snapped through Sanna, tightening her spine. No more of this. She yanked her shoulders back.

"Excuse me, Mam, but Luteis is *everything*."

"Sanna—"

Sanna shoved her chair away, pressed to her feet. A gentle burn of heat radiated into the house from outside. She could hear Luteis moving closer.

"Thank you for breakfast. I'll be back for the handfasting."

With that, Sanna fled.

Six

Isadora

Beams of sunlight woke Isadora.

She blinked awake to a tangle of dawn dancing in her eyes through the window. With a stretch, and a squeak, she elongated her arms over her head. Her toes unfurled along crinkly, cotton sheets. With a deep inhale, she recognized the scent of . . .

. . . vetiver.

A startled gasp brought her all the way awake.

She bolted upright.

A mostly unfamiliar room sprawled in elegant tones of dark wood, painted forest murals on the ceiling, and expensive curtains. Recollection served at the same time, and she sat there for several moments, a befuddled mess.

"The good gods," she muttered, shoving hair out of her eyes. "There isn't enough tea in the Central Network to help me cope with this."

A glance to her right confirmed that Max's side of the bed, which might as well have spanned a house itself, was empty. The heavy damask curtains were tied back, allowing sunlight to filter through glass window panes. He must have left for the castle already. The urge to slip into the paths, see what lay ahead, ran through her. She punted it off.

No, the time had come to live, not assess.

She'd check the paths later.

Isadora scooted out of bed, drew her shawl off the back of a chair and twirled it around her shoulders. Who put the shawl there? She hadn't worn it last night nor pulled it from her bag. She shuddered in the cool air and stepped to the window.

A quick peek revealed the grounds she'd studied in the dark. Patchy snow spread all the way to the edge of the forest, where wild things overtook the tame land. Brittle vines, spiny undergrowth, trees, all manner of shrubs, cluttered Letum Wood in a warbling line. Fog lingered, burning away as sunlight appeared behind rolling clouds.

The flick of a horse's tail drew her gaze toward the stable. Was that a small cemetery tucked on the other side?

She stepped away, found a pair of slippers on the floor next to her bed. They felt like a familiar embrace as she stepped into them.

Slippers?

Had Max . . .

The trailing question disappeared. Her bag lay open on the floor not far away, only a few things unpacked. Her shawl, slippers, and what other toiletries scattered the room, strategically placed where she'd be most likely to use them. Max must have taken the time out of his morning to unpack her things.

"You know me well," she murmured, impressed despite herself. Perhaps their time together in the Southern Network worked in their favor as a marriage precursor. A piece of parchment lay on top of her day dress, which draped the divan. His handwriting filled the interior in neat, stacked lines.

Isadora,

*I've taken the liberty to unpack a few of your things,
should you need them, in an attempt to ease your transition here.*

*If you want to explore when I return home from work,
I'm happy to give the official tour, but you're not
restricted. You can go anywhere you like. I feel it's fair to
give some warning. Wildrose is not what you might
think.*

*Faye may return to retrieve a few things. Don't be
alarmed if you see her. Pearl might also pop in. She has
a habit of turning up at odd times. If you need help with
anything, see Tavish in the stables. Ean may also
wander through the kitchen.*

I will return for dinner.

—M.S.

Isadora rolled the little letter into a tube and tapped it
against her lips as she considered.

The name *Faye* had bounced around the Advocacy once
or twice, mostly from Lucey, but no one really knew anyone
else in the Advocacy. There could be correlation between *this*
Faye in Max's letter and *that* Faye with a reputation in the
secret society, but she didn't know for sure.

She'd been apart from the Advocacy for months now,
though Max had never let her integrate very deeply. He'd spent
most of their time bossing her around, yet managing to help
her understand her magic better. A thrill of amusement
slipped back through her.

Handfasted.

Ha!

On a whim, she sauntered out of the master suite, note in hand, and down the stairs. Daylight changed Wildrose irrevocably. Her white nightgown kept her decently covered, and he said not to expect anyone. Tavish, whoever that might be, would hopefully remain in the stables unless sought out.

Wildrose could reveal its own history.

———

Wildrose Manor held many shadows and even more secrets, as far as she could tell from a cursory walk-through. Isadora kept her shawl drawn tight, Max's letter in hand, as she breezed down the halls, glancing through open doors. His warning rippled through her mind with each step.

I feel it's fair to give some warning. Wildrose is not what you might think.

A vague sense of familiarity lingered in the old corners, the tall chandeliers glimmering against squared ceilings. Walls of elegant paintings stretched down hallways. The wooden floorboards creaked under her weight as she strolled by. Flat tacks kept dusty carpets pinned to the wooden floor beneath. Every now and then, she passed a vase. A bust. A handful of books left on a shelf within reach.

Quiet streams of light fell through tall windows, all of them the same size. Everything in Wildrose appeared intentional. Four-poster beds. Quilts with hints of time lingering in their designs.

Isadora hummed as she wandered, just to hear something.

A rustle of sound drifted up a stairwell on the second floor, after she passed a room that smelled like pipe tobacco and harbored countless wooden boxes. She paused, ear tilting the direction of the noise.

A whisper.

Isadora hurried silently down the carpeted stairs. She knew

that voice, didn't she? With a spell, she transported to the bedroom, swapped her nightgown for her day dress, and returned. The noise continued.

Was it Faye?

On the first floor again, she found herself near the kitchen. It tucked against the back corner, not far from a hidden wood-shed. The flutter of a light blue fabric and dark skin passed barely within sight in the interior of the cooking room.

Isadora stepped into the doorway.

She didn't recognize the woman in front of her, though she knew the song under her breath. Max had only allowed her into the headquarters of the Advocacy once or twice during her tenure. He was oddly protective of it. When she was there, she heard that song.

"Faye?"

The woman gasped, whirled around. She had friendly eyes set in a kind face. Her thin cheeks gave way to a broad nose. Eventually a smile.

"Isadora?"

"Yes," she said slowly. "Are you Faye?"

"I am." Her white teeth grinned. "I'm surprised you could tell, after all the transforming I did for the Advocacy."

"We've met before?"

"Yes."

"Oh. Well, it's good to officially meet you. I suppose there is a little familiarity . . ."

Faye laughed, an easy, tinkling thing. "I always kept my hair the same, though it was fun to vary the hue of my skin and my cheekbones. I didn't know what it was like to be pale until the Advocacy necessitated such drastic changes!"

The strange sensation of a known voice in an unknown face washed through Isadora in a wave.

"So you know me?"

Faye hesitated. "Well, yes, to some extent. Mostly as Max's

protégé, as he didn't often take witches under his wing personally."

A fact she'd suspected, but never confirmed.

"I see."

Faye gestured to her with a wave. "And now as his wife! Congratulations, I think?"

The exploratory question nearly sent a weak laugh through Isadora. This entire experience felt surreal.

"Max told you, I presume?"

Faye chuckled, set aside a basket filled with napkins, wooden spoons, and other sundries.

"No. Well, yes." She tilted her head. "What a difficult web the Advocacy spun. Charlie told me. Max and I don't have a lot to say to each other, though we're friends. Of a sort. Anyway, I know that you handfasted to help us see the political climate through, and then . . . all the rest."

Faye ended delicately, a fact that eased some of Isadora's concern. The role she played in the closing out of inter-Network hostilities had her nerves on edge. Such power as a Watcher surely wouldn't go unnoticed.

What that might mean, though, she couldn't fathom.

"I'm not sad to see the Advocacy dwindling into quiet repose these days," Faye continued, reaching for a dry rag. "Lucey aside, anyway. She's been quite busy closing down the dwindling business, and the upkeep of those vagabonds that still need some help. Anyway, you and I have much to get acquainted with. What do you say to a drink of tea and a nice chat at my new place? I'd love to show it off to someone."

———

Isadora followed Faye's transportation spell to a quiet home on the far outskirts of Chatham City. Smoke, trees, and buildings littered the skyline from the top floor of a four-story house. A young orchard, a towering fence, and a pond ringed the periphery.

Hidden in the distant folds of Chatham City was a teeming pot of humanity. Chatham Castle stood stalwart above all, a behemoth Guardian in the sky, set against an even greater backdrop of forest.

The air smelled like cinnamon. Several boards lined the walls, filled with oddities that created a cozy home. Jars of different colored sand, of varying heights and widths, spread in a rainbow against the wooden walls. No divan. Giant pillows cluttered one corner, built up to a snug nook. Isadora wanted to grab one of the thin books and curl up around a fluffy pillow.

"You have a beautiful view," Isadora said.

"Thank you, I thought so. I rent this floor from the elderly couple that lives below. After so many years at Wildrose, I wanted to be able to *see* something. Witches, mostly. While I loved my time in the country, I wanted a bit more . . . presence . . . to my day. I can't lie, I'm quite fond of the markets and walking around the city. Charlie hates that I go alone, but . . ."

Faye shrugged, the smirk on her face clearly stating that Charlie's opinion was his own problem. Isadora hid a smile.

She might have just found her new best friend.

"I see."

Charlie. The thought ruminated in the back of her mind. Amongst all the other shocks in her recent life lay that of the High Priest, Charles, actually being the hidden Advocate all these years. A brilliant man, posing as a dunce.

Isadora turned away from Chatham City and its grayish splendor. Faye bustled around a small table. A wide bed, a set of two chairs, two plates, a pair of shoes too large to belong to a small-footed woman like Faye, and a hint of something masculine in the air, stacked several pieces of a growing puzzle.

"You and Charlie . . .?"

She allowed the implied question to gather its own power. Faye laughed again, softly this time.

"Yes. Me and Charlie."

"Oh."

"He's unexpected in most ways, isn't he?"

"Very," Isadora said with a breath. "I . . . I'm still trying to take it all in, to be honest."

"He told me you handled the truth about his role as the Advocate well. You're in a very exclusive circle. The witches that know the truth about him are small, but growing."

"Word of—"

"Yes, word of the Advocacy and his role in it will eventually spread, but he wants to delay that for now. There's more to figure out in our world than who the High Priest is or pretends to be."

Is there? Isadora wanted to ask. As brilliant as it was that Charlie could save so many witches, she couldn't help a sense of uncertainty. Could they trust a witch so capable of great deceit?

Faye watched her closely.

"Max hasn't told you about how he met me and Charlie, has he?" she asked, and Isadora was grateful for the diversion.

"No."

"Has he told you about his family in the East?"

"A little. When we were in the Southern Network he told me a little about his pere and mere but . . . details are vague."

Faye sighed. "Well, that's expected. Charlie told me not to meddle in things with you and Max, but I think you've been put into an unfair situation. Max isn't likely to tell you the details that I have about him, Charlie, Wildrose, and Ranulf, but I think you should know. If you're going to stay with Max, anyway."

"That's the question he and I need to answer, I suppose."

Faye studied her, then nodded. "Yes, I guess you will. Do you love him?"

"I do."

"I can tell. Do you trust him?"

Isadora could only stare, shocked into silence. She didn't know. The kind gesture of unpacking her bag, his openness in letting her roam Wildrose. Even the plea in his voice when he asked her to stay . . .

"I don't know."

No shock crossed Faye's eyes. "Well, I don't blame you. Max and I rarely see eye to eye. He can be a difficult personality, and I can be headstrong, but we've figured it out because of our love for Charlie. If there's any witch that might speak against Max, it's me. But even I will vouch for his character, though he's far from perfect."

Sensing a confidant, Isadora said, "I'd love more information. I . . . I don't know what I've gotten myself into. The handfasting was just supposed to be in the Southern Network and now . . ."

She shrugged, at a loss.

Faye put her hand on the back of a chair and pulled it out.

"Sit, Isadora," she said more firmly, in a command Isadora had no reason to refuse. "We might as well start at the beginning, when Charlie, Max, and I came together at Wildrose Manor. I won't tell you everything—that's not my place—but I will tell you the beginning between the three of us. That much will help."

Seven
Maximillion

The sound of silence met Max when he returned to Wildrose. Not surprising. The paths had revealed a mostly quiet night ahead. Darkness had long since fallen, casting shadows on the forest, and he regretted his late return.

He transported to the same spot he always did on the front porch, then glanced up. The friendly burn of several candles in the master suite assured him that Isadora was inside. A promising first sign. Part of him had worried she'd run away in the quiet hours while he'd had to work.

Trepidation overcame him as he stepped through the double front doors and into the manor. His conversation with Charlie that morning had unseated him all day, the annoying twit. He'd stressed about Isadora far more than he would have if his best friend had just kept his mouth shut.

What if she didn't like Wildrose?

Would his political world and all its expectations be too much for her?

She had proven herself worthy of an Ambassador's wife in

the Southern Network, but that had been for a short time. Now, it would be forever.

He'd all but asked her to share their lives, then left her to figure out that life alone. Such a thing couldn't be helped. Pressure from the closing of the borders, the finalizing of the Mansfeld Pact, put a prodigious weight on everything at the castle. Indeed, he'd been lucky to escape long enough *to* ask her to stay with him.

Or maybe that was his own preoccupation talking.

"Isadora?"

Distantly, a voice replied.

"Up here!"

Well, she spoke. That also meant something. Max spelled his briefcase to his office on the third floor, then transported himself to the landing outside the master suite. A lazy use of magic, but after an exhausting day, he couldn't help it. Such actions had nothing to do with an urge or excitement to see her.

Of course not.

With more eagerness than he thought he possessed, Max pushed through the doors. She sat on a divan, legs tucked up on the cushions. A blanket wrapped her shoulders and a book lay on her lap. He blinked, studying the inviting picture with a stab of longing.

By the gods, what he'd give to be that blanket.

She smiled. A hesitant little thing, riddled with wariness. "Max?"

"Isadora."

He chastised himself the moment the word crossed his lips. He sounded like a board. Something amused her, for her lips tweaked up at the edges. She closed the book, set it aside.

He let the door shut behind him and advanced. Questions stalled in his throat. She'd always been better at this sort of thing. When they were in the South, she ignored his bluster and somehow got him talking.

Wily wife.

She straightened, tightening the blanket around her. A friendly fire crackled in the hearth, tossing golden light that danced across her skin, a wild and lovely thing all at the same time. Curiosity filled her studious gaze.

"Well?" she asked, hiding a yawn. "How was your day?"

He drew in a breath, let it out. The action released some of the ire that simmered.

"Busy. Very busy."

She patted the cushion next to her. Relieved at the invitation, he obeyed. Another knot in his chest loosened as he stared at the fire. She retracted her legs, allowing him more room. He resisted the urge to snatch her lovely ankle, feel if the skin was as soft and warm as he dreamed, and tug her onto his lap.

Isadora's bent elbow propped on the edge of the divan. She leaned her head on it. "Tell me about it?"

He hesitated. "It's bureaucratic nonsense. You really want to hear?"

"It was bureaucratic nonsense in the Southern Network, too, yet I still enjoyed your updates then."

The reminder wasn't lost on him. They had some footing.

We're not totally new at this, she seemed to say. *Remember?*

His shoulders lowered further, making him realize how high and tense they'd been in the first place. Taking the offered gift, he nodded once.

"Indeed."

Gradually warming into the retelling of his day, and glossing over the part where Charlie visited, he gave her a general accounting. She poked questions here and there, murmured exclamations of surprise, and rolled her eyes at the antics from the West. Dostar, as always, remained difficult.

When he finished, he felt oddly loose against the couch. He turned to face her more fully. She gave a petite yawn, eyes crinkling in a charming way. She made a sound under her breath as she stretched. Her leg elongated, slipping onto his. The sleepy way she blinked made it seem like she didn't even notice.

He couldn't *stop* noticing.

Her skin burned through his pants, into his leg, until he wanted to pull her in his arms and teach her what heat hand-fasting could *really* bring.

The good gods, he'd never get enough of her.

"And you?" he asked, gratifying himself with an even cadence.

"Oh, nothing much. Except I did run into Faye. We had tea at her new place. It was . . . very enlightening."

Her leg withdrew again. Max didn't even ask what that meant because he stiffened and all the angst returned in a flash. Isadora sat up. A sense of reckoning lingered in tension she couldn't hide.

All he could manage was an uttered, "Faye?"

"The real Faye, I should clarify, as I vaguely recognized her from Advocacy work. We talked for hours about . . . " A hesitation, then, "about how you, Charlie, and Faye all met."

"Demmet," he muttered.

Faye was no enemy. She ran Wildrose when he could not and did it with impressive skill and alacrity. Charlie adored her to a nauseating effect. She'd earned Max's respect, no small thing, but they weren't amicable. Out of any witch from whom Isadora might receive his past, *she* was not the one he'd choose.

Isadora laughed, but the mirth was short-lived. "Yes, well, she had the same sort of thing to say about you. Mostly good things, in case you're worried. Just . . . more things than I expected."

"Like what?" he snapped.

Her gaze cooled. "I'll tell you when you talk to me like your wife, not one of your Assistants at the castle."

He turned away, duly chided. "Forgive me. Please, if you would, allow me to know what Faye shared?"

Isadora tucked her arms around her middle, securing the blanket more firmly with them.

"Mostly your love for the Advocacy, for Wildrose. For . . . Charlie."

"Oh."

The conversation paused, bated with thoughtful silence. In some regard, Faye had done him a favor. Broken the ice on a subject that felt too overwhelming to tackle. With all he held on his plate, how could he crack open history so Isadora might understand?

"Faye said nothing bad about you. Just . . . surprising. I feel as if there's a man hidden beneath all the folds that make you who you are. One who I don't really know."

To that, he had no response. Sometimes he felt the same way. As self-possessed as he attempted to be, could anyone truly know themselves that well?

He harbored doubts.

"Has learning such information frightened you?" he asked.

Isadora stared hard at him as she mulled that over, then slowly nodded.

"A little."

"Why?"

"Because I don't think you would have told me. Would you?"

He paused. "I don't know. Eventually, it seems likely."

"But you had no plans?"

"No."

"And that," she said softly, "is why I realized, when talking to Faye, that I'm not sure I trust you."

His head snapped up. Eyes met hers. She held his gaze, a mixture of certainty and terror in their depths.

The good gods. She didn't trust him?

"Why not?" he rasped.

"The night of the dance in the Southern Network," she immediately countered. "You told me about your parents and I opened my heart to you. You closed it down. You said, and I quote from memory, *when this is over, we'll return to our lives as acquaintances. Our professional relationship can go back to the way it was.*"

His jaw hardened. Oh, he remembered the words, and she left out the ones that mattered most.

You will be free to find a man who truly deserves you.

He most assuredly didn't deserve her.

Max shot to his feet, wounded. Well, she would be honest with him. At least they'd proven that.

Isadora froze into position on the couch.

"Trust is an expensive commodity," he said as he strode to the fireplace, snatched the poker. Vermillion cinders stirred as he poked at a falling log. "We've been handfasted for all of a day, if you ask me."

Another long pause.

He felt out her silence with a sick feeling in his gut. Was this the end already? Had Faye told her enough that Isadora already wanted freedom?

A cold feeling struck him. Had Faye mentioned Bella? Or, heavens forbid, Caterina? The lack of deepening suspicion and disgust from Isadora told him it was unlikely. That would have been a step too far, even for Faye.

Before his mental spiral grew weight, Isadora spoke again.

"I'm inclined to agree with you, Max. Yesterday, we chose to remain in a sham of a handfasting, which may give us a single day to say we've been together. Except I wouldn't say that we're handfasted. Not truly. Not . . . *yet*."

He spun.

"What is it you want, Isadora? Tell me straight."

She stood. The blanket fell away, revealing strongly held shoulders and a proud chin.

"I want three months."

"Three months?"

"Yes. In that time, I want us to decide if this is something we can do for the rest of our lives. To give a valiant effort. Do I have a place in this giant house? Can you fit with my family? Is it possible for Maximillion Sinclair to love another witch?"

His throat bound up.

She didn't know.

How couldn't she know how much he loved her? If possible, the wound deepened. He turned back to the fire. She was too enchanting tonight. Standing there with such certitude, like a bossy know-it-all hiding a terrified woman. Oh, he could see her fear, lurking back there, so poorly disguised.

Of course, he hadn't said the words. *I love you* hadn't crossed his lips . . . ever. A declaration of need for her had, of course. He recalled every word that begged her to remain with him.

But if you didn't want to go. If you wanted to stay. With me. Then . . . I believe we could build something together. Something . . . peaceful and real and . . . not empty and cold.

Not love, though.

He'd never said those words out loud to any witch. Not even Charlie. She didn't know what she asked.

Or maybe she did.

"It's a fair request, Isadora. You shall have your three months. I ask only that you establish expectations for me. What do you want in all that time? What am I to do? What sort of husband does Isadora Spence desire?"

He didn't face her—on purpose—but even without being able to see her, he sensed her slumping shoulders. Her disappointment.

"Thank you. I . . ."

Her voice faltered, but not with tears. Something else altogether. He didn't understand. He gave her what she wanted.

Though he wanted to ravish her with a kiss that would wipe all this lingering malady, instead he set the poker down. The awkwardness in the air, as thick as soup, maintained too tight of a shroud around him.

"I want to act as if we're courting," she said. "As if we're truly trying to discover whether our lives are compatible. Without . . . greater expectations."

Her gaze darted to the bed, then back.

Ah, now he understood.

He drowned in emotions he couldn't identify. The earlier ease of intimacy had all but been erased. Her demands were fair. In fact, he should have thought of them himself.

He hadn't.

That meant something, too.

"You shall have your courting. In the morning, I'll follow up with a plan and some ideas to get to know each other. Forgive me," he said, as crisp as a new fold. "I have a few items of business to finish in my office, and then I'll return to bed. Don't feel as if you must wait up."

Before she could respond, he faded into the hallway, drew in a shuddering breath, and retreated to his office.

EIGHT

ISADORA

Of all the intractable, idiotic men!

Silently, Isadora fumed. She paced across the floor in front of the fireplace with burning indignation.

Business in his office?

No dinner?

Not another word of caring?

With a growl, she flung the blanket onto the couch and stalked toward the armoire. There, she paused. His clothing filled half the space. Last night, he must have made room for her before they silently went to sleep without speaking.

Her side?

Barren as an empty bowl.

She had only three dresses to her name, and one of them was a work dress not fit for anything but gardening or cleaning. In a place like this? She'd wear it all day and still not run out of chores.

Setting that aside, she reached for her only nightgown. A job. That's what she needed. Something to distract her that provided currency and stability and . . .

Oh.

Wait.

Maximillion had all those things. If they were truly hand-fasted, didn't that give her access to his currency? The idea welled up with a sticky feeling that didn't feel entirely right, either. Besides, she didn't have time for a job with Mam hand-fasting Elliot, Sanna wandering Letum Wood with a dragon, and figuring out her relationship with Max—which stood on a precarious ledge of slippery questions.

Setting it on her mental list of *things to figure out soon*, Isadora dismissed the concern.

Her nightgown was simple, but clean. No holes or patches required, which was more than she could say for her work dress, and both pairs of shoes. Where had all the clothing from the Southern Network ended up?

A petite desk in the corner drew her gaze. She summoned a pencil and piece of empty parchment, then set it on the coffee table and began to scrawl out exactly what he'd requested.

A list of demands, like a hostage negotiation.

1. Court me as if we weren't handfasted so we can get to know each other. We should ask lots of questions.

2. Prove whether our lives can merge.

3. Meet Mam and Sanna together.

The urge to add *come with me to Mam's handfasting* was almost too strong to ignore, but she sent it away. No, she wouldn't throw him into the Dragonmaster families in such a way. Not with so much happening in the Network. She wasn't unsympathetic to his pressures at the castle.

Eventually, though, a meeting must occur.

4. I want you to . . .

The last drew away. *Not be afraid to touch me.*

She used a spell to remove the ink and scowled at the paper. The man had been as loose as a rock when she'd slipped her foot onto his thigh, just to see what he did. He'd stared at it, eyes dilating, for half a breath before ignoring it entirely.

Was he unaffected?

Their passionate kiss in the forest only a few days ago led her to think otherwise. Why suppress it?

The hours-long conversation with Faye had revealed more than Isadora expected. His deep relationship with Charlie surprised her most of all. So, the dolt *was* capable of caring. It should have made her feel better, but it only confused her more.

Like throwing open an attic filled with ghosts and shadows that wouldn't budge. They remained stolidly in place, stubbornly steadfast. Trust Max to have ghosts that refused freedom.

Well, the truth remained. She loved the bloody man. Despite his imperfections, just the smell of him made her heart race. His troubled gaze, so bullheaded and assessing at the same time, made her want to soothe his panic away. She couldn't help but think he truly didn't *know* what he did wrong, the fool.

He wanted expectations?

She had them.

She scrawled a finish to the final one on the list.

4. I want you to tell me you love me. In words. Out loud. And mean it.

Satisfied, she dropped the quill, folded the paper, and sent it to him with a spell. Let the daft man chew on *that* for the night.

With a flop, Isadora landed on the mattress, summoned the blanket, and tucked herself into bed with a sleepy yawn.

NINE

SANNA

"How am I supposed to write a letter to Isadora in the middle of the forest?"

The muttered question fell on unhearing ears. Luteis had long since fallen asleep. She curled a little tighter to his warmth, crinkled the broad leaf she held in her palm.

No ink, no quill. No method to send the letter to Isadora, either, even if she could write it. Perhaps magic wouldn't be the worst thing . . .

Her thoughts turned.

She could make charcoal and scrawl a message on the leaf. She'd done it before. Lighting a fire without Luteis's help was out of the question, though a conflagration was unlikely with the forest so wet.

Well, she could *clear* an area, start a fire, and use the resulting charcoal. But that would wake Luteis, and he needed to rest. She didn't want to stumble around the forest, either. Besides, it would take awhile to get the flame started, and the burned wood had to cool. After touching it, she might accidentally wipe it on her face and never know.

Did that matter?

Sort of.

She shook that aside. No, she'd never cared what she looked like before. She'd run all over Letum Wood with soot and charcoal and mud stains in the past, and it hadn't mattered.

Except everything felt different now, especially the little things. She didn't want to look like a heathen just because she couldn't see. When she had sight and she appeared a bit wild, it was different.

Less about capability, more about choice.

Mam's words darted back through her mind. *Luteis isn't enough.* Hearing them again, in a looped refrain, set her teeth on edge. Oh, she'd never forget such a comment. Of course he was enough! He was the reason she had no sight in the first place. He was her eyes.

Her heart.

Luteis would always be with her.

Al . . . always.

Mired in her faltering thoughts, Sanna squeezed her eyes shut and tried to remember. What had Letum Wood looked like at night?

Her eyes opened.

This, in fact.

Utterly dark.

With a sigh, she turned so her back pressed to Luteis's leg. Shifting brought a wave of cold over her shoulders, but his radiating heat ebbed it away. Unbidden, Mam's words returned.

Sanna growled. She needed to find Isa, talk to her. Her sister would be able to make sense of what Mam said, because she couldn't.

Handfast Elliot!

Interest in Jesse?

Necessity drove such maternal machinations, surely. Sanna

could understand the motivations behind it. Yet the thought of Mam handfasting anyone *but* Daid stymied her, leaving a rock on her chest that made it harder to sleep.

If she only had a spell . . .

Talis, the previous brood sire for the Dragonmaster community, had outlawed magic out of fear over what it had done to dragons in the past. He prevented witches from learning incantations, lest poachers more easily find them and danger alight upon them again.

Now, Sanna wondered . . .

The urge to use it felt wrong. She harbored the desire carefully in her chest, still too afraid to speak it. Talis was long dead. She watched the light bleed from his eyes after Daid delivered the killing blow. Talis wouldn't know, nor be able to punish her. Isadora used it constantly. So did witches outside of Anguis.

Still, a fear of magic persisted.

Sanna closed her eyes, snuggled so close to Luteis she felt the pattern of his scales along the ridge of her spine. His long wing shuffled, folding farther over her in toasty protection.

Finally, she fell asleep.

———

The exasperation in Isadora's voice woke Sanna before a nudging along her foot.

"Really, Sanna?"

Sanna blinked awake, pulled from groggy dreams half-filled with fire. She stretched, arms elongating.

"What?"

The noises of Letum Wood had woken back up. Calling birds, settling tree branches. Wind rushed by, whistling through the thin undergrowth to beckon winter closer.

"Why are you sleeping on the ground, when you can have the whole attic to yourself at Mam's?"

Sanna pushed up, grounded by the gritty feel of dirt against her palms. "I just . . . wanted to be with Luteis in the trees. Some of us like sleeping outside."

Her slightly muffled reply must have come from behind a scarf. "It's freezing out here, Sanna!"

"I'm with a forest dragon. He's so warm. Besides, I'm wearing my coat."

"It's not all that safe."

"Letum Wood has never been safe. And you didn't protest before," she hastily added.

Isadora huffed. "I always protested, you just didn't listen. It's even *less* safe now that you don't have your sight."

Sanna unclenched slightly. At least Isadora addressed the issue straight on. Unlike Mam, who didn't like the words *blind* or *sightless* or *can't see.*

"You're kidding, right?" Sanna pushed to her feet, woozy. Luteis shuffled at her back, his teeth snapping together at the end of a yawn. "I snuggled a forest dragon all night. What was going to approach me?"

Correct, Luteis said with a huff.

Isadora sighed. "Right. Well, I suppose there are worse places to sleep. Though it still doesn't seem wise to wander in the winter. But you're an adult. The decision is yours."

"I sleep better when I'm with Luteis, anyway, than on a lumpy mattress or inside where it gets hot."

"I came to check on you."

"I'm fine. Figuring my life out, as you can see."

Isadora paused. Sanna could still recall the way Isadora's eyebrows used to come together, wrinkling her skin and nose, when she fell into thought. Did she do that now? The silence broke with a quiet declaration.

"Mam told me what happened yesterday, when she talked to you."

"Weird, isn't it?"

Another pause, this one gratifying. At least she wasn't the only one having a hard time thinking it through. Isadora's arm came through Sanna's and tugged.

"Come on, let's walk together. I have a feeling you don't get to just *walk* in the forest much anymore, and there's a small game trail. Luteis," she called over her shoulder, "you're always welcome."

Your sister, he drawled, *is also welcome at my perch anytime.*

"Luteis says thanks."

That's not exactly what I said.

She ignored his precision.

"Let's walk," Isa suggested.

A thrill darted through Sanna. No, she didn't get to safely *move* much. She missed the way she used to run across tree branches, slide on the moss. Thinking about it brought a lump to her throat that she swallowed back.

She gratefully kept up at Isadora's side, hand on her elbow.

"Root on your right, then you're clear for a bit," Isadora said crisply. "Now, let's talk about Mam and what she said."

"Handfasting Elliot. Can you believe that? Did she mention her plans for me and Jesse? Weird!"

Isadora swayed to a stop. Sanna lurched at her side, then spun to face her.

"What?"

"Yes, there's news of Elliot," Isa said impatiently, batting Sanna's arm with her other hand. "And Jesse, too. Honestly, Sanna, neither of those should have come as any sort of surprise to you. But that's not what I'm here to talk about today."

"It's not?"

"No! I'm here to discuss you and Luteis and . . . whatever you're doing living out here in the forest. Mam said you could have her old house to yourself—the entire thing—and you didn't want it. That's what I wanted to talk about."

Sanna scowled. "I'm not going to live next door to Mam for the rest of my life."

Isadora tugged her firmly along again. Sanna stumbled, righted herself, and forced her legs to move. Luteis pushed lazily to his feet. The clacking of scales rippled through the air as he shivered. He seemed to lumber to their right, where he'd follow, unseen.

"Can we talk about you and Max first?"

"Nice try," Isa drawled. "No. Eventually, yes. But first, we're going to talk about you living in the forest. Let me make one thing clear: I think you should live in Letum Wood."

"Really?"

"Yes. There's no reason losing your sight has to stop your life. I don't think you should do it without help, though."

"I don't need help."

"You do."

"I have Luteis!"

A brief pause likely indicated a roll of her eyes. "Witches live perfectly functional lives without their sight all the time. There are resources available to you out in the Network. What if you learn a few things, then come back?"

A shudder rippled through Sanna. She did *not* want to talk about this. This conversation led down other paths, like going into the Network and talking to strangers. Sensing that steel in Isa's voice, however, she had little choice. How would she escape?

Run into the forest?

"I'm not like other witches. I wouldn't belong in the Network."

"That is an eternal truth I shall never dispute. Nevertheless, neither are you so different that you couldn't learn to be independent. Lucey knows other witches without sight. She's helped them as an Apothecary."

"So?"

"She could introduce you."

"Then what?"

Isadora blew an exasperated raspberry. "They could help you adapt to your changing vision."

Silence swelled between them, loaded and painful. She didn't want to think about this. Letum Wood was her only escape. She had Luteis here. Though she couldn't see her beloved trees, they still made her feel safer than life in the villages.

"I'll think about it."

Isa's lack of immediate response meant she understood exactly what Sanna wanted to do—throw her off track.

"Will you really?"

A note of hope, concern, surprised Sanna. Of course Isadora would worry about her. She'd expected as much. But to this extent?

"Yes, I'll . . . think about it."

Eventually.

"And magic? Will you let me teach you a few spells yet?"

"No!"

"Sanna!"

"I said I'd think about it! One thing at a time, Isa. I'm still just . . . I'm figuring it out, all right? You have to let me do it at my pace. It's overwhelming otherwise."

Isadora sighed, an aggravated thing. "Fine, but if you don't, I'm going to send Lucey here with a blind witch anyway. They should be able to teach you some helpful spells, if you won't let me."

"You wouldn't."

"Watch me," she muttered.

Sanna smirked. "Shall I try to?"

"Oh, you know what I mean. I'm serious, Sanna. I'm holding you to it. I know you didn't ask to lose your sight. I know it's not fair. You deserve to still see, and you lost your sight attempting to save your dragons. None of it makes sense, and I'm angry at all of it. You must be livid. But that doesn't mean your life—the one you wanted—is over. You can still be Sanna of the forest *and* a blind witch. You need to know that."

A traitorous flare of hope brightened the cold chambers of her heart. Isadora had put into quick words everything Sanna both feared and desired. Her agony culminated in the fact that she didn't ask for blindness. She served the creatures she loved the most, and lost everything.

"Thank you." Sanna's chin tilted up, voice thick with tension. "I vow it, Isadora. I'll think about it. Please, give me space?"

"I will. I promise."

"Thanks. Can we talk about you and Max now? I mean, it's only been a day . . ."

"Max and I . . ." Isadora trailed away.

A raspberry followed, eradicating the tension that built up with the question. Sanna held her breath, startled by how much concern she held for her sister. Technically, she hadn't met Max yet. Not really.

The thought of Isadora handfasted to a stranger didn't sit well.

"What are Max and I?" Isadora cried. "I don't know, Sanna. We're a handfasted couple that hardly knows each other, living in a manor that's too big for both of us, and neither really know what sort of life we want to live. Last night, he agreed that we can give this a three month trial period, so that's what we're doing."

"Three months?"

"I suppose that I'll know by then whether we can live together or not."

"Does he love you?"

A lonely pause followed. "I hope so," Isadora murmured, "because I so badly want this to work. And that's exactly what I'm trying to figure out."

"You love him, don't you?"

"Hopelessly."

"You deserve someone to love you as much as I love Luteis."

"I know. I adore him, Sanna."

"But—"

"I know. I know. The question is whether he can give the same back, as Luteis does for you. Brokenhearted or not, I won't stay with him if he can't say the words. You know, you're not the only one stumbling around in the dark these days. Sometimes, I think all of us are a little bit blind."

TEN
MAXIMILLION

I sadora's letter burned at the bottom of his desk like a secret flame. He ignored it, but not really. It filled his head constantly, like living in a nightmare.

Normally, the ring of glass paned windows and snowy vistas of his turret office provided a sense of escape and a reprieve from the pressures of his work. Today, the world felt too bright. Too cold. Too close. He longed to curl away and . . .

What?

What else would he do if not this?

He paced in front of his desk, chewing on his bottom lip.

Oh, Isadora's list of demands last night had been fair enough. Meet her family, court her, ask questions. He felt proud of her thoroughness, and grateful for such straightforward expectations. One couldn't blame her for what she wanted.

Until he read the last one.

. . .

4. I want you to tell me you love me. In words. Out loud. And mean it.

She could have asked for anything else, and he would have given it to her. Wildrose. All his currency. Passion and tenderness and a life together.

Not that.

He ran his tongue over his front teeth, considering the sound and shape of such words. They way they did—or rather, did *not*—roll off the tongue. *I love you.* He'd never heard them before, except maybe from Charlie. Ranulf and Pearl had implied the words often, but never outright said them.

They were more than words, anyway. They were a covenant heart-tie. A forged bond. An everlasting promise to be something to the other.

The deepest of oaths.

He muttered a curse under his breath, shook his head, and glanced up when a rap came on the door. Wally called through the wood.

"Ambassador?"

"Yes?"

"The new Ambassador to the Eastern Network has arrived for your initial meeting."

Max cursed again. Of course. His aunt Serafina, the reigning High Priestess of the East—though he doubted that would last for long in an insufferable place like the Eastern Network—had swept out the old Network Council and structure of her husband, Dante. She'd spent the last week and a half placing new witches into power in a generalized reform.

Max strode to the door, gripped the handle. He closed his eyes, pulled in a deep breath. Felt the cool air curl through his lungs, dissolving into the space, before he let it back out.

Tranquility arrived.

He stuffed aside thoughts of Isadora, courting, and other concerns for later. The door opened. He gave a cordial nod to a slight male witch with spectacles perched on the end of his nose.

"Ambassador Vargara, welcome to my office."

ELEVEN

SANNA

The smell of flowers thickened the air.

Sanna tilted her nose back, startled by the fragrance. Flowers this time of year?

Luteis, are there flowers here?

Yes.

What colors?

Blue, orange, and yellow.

Those are Mam's favorite, I think. The smell is familiar. Like citrus and honeysuckle.

What a fortunate coincidence.

Unlikely to be a coincidence at all, but Sanna didn't voice that. Mam, or someone else, must have used magic to make the flowers bloom.

The sound of giggling children, and a cry from farther away, bounced off the close spaces of the lower floor where Mam and Sanna lived. Sanna shrank back into the hallway, away from the chaos. She counted at least four voices, but there could have been more. More than five and it became too overwhelming to keep track.

Luteis couldn't follow her in here, and he didn't like

peeping in through the windows. In fact, no one liked a giant dragon squinting at them. Which only made it more difficult to understand what she didn't see in the room.

These old houses in the Dragonmaster village, at the base of the Circle of the Ancients, had been a quick, safe refuge when they needed it the most. The remaining Dragonmasters had fled from burned Anguis and set up a new community here, one that made it easy for Elliot and Mam to merge lives. Elliot and his children lived just next door, so Mam didn't have far to go.

Which meant Sanna *could* stay here in this big house. Technically, it gave her what she wanted most. A place to live.

Except, not really *with* her dragon. Nor with her desired privacy. She didn't want to live right next to other witches who would intimately know her daily routines. Mostly, she didn't want to need them.

She craved the freedom of her own place. The ability to do what she wanted with it, piece it together. The walls would be shorter, not quite this tall, as she didn't need a lot of space.

Only a couple of weeks had passed since her sight completely disappeared, which meant that the hope of living alone might be asking too much.

Did she know how?

Had she adapted enough to her changing sight to be alone?

Weeks or not, it felt like an age.

Isadora's plea to her to consider learning from another blind witch continued to ring through her mind. Not a *bad* idea, certainly. But it would require her to go into the Network. Unless the witch would come here?

No. Elliot wouldn't like that. Neither would Mam. They wouldn't want others to know they lived here, even if the witch wasn't a threat. Besides, could blind witches transport?

How long would it take a witch to arrive here by walking? Someone would have to escort them . . .

Sanna shook her head.

Too many questions.

Hand ahead of her, she stepped toward the staircase on her right. Her right hand found the wall before her left found the banister. She walked up, toward Mam's room. At the top, she called out.

"Mam?"

A door breezed open to her left with a stirring of air. Sanna turned toward it. Mam spoke, her voice thick with tears.

"Sanna?"

Arms wrapped her. Sanna jolted, not expecting it, but didn't pull away. Mam gave a little cry into Sanna's shoulder.

Awkwardly, Sanna patted her back.

"Mam?"

"I'm sorry. I'm just . . . I'm emotional today. Come inside. Isadora just wrote. She should be here any moment now."

Mam grabbed Sanna's wrist and tugged her in. She stumbled to a stop, momentarily disoriented until she could find the wall on her side. The rustle of a dress followed. When Mam spoke, she sounded quieter.

"What's wrong?" Sanna asked.

Mam sniffled. "I miss your Daid, that's all."

"Daid?"

"Isn't that strange?" Mam laughed, a breathy bundle of tight, strung-out nerves. "I'm handfasting another man, yet I can't stop thinking about Rian. I just . . . I miss him."

"Me too."

"He would have wanted this, I think. Elliot is a good man, and it's not like we plan on having children. I'm beyond that now and with his four and the three that Adelina left behind, we already have so many mouths to feed. This is companionship and survival and . . . I'm not so afraid when Elliot is with me."

The conviction in Mam's voice struck a deep chord. Sanna sobered, washing away her frustrations. Her fears. Because of Luteis, she never thought of what it must be like for Mam to live without Daid on a day-to-day basis.

"Mam, I'm sorry that I left the other day."

"Oh, I expected that," Mam drawled wryly. "I'm always upsetting you, Sanna."

Sanna hid a wince. She deserved that.

"I'm happy for you and Elliot."

"Are you?"

The uncertain question also made her wince, but perhaps she deserved that, too. "Yes, I truly am. I'm sorry that I didn't act like it at first. It just . . . it surprised me, that's all. I don't want you to be alone and I want you to be safe. Elliot is a good man. He was like a daid to me after Daid died. Both of you are grieving. It . . . makes sense, as you said."

A warm hand came to her cheek. Sanna leaned into it.

"I know, *amo*. There has been so much change for you. My hope is . . . at least . . . this is one thing that might help you?"

Sanna kept her body from stiffening by sheer willpower. Would their handfasting help her? She could see why Mam might think so. If Mam lived with Elliot, Sanna could stay in this house by herself, close to others that might help her.

She could.

But that wouldn't take her away from the constant whispers. The questions. The awkward silences when she walked into a room and no one knew what to say. Or if one of Elliot's children grabbed her arm in an attempt to help her when she didn't need it.

There was too much history behind all of them for her to stay here. To them, she was a fallen Sanna of the forest. The one who used to run on the branches and understood the dragons. She had once been a leader.

Now?

She needed something new.

Fresh.

Hers.

Yet, she couldn't tell Mam that. Not today, on her hand-fasting day.

"Mam, you're doing the right thing."

A clear voice came from the doorway. "Yes, you are."

Sanna whirled, grateful Isadora had arrived. She wished only that she could *see* her. Did she dress up for this day? Had Maximillion bought her new gowns befitting an Ambassador's wife? Isadora approached, slipped her hand in Sanna's. Mam let out a peep of a sob.

"Happy tears!" she insisted, hugging them both. "These are happy tears."

"Of course they are, Mam," Isadora said with a little laugh. "We all miss Daid, but we're happy for you and Elliot. Daid would approve. This will be so much better for all of us in many ways. Sanna and I are here for you through all of it."

Isadora pulled Sanna closer, her fingertips digging into Sanna's side. Sanna leaned into her sister's firm hold, not sure of who held up who.

A long minute later, Isadora pulled back. "Now, let's get you handfasted and have a little party! I might have been snooping, but I thought I saw a Leto nut cake down there and I. am. starving. Also, Max sent a few treats as a congratulation. I think you all will be pleasantly surprised."

———

Twenty minutes later, Isadora squeezed Sanna's hand. "Mam is lovely, standing next to Elliot," she whispered in her ear. "He has his best clothes on—they're still quite patchy, but you can tell he tried—and what little hair he has left is brushed to the side. It's horrible, Sanna. Truly."

A giggle interrupted her. Sanna rolled her lips to keep from laughing as Isadora tightened her hold on Sanna's fingers.

"You would die laughing if you saw it, but don't tell anyone I said so. He looks so proud. Mam's tears have dried up. She's all smiles, and she seems quite content. Oh, they're starting their promises. Elliot has taken both of Mam's hands and he's holding them so tight, his knuckles look white. I think he's nervous. Oops! I better be quiet."

According to Isadora, witches in the Network had another witch handfast them, instead of just doing it themselves the way the Dragonmasters did. Elliot spoke first, promising Mam protection, shelter, and companionship. His deep voice rang through the room.

Mam's more demure, raspy voice followed with similar vows. They ended as quickly as his. Though simple, they were heartfelt.

Commotion broke on the other side of the room after a short pause. Elliot's five children—only Lucey wasn't present —and the three Parker kids whooped and cheered.

"Just kissing," Isadora said with a laugh. "That's all you're missing."

Kissing? Sanna fought back a wave of nausea. Gross. She didn't want to think about Mam and Elliot that way. Isadora stood up, prompting Sanna to do the same, and everyone clapped lightly as the clomping of feet went by.

"Where are they going?" Sanna asked. Isadora kept their arms looped together as she half-twisted to look behind her.

"To throw the herb sachet out the door for good luck! Might as well wait in here. They'll be back, and there's not much to see."

"Literally," Sanna said dryly.

Isadora laughed.

Elliot's children thundered after the happy couple, shouting. Above it, Sanna heard Mam laughing and calling out in response. Slowly, Isadora sat back down and Sanna followed. Relieved for a moment of quiet, Sanna tried to reorient to the room. Her hand reached out, feeling in front of her.

Nothing.

"Where is Max?"

"At work."

A hint of shock filled Sanna's voice. "He couldn't make it for this?"

Isadora stiffened ever-so-slightly, though her tone remained light and unbothered. "Not with final Network negotiations around the Mansfeld Pact hitting a new crest. He sent a gift for them, but I didn't ask him to attend. It seemed . . . like too big of an ask."

Movement seemed to indicate motion, as if Isadora had waved a hand toward something.

"The gift is from his Assistant," Isadora continued, a bit aimlessly. "It's a beautiful bouquet of flowers from a hot house somewhere and a card. Mam's favorite flowers, even."

Ah.

So that explained the smell.

"He also sent some treats from a bakery. There's not much sugar, but they managed to scrape together some sort of frosting that's delicious."

"That's very kind."

"I thought so, too."

They fell back into silence as feet returned amidst peals of laughter and low, rolling chuckles. Somewhere in that mess, Jesse would be helping his siblings. She thought she heard his voice making a few commands, but ignored it. In the chaos, they hadn't spoken yet. That was fine. With Mam's motivations at the top of Sanna's mind, she wasn't sure she wanted to talk to Jesse right now.

A body lowered onto the chair at Sanna's right and an arm squeezed her shoulders.

"Thank you," Mam whispered, "for being here."

A kiss pressed to Sanna's temple followed, and Mam retreated again. Calls for food in the kitchen sent the plethora of noises back out the door. From the forest came a familiar sound of scales sliding across ground, fluttering, giant wings. Luteis' serpentine voice followed.

Has the ceremony finished?

Yes, I believe Mam is feeding those who came.

"I better help Mam," Isa said. "Do you want to come into the kitchen?"

"Not really."

Isadora paused, hand still on Sanna's. "What do you want, Sanna?"

My eyes back.

To see the forest, not just smell it.

My home.

"I don't want to be here," she said slowly. "Can I have a break? There's . . . a lot of noise and . . . I'm overwhelmed."

Isadora squeezed her fingers. "Go with Luteis. Take a break. I'll help Mam and keep her occupied. Come back in an hour. Things will have settled by then."

With relief, Sanna stood up.

"Two chairs," Isadora called. "Take a right."

Fumbling to find the backs of the chairs, Sanna worked her way slowly to what she presumed was the middle of the room. A cool rush of air led her to the right.

I'm here, little one.

Coming.

Hand ahead of her, Sanna stepped out of the house and into the forest, feeling the soft earth at her feet in relief. A rush of heat slid past. She reached out, touched the edge of a waiting wing, and followed him into the trees. Somehow, Mam's handfasting threw into sharp relief exactly what Sanna wanted, and it wasn't the Dragonmasters.

Once at Luteis's side, his tail wrapped her wrist. She followed it, climbed carefully up his back, and settled at the juncture of his neck.

"Luteis, I know what I want."

What is that?

"To build my own house in Letum Wood and live there with you. No more mumbling about it. We're going to *do* it."

Twelve

Isadora

Mam lifted an inquiring brow when Isadora entered the kitchen after making sure Sanna made it to Luteis without harm. Elliot dealt with a skinned, bloody knee and hiccuping cries on the other side of the room.

"Sanna is fine," Isa said to Mam's silent question. "Just needs a break. I think the noise is overwhelming. Luteis was waiting outside."

A crestfallen expression followed. Mam erased it behind a courageous smile.

"Thank you, Isa. I've managed to pull together something of a nut cake, as you saw. Doesn't have much air to it—it's more like a dense bread—but it's lightly sweet from some honey we managed to scrounge together."

"Looks delicious!"

With a spell, Isadora conjured the pastries Max had paid for. An idea that she suspected came from Max, but Wally executed. Mam reared back, eyes wide.

"Oh!"

"From Max." She smiled, hoping it didn't show the trepidation she felt around saying *my husband*. "He apologizes for not being able to come, but Network affairs are hard for him to break away from right now. And he hasn't officially met the family. Would have been weird to pull attention away from the handfasting and onto him."

Mam touched a triangular pastry with awe. "Tell him thank you."

Though Mam had been raised in the Networks, she hadn't left Letum Wood or the Dragonmaster families in decades. A quick nod affirmed Mam's appreciation. Isadora thought of summoning the flowers he sent from the other room, but decided against it at the last moment. Later, she'd notice.

To Isadora's surprise, she missed Max and wanted him by her side. The moment to introduce him to her family would come. For certain, it wasn't now. Not at the merging point of two grieving families and a broken community. Dragons parted from witches forever. Their leader sightless as a result, struck low.

As little change as possible is what the Dragonmaster families needed.

The pastry crumbled a bit at the end when Mam broke a piece away and placed it on the tip of her tongue. Her eyes closed.

"Oh," she murmured. "That is delicious. So very rich and flaky."

"I'm happy to hear that."

Normally, it would shine with a light glaze of sugar across the top, but lacking supplies from all of Greta's wars made sugar difficult to forage. It might take months to rebalance food supplies, if that could be done at all. With borders closing and exports shut down, all lay in chaos.

Isadora reached for a wooden plate, sanded smooth and square, as Mam pressed a sharp knife into the pastries. A pathetic wedding cake, indeed, but better than water and limp, bitter greens.

"You looked lovely up there, Mam."

Mam gave her a humored glance. Elliot slipped out of the room, gathering the hiccuping child by the hand and leading them out.

"Thank you," Mam said, her gaze following him. Once gone, she said in a lower tone, "Well, what are your thoughts about all of this?"

"That you're wise."

Mam kept a careful eye on her as she balanced a thin slice of Leto nut cake on the knife edge. She carefully placed it onto the waiting plate.

"You're not . . . upset because Elliot isn't your father?"

"Of course not, Mam. As you're aware," she drawled. They'd had this discussion before, but insecurity lingered in Mam's eyes.

"Well." Mam shrugged. "Saying it and seeing it are two different things. After the year or two we've had . . ."

She trailed away. Isadora understood the quiet resilience in Mam's voice. The need for safety, yet approval. The feeling that she was no longer a child in Mam's eyes propelled her out of the moment with a sense of shock.

Did handfasting Max change the dynamic, or was this a simple result from growing up?

She couldn't help but wonder how Mam felt about Sanna. Did she view Sanna as an adult, or as an adult child? The difference spanned a vast chasm. Isadora pulled another plate off the stack, held it up.

"Tell me about life with the Ambassador of the Central Network."

"Ah . . . he always surprises me. He lives in a lovely estate named Wildrose Manor."

"He?"

Heat blossomed across her chest. "We, I mean. We live in Wildrose Manor."

A hint of a smile threatened at the edge of Mam's lips. "A manor?"

Isadora nodded.

"Sounds intriguing."

"It's very . . . vast."

Mam paused, eyebrow lifted. "You don't like it?"

"I do," she rushed to say. "I do. It's just . . . so big. I'm used to small and cozy and easy to clean."

A chortle rolled out of Mam as she sank the knife into her rounded cake. "Yes, you are the daughter I always knew. Pragmatic and in no way interested in housekeeping."

Isadora fought with a smile.

"I suppose it doesn't matter what size it is, it's just . . . not home," Isa said softly. Mam paused, reached over. Her hand rested on Isadora's arm.

"Not yet," she whispered. "But I think you'll soon find that home isn't a place. Home is where your witches are."

"What if he's not really mine?"

Barely repressed curiosity filled Mam's gaze, but Isadora shook her head. "Never mind. That's not a fair question to ask. Not yet. It's too soon in our handfasting to tell. Anyway, can we talk about something else?"

"Sure."

Contemplative quiet followed while they plated a slice of cake, and part of a pastry, for each witch present. The time loosened Isadora's bunching nerves. Talking about Max with Mam was . . . so strange. Like mixing oil and water. Her two lives would never truly merge.

"Mam?"

"Yes, Isa."

"Will you be happy?"

Mam paused, seemed to think about the question, and said, "I am content and that's all I ever wanted after Rian passed. Elliot is a good man. His children are well-behaved.

There will be companionship and mutual respect and warmth. It's enough."

Something cold settled deep in Isadora's stomach. Authenticity rang from Mam's words. Isa didn't doubt that, should Mam have the chance to change the past, she'd bring Daid back from the dead and forget Elliot existed. Since that was impossible, Mam had to make do with what she had. A relationship built out of practicality and trust.

Eventually, could she forge something like that with Max?

No, her heart whispered. *It's too late for that.*

Indeed, she loved him far too much for practicality already. Resolution filled her with renewed strength. Maybe she didn't love Wildrose, nor feel as if it were home. Maybe she didn't understand her husband or how their two impossibly different lives would ever mold together.

But by the gods, she would die trying. No matter what came of her experiment, she would figure out if love was enough.

THIRTEEN
MAXIMILLION

Max straightened his jacket, itched his nose, and ignored the pull between his shoulders. Despite his fidgeting, dressmaker Bella still stared at him with wide eyes, mouth slack.

"You're jesting."

"I'm not," he muttered.

Her astonishment deepened. Wide-eyed, she leaned on the table that rested between them. She must have used a potion to elongate her eyelashes, for he'd never seen eye fans that wide.

Bella straightened. "Handfasted?"

"Happily so."

She set her hands on rounded hips, ignoring his dry tone. A rolling laugh followed. "I heard rumors, of course, but thought it drivel. You know how the gossip columns stir up anything for a read. I mean, if there was any witch I had assumed would never . . ."

In her daze, he couldn't help but wonder what he saw in her before. An outlet, perhaps. Unfair of him, but true nonetheless. Bella had been a safe arm through his when social etiquette required a companion. She achieved her equally selfish purposes through him. Societal advancement, for one. After being seen on his arm for one gala, her dressmaker's shop had been flooded with new customers for weeks.

She required no idle chat, asked no questions, and showed herself presentable for every occasion.

As well as . . . other necessities.

"Do you love her?"

He scowled. "Not your business."

She laughed. "Oh ho! Now it's none of my business?"

"My emotions are of no concern to you."

Bella's brow lifted. "Not at all," she cried. "Except for how well I know you. Does the poor lass know what she's gotten into?"

"Obviously," he gritted out from between clenched teeth. Bella hit a little too close to home—and the somewhat turbulent atmosphere at Wildrose—with such a question.

"Don't send her on a chase, Max. You bottle all things up. Don't do that with a wife, if you really care."

"Your advice has not been requested."

Bella smiled like a cat. "And yet," she drawled, "I'm giving it."

"There's more than one way to show love that doesn't involve the words."

"Right. Speaking to another woman about your wife is surely the secondary route for deepest affection."

"Bella . . ."

His warning fell on deaf ears. She laughed to herself. He almost didn't come here today, fearing a jealous woman. Bella was too detached for anything like jealousy, but her surprise was deeper than expected.

"Who is she?"

"No one you'd know."

She rolled her eyes. "I'll find out, Max. You know I will."

"I know."

"You're not going to tell me?"

"Why? You have your sources. There are better things to do with my time than fuel your lust to know the latest news."

"Then I'll seek it out on my own and stir up all sorts of publicity while I do it."

Ah, the Bella he knew best. Cutthroat, and effective. He hesitated. In fact, he *didn't* want that. Who knew what manner of unsavory rumors Bella might land on and then spread herself—in the name of thwarted positions. Bella might not hold envy, but she didn't enjoy being usurped either.

"I'll bring her for a fitting."

Curiosity glittered in her coy stare. "Here?"

"Give me a slot and I'll make it happen. You can satisfy your questions with your own eyes, instead of mongering amongst the dregs of society."

With a nod, she agreed. "I shall look forward to meeting the woman who secured your safety. How *else* can I help you, Max? Surely you aren't here to bring the good news?"

"I came to ask you for . . . a favor, I suppose."

She waved a hand, blinking fast, as a wordless indication to continue.

"Ah . . ."

Realizing his stupidity too late, Max fought to find the right words. *I don't know how to court my own wife* was a little too close to home. As well as *I've never done this before and have no idea how to do it.*

There were some things Bella didn't need to know.

"I've been away quite a bit," he finally said. "I'd love some ideas for how to . . . do something special for her."

An eyebrow rose, finely blonde but lined with a darker brown to highlight her face shape. She'd once explained all her preparations before one of their social events, and the sheer time requirement boggled him.

"So you came to me?"

"You're a woman of experience and wisdom in the ways of women. I need a few . . . ideas."

"Have you asked her what she'd like?"

"I'd like to surprise her."

"Is she a typical woman?"

"In what way?"

She chortled. "Does she like romance? Can you sweep her off her feet with flowers?"

"Oh." Max raked his mind, completely unmoored by the question. Isadora didn't strike him as the usual romantic type. She came from a background of witches who handfasted for practical reasons, from what he could tell.

And yet . . .

"I would consider her a romantic, yes."

"Well, a candlelight dinner is always nice."

"Where?"

She shrugged. "Somewhere nice? You know all the fancy restaurants in the city. *The Castle Faire* is good for their desserts, but their menu is quite . . . lacking . . . with all the wars and things. To that end, ignore the fancy dinner idea. What about a quiet picnic?"

"A picnic?"

"Maybe she'd just like to be alone with you?"

"It's winter, Bella."

"So take candles."

"In the cold?"

"Warm her with your passion." She winked. "I know it's hot enough."

He growled. "This is not helpful. If I wanted to freeze her out of my life I could take her on a picnic in the woods in the depths of winter. I'd really rather she stayed around. We need something . . . romantic and pragmatic, I think."

Nonplussed, Bella leaned back. "Then good luck figuring it out, since you're so open to feedback."

Max let out a breath. "I'm sorry. I just . . . I'm not sure how to do this."

Bella paused for a long while, studying him. With an exasperated breath, she leaned forward. Loose, blonde curls slanted onto her slender shoulders.

"Max, get out of your own way."

With that, she straightened up and stepped back. The *ting* of a bell announced a new customer. Max turned his back to the door and transported away, deeper in the quagmire of how to tell his wife he loved her.

Without saying the words.

Fourteen

Sanna

What is it you're seeking in the . . . place . . . where you want to live?

A twig popped out of nowhere, smacking Sanna in the nose. She reached out, cracked it in half, and shoved it away. Her eyes welled up with tears that she blinked back.

Mori, that stung!

The swish of Luteis's tail was a comforting sound as she crept forward again. "Sorry, what did you ask?"

Patiently, he repeated. *What is it you're seeking in the place that you want to live?*

"Somewhere in the forest?"

You must be more specific if we are to create a plan.

Sanna sighed. "Somewhere *far* in the forest. I don't want to worry about other witches finding me."

On this we are agreed.

"A place with an open clearing, perhaps? Somewhere near a tree, with roots. A stream, too. The roots in the ground, the tree, the stream, can help orient me to where I am. I can hear the stream and know where to go. Memorize the roots, maybe? They don't move around like rocks might."

She trailed away, head cocked. No sound of water here. Luteis's tail twitched by her ankle.

We may need to try somewhere else. How big is this house that you want?

"Small. It's just me."

What about whelps?

Her nose scrunched. "No, thanks. No whelps for me."

Hmm . . .

He grumbled his displeasure. She ignored it. If Luteis wanted whelps, he could have them himself. She wouldn't say no to a baby dragon. Their fire was wild, but they had a sweet temperament until they were one or two. She wouldn't be able to trust them in her home after that.

A sniff came from behind her.

This way, little one. To your right. I think I smell water.

She obeyed, turning a sharp right that he corrected with his tail on her shoulders. Hands swinging around in front of her, she continued in that direction.

Will you need help from other witches?

"With what?"

Witch things.

The vague reply made her laugh. "Do you need help from other dragons with dragon things?"

No.

"There you go."

You always have me to protect you and hunt for you.

"Thank you. I hope so?"

But I cannot do witch things.

"I never expected it. I *can* take care of myself, Luteis."

He harrumphed. *I am not doubting our ability, simply inquiring to make sure all aspects are accounted for. To witches, it appears that selecting a home is an . . . important thing. To dragons, the entire forest is our home. This isn't a ritual in which we participate.*

"True."

Notify me if I miss anything important?

She stifled a smile. "I will."

The rush of a brook trickling by filled her ears. Sanna peeled several bushes out of her way, then paused. Something wet tickled the bottom of her feet, suddenly cool. The air changed, taking on a different scent. Vaporish and musty. She tilted her head back to sniff.

"Water?"

Indeed.

"Good work, Luteis. You found a stream. That's a great start."

The lapping sound of him drinking followed. He stopped. *Brackish.* Luteis sneezed. *It is not delicious or refreshing.*

"What does it look like here?"

A swamp.

"Oh."

I might not mind, if you don't. Except the water has a foul taste and odor. Forgive me, I do mind.

"Is this a pond? Standing water?"

Both?

"What do you see?"

Water.

Sanna nearly growled. Isadora instinctively saw the details for her out loud. A dragon might, she supposed, need a bit more coaching.

"No, tell me what you *see*. How many trees? Are they mossy? Boulders? How much water?"

A pause followed for so long that Sanna wondered if he heard. Had he slithered away to look at something and she didn't realize it?

These details are important to you?

"Yes."

Why? You cannot see them to appreciate beauty or not.

"Well . . . I . . ."

The silence continued to stretch. Sanna's shoulders relaxed down. "I guess it doesn't matter, but if it's a really wet place, it wouldn't be good to build a house. There might be more rodents or the wood of the house would wear away. Not to mention bugs in the summer. If this is a bog, they'd be unbearable."

This makes sense. So, you require me to see for you in order to determine if this is a good place for a dwelling?

"Yes. I hadn't thought of it, but yes."

Another pause.

"So?" she cried when the silence stretched too long. "What do you see?"

I see rocks. Dirt. Some water with floating green things. There are many small trees, bushes.

"Probably not a good place to live, then, if the water is stagnant."

It appears to have little movement.

Sanna stepped back. "All right, where else can we go? Maybe this leads to deeper water somewhere?"

Upstream. There may be more free-flowing water for your witchy stomach, which is quite weak.

She let that slide.

"C'mon," she murmured and braced herself for a jarring ride on his shoulders. "Let's go upstream, then."

———

Luteis slinked along the forest with smooth steps. Sanna barely stirred on his back. The forest soared in a canopy overhead that she no longer saw. She couldn't touch it—it was too far away—but sensed it hovering.

Waiting.

Existing in the nuance of sound.

The bump of riding on Luteis' back, at the junction of his body and neck, soothed her. Hours of searching had passed. She couldn't tell what time of day it was, but her growling stomach indicated she missed lunch.

Where she would find food out here in the winter, she couldn't imagine. With his firm scales under her legs, and the smell of Letum Wood a surrounding embrace, the too-large world became a little familiar again.

Even if it was scary.

Lower yourself, little one.

She hunched over, kept her fingertips high. A branch passed overhead, the mossy edges grazing her hand.

"Am I clear?"

Yes.

He lumbered on. Sanna straightened.

"Any luck?"

We are following a stream. Can you hear?

"Sometimes."

Along this stream are many bushes. In the summer, they'll be far thicker than now, and there are already too many.

"Thank you," she said quietly. "When you describe it, it's easier."

I shall strive to improve on the skill, little one.

She touched his flank in silent appreciation, then lifted her shoulders in a bolstering breath. "Well, we just started searching and it's only been a day."

Correct.

"Let's keep going."

As you wish.

His placid stroll was soothing in itself, particularly in the quiet. Only one bird whistled by. Most of them had tucked away for the winter, or escaped to warmer climes.

I will head more to the east, he said, more to himself than to her. *There is another branch of the stream there to check. Would you prefer that I walk or shall I fly?*

Her hands curled into fists. The thought of flying was . . . well, something she wasn't ready for. Flinging into the sky, unable to see didn't sound as fun as before.

Her response was a rasp. "Give me time?"

Always, little one.

Onward, he strolled.

Minutes later, Sanna could bear the silence no more. "Isadora agrees with Mam about me needing to find help. Another witch to guide me as I adapt to being blind."

So I heard.

"What do you think?"

He harrumphed. *I was tempted to be insulted in their lacking belief around our relationship, but I understand their concern. If I had a whelp, then I would also be afraid for it.*

"Thanks. I think."

What do you desire, little one?

"My old life."

That's not possible.

"I know, which is why we're searching out our own new life. A different version of the one we wanted before."

Do you know what this new life will look like? Beyond your special witch-dwelling.

"Not exactly. All I know is that I don't want to live with Mam and Elliot, and I definitely don't want to live in a town or a city with witches surrounding me that I don't know and can't see. Particularly without you," she added morosely.

The thought sent a shudder through her.

We are agreed. Can you build this . . . home?

"Not alone."

Could we, together?

She snorted at the thought. All the timbers, nails,

hammers that such work required would be hard to find, not to mention use. What a nightmare for a dragon to construct a house. One wrong sneeze from Luteis and the whole thing would burst into flames.

"If we built it from stone, perhaps?"

He growled in his throat, a thoughtful sign. Until this moment, she hadn't considered the option, but it sounded better than flammable wood with him around.

Where would we find such stones?

"In a quarry?"

What is this quarry you speak of?

"A place where you find rocks, I think. I've never been to one officially. Daid used the word a few times, but I don't think there is one in the forest. Maybe in the North? The mountain dragons would know, for certain."

They do have large boulders there.

"Very large boulders."

A whimsical smile found her face as she recalled the stony mountains, stark ridges, of Selsay's domain. The buttresses of rock defied all understanding. Thinking of the mountain dragons made her think of the forest dragons. Cara, Junis, Elis. They'd all but faded into the forest, forgetting her.

She longed to see them again.

Could we speak to Metok about this . . . quarry?

"I don't know. I assume we'd have to fly there."

Lower yourself.

Sanna obeyed. The sensation of something passing overhead followed. She fell into deeper thought, straightening when he indicated it was safe with a rumble.

How big will this dwelling of yours be?

"Smaller than Mam's house."

More than one height?

"Um, no? I guess not. I don't need a lot of space."

Do you plan to mate?

"Ugh. No."

There is disgust in your voice. You don't find this agreeable?

Thoughts of Jesse and handfasting and all the closeness that came with another witch in her life swelled up at once. Not all of those thoughts were fair. Jesse was a wonderful witch—a close friend. Just . . . not someone she wanted anything close to a handfasting with.

"Not really."

Is this unusual?

"I don't know."

Hmmm . . .

Sanna fell quiet. She had anchored herself almost entirely to Luteis, hadn't she? Thoughts of husbands or babies or other witches in her life, outside of Mam and Isadora, hadn't even occurred to her.

She shifted, uncomfortable with the thought.

We can't have your witch-place too close to the stream, he continued, oblivious to her own thoughts, *as flooding might be an issue. You're certain you won't need access to other witches?*

"No."

I have my doubts.

"We can live out here with just the two of us. That's what you wanted to do as nomads, right?"

He paused, then said, *There is much planning to do.*

Her nose wrinkled. Indeed, more than she'd expected. Now that he plagued her with questions she wasn't ready to answer, she wasn't sure where to start. The overwhelm of beginning again made her want to tuck into his side and cover up with his wing.

That would accomplish nothing, but the urge proved strong.

"We'll answer those questions when we must," she said firmly. "For now, we need to find the perfect spot. Close to a stream, but not too close. Not much undergrowth, or at least small enough amounts we can clear it away. We'll figure out wood, stone, windows, hearths, all that later."

I am impressed, little one. Your organizational skills have increased since you met me.

Sanna chuckled, hardly able to help it.

"Thanks, I think."

One last question?

"Yes?"

Do we need to fear other witches? Would other witches be more likely to harm you because of your lacking sight? I have felt deep concern over this, but am not sure if witches would be less inclined or more. Dragons don't prey on the weak. There is no honor in it.

The curling fear in her chest increased twofold.

"Yes," she whispered. "Witches don't have the same amount of honor as dragons. That's why I want to live in the forest, Luteis. Deep in Letum Wood, where other witches can't find us. The distance alone would keep me safe. You wouldn't have to worry about me as much."

I can see the benefit.

His drawling tone left something to be desired.

"But?"

My concern rests primarily with your lack of scales. You become cold quite easily, and you lack internal fire. Will a house of stones keep you warm? Wouldn't it be better to remain with me where my wing provides certain heat?

She laughed. "There would be a fireplace."

That you could run yourself?

Sanna faltered. "Well . . . y-yes, of course." More confidently, she stated, "Even without sight, I'm positive that I can start a fire."

A moment of thought preceded his reply.

In this, I believe you. You have always exceeded impossible odds. We will always be together, so I can always conjure fire for you. With any luck, I shall outlive you.

"That's . . . bleak."

Is it? True surprise filled his tone. *I thought it was obvious. I'm only fifty-something years old. My ancestors often lived to one hundred and eighty, which is beyond the age of a witch.*

Sanna lifted both hands. "See, Mam!" she called, though Mam would never hear. "Luteis will always be enough!"

Her hands rested on his warm scales, burning brightly below her palm. Quietly, she whispered, "Always enough."

He purred as they ambled into the forest.

Let's resume our search for the perfect witch-place. Tell me what you want, and my eyes will find it. Together, little one, we'll prove all of them wrong.

Fifteen
Isadora

Despite having all of Wildrose in which to eat, including an elegant dining room with stools for chairs and a chandelier made out of tree branches, with green candles to burn, Isadora chose the kitchen.

The snug space heated faster. Not to mention an easy-to-access woodpile just outside the kitchen, thanks to the young lad Ean, whom she hadn't yet met. A table on the far side provided plenty of space for both Isadora and Max. Using the kitchen lessened the need to clean another room later.

How Faye kept up with this place, she'd never fathom.

Isadora's cup clinked gently when she set it back on the saucer. Blunted morning light brightened outside. Max peered at her from over the top of his coffee. She met his gaze, eyebrows high. He lowered his cup, gaze filled with smoky question.

"Well?" he asked.

His deep rumble flipped her stomach. Isadora swallowed. He'd been working like a madman for days, barely home except to eat dinner and fall into bed. Sitting with him in such a normal setting stirred her up inside.

The rhythm resembled the one they shared in the Southern Network—perhaps a prelude to what life with Max would be—and had been soothing while she grappled to find her footing in a new world.

Yet again.

"Well, what?" she asked, then sipped. The taste of lavender and honey flooded her mouth. Max set aside the newsscroll, stretched an arm over the chair next to him.

"What do you think of my idea?"

In fact, she had fidgeted over his idea for the last ten minutes. *You are in need of more dresses, I've noticed,* he said when she entered the kitchen. *Would you be interested in shopping for them together? I have some opinions on current styles.*

The offer had been arresting and . . . sweet. Max spotted a necessity, a detail she hadn't pointed out to him, and offered to go with her. Such an event would have been mildly daunting on her own. Mam had always sewn her dresses. Though she'd experienced much of Network life the past two years, there were things that still terrified her. Basic things, like dress fittings.

Besides, Chatham City dressmakers were known for intensity of purpose in their work, and their social power. They were teeming hothouses of gossip. Maximillion's offer to go with her might have been a way to make a statement about their handfasting.

Or it might be an offer he felt obligated to give, considering the list she sent him days ago. If nothing else, he tried.

She'd honor that.

Isadora swallowed another mouthful of tea, not tasting its comforting palette anymore. It went down like a gulp.

"I think," she said slowly, running the edge of her finger along the rim, "that it's a good idea. If you go with me?"

Max paused, ceramic mug halfway to his mouth. He lifted an eyebrow, as if startled that she accepted. She fought back a chuckle. Oh, how hard he tried, even if sloppily executed. He set the mug back down.

"Then the dressmaker is prepared to see us at noon today. I managed to procure an appointment."

"Aren't wait lists six months long?"

"Yes."

Her fingers toyed with the end of her sleeve as she waited for an explanation that didn't come. She refused to feel embarrassed over the disheveled state of her clothes. No one wore fresh fabric or finery these days. No one *she* knew, anyway.

Some hesitation rose.

The dissolution of all the border wars had eased food demands on the Network, allowing more to distribute to the populace instead of the Guardians. Disbanding Guardians and the remnants of so many battles, however, left haunted witches everywhere. Textiles were far from resuming their usual market.

If nothing else, going to the dressmaker provided the perfect opportunity to satisfy a burning question: could they survive routine life *and* extraordinary circumstances?

Mundane events would constitute most of their marriage, she'd wager. Handfasting was more than a string of wild, unanticipated happenings in different Networks.

"You have an eye for fashion, Max, whether or not it's something you'll admit to yourself. I look forward to your opinions and I trust your fashion sense."

He blinked, his lip twitching with the words *I trust.*

Though, I still don't trust you with my heart, she silently added.

He hid a glassy expression behind another sip of coffee. The flashing headlines from a *Chatterer* scroll illuminated the table near his breakfast plate. Max had woken early and set out several fried eggs, bread warmed over the fire on a grate, and a small crock of salt and one of butter.

Max had the capacity to care for himself—and her—that she'd never credited to him. Just because the man commanded Assistants and servants in the castle didn't mean he required them at home, a revelation that surprised her.

To great effect.

"I am happy to accompany you, fashion opinions notwithstanding."

"Well." Isadora lifted her teacup in silent salute, smiling. "I suppose I'll see you later at the dressmakers, Max."

She ended in a chortle.

He ignored her.

———

Bella's Dressmaker Shop was a narrow building set in between a painting boutique and a tobacco store. The air smelled like pipe leaves and turpentine.

Bright candlelight illuminated the interior. Sparkling mirrors made the thin store appear wider than normal. Along each wall, dresses. So many dresses. Most hung on velvet hangers, others on wooden. Flounced, petticoated, thin, silk, cotton. An overabundance of options awaited.

Isadora stalled in the doorway.

Max put a hand on her back. "Believe it or not," he murmured, "they won't eat you."

His cloying tone—one could almost say he *joked* with her —sent a thrill through her toes. Max pressed forward, bringing her with him.

"Miss Trusseau?"

A woman with wide, blonde curls and a pert nose popped into view. She sat behind a table littered with fabric and spools of thread. With a squeak, she straightened up.

"Welcome back, Max."

Max stiffened through the arms. "Bella. Good to see you again."

Color infused Bella's cheeks as she bustled over, a simple dress hanging off of ample hips. With curiosity, she studied Isadora. Her gaze lingered on Isadora's shoulders, chest, and hips, leaving a calculating sensation in the air. After inspecting Isadora's current fashion, Bella regarded her face.

A softening surprised Isadora.

"What has brought you here?" Bella inquired. Astonishment thickened her tone. A piece of lace drifted behind her left shoulder, trailing out. Fluffs of fabric and bits of string clung to the edges of her skirt.

Max opened his mouth to speak, but Isadora beat him to it. "Bella Trusseau." She stepped forward, a hand outstretched the way most Network witches appreciated. "I've heard so much about you. My name is Isadora Sinclair."

"Hopefully good things?"

"Yes, all of them."

"I've heard—"

Max stepped forward. Professional courtesy frosted his voice as he said, "Bella, my wife is here for a dress. Several of them. Will you be able to help her? We'll need a full collection, from formal wear to day dresses." He glanced at Isadora. "Something for outside as well?"

Gratified that he'd know her preferences, Isadora nodded. The awkwardness of how much currency this would cost lingered in her thoughts, but she let it go. If they were to remain handfasted, it would be *their* currency.

She had to think that way now, odd as it seemed.

Something in the situation lifted the hair on the back of her neck. Bella's darting gaze hid bewilderment—perhaps pain. All of a sudden, Isadora remembered Max's willingness to come with her to *this* shop, where he'd procured a slot despite a six-month waiting list.

There were other dressmaker shops, of course, but Bella Trusseau was known to be the most popular, according to rumors. Bella's broad range, yet affordable prices, sent regular witches and High Priestesses here alike.

Was Max making a statement today, or satisfying some of his own curiosity?

Bella drew in a deep breath, shoulders expanding with the motion. Her chin elevated. All vestiges of curiosity stuffed away.

"We have many styles that may be of interest to you, Mrs. Sinclair. If you will come with me, you may see them." She sent Max a hard glance as she bustled toward a back closet. "You may stay here."

Max returned her glittering stare.

Isadora froze.

She didn't want to go anywhere with that woman, and she didn't want to be in this store. Not with two hostile witches that seethed animosity. Bella continued across the room, shoes clacking in their path. As if reading her mind, Max leaned over to whisper in Isadora's ear.

"I'll explain everything once you have a satisfactory wardrobe. I promise."

The strength of his voice relieved some of the prickling hesitation. She glanced up. He met her gaze, his own unyielding. Not even a goddess could read a stare like that.

"Is there nowhere else?"

"There are other shops if you don't find anything you like, but . . . let's just say this meeting had to happen first if we are to satisfy your list."

A dozen questions surfaced with his reply, but Isadora ignored them. His pleading look asked for more than silence. He wanted trust—for at least an hour.

She warred within. She'd much rather call this confrontation for what it was: a reveal of his wife to society.

"I'll choose to trust you until you can explain."

His hold on her arm loosened. He nodded her toward the back, then peeled away to a bright pink divan near a cluster of mirrors and an elevated platform. His greatcoat billowed as he lowered to the edge of the seat, his jaw tight, knee bouncing.

Isadora found Bella at a long rack of dresses on the other side of the room. Bella glanced at her out of the corner of her eye as she approached, then swiveled with a stiff smile.

"How about this style?"

Isadora braced herself.

She couldn't wait for this to end.

Sixteen

Sanna

I t will be quite dark tonight, I predict. There will be no moon.

Sanna chuckled.

"I agree. Very dark."

Luteis snorted with amusement.

I'm hungry and desire more food. Will you . . . He hesitated. Sanna shifted on the leaves where she lay, a twig poking her between the shoulder blades.

"Will I what?"

Go with me?

She froze.

Since losing her sight for good during her confrontation with Deasylva, she'd avoided flight. She'd ridden Luteis back to the Central Network from the Western Network, but recalled none of it. The jeweled sky, glittering with stars against the velvet backdrop, didn't exist for her anymore.

The thought of hovering so far above the ground, unable to see . . .

"What other alternatives are there?"

You might stay, but it wouldn't be safe, either. You could wait for me at your Mam's home. I would be happy to take you there. We're only—

"No, I don't want to stay here without you, and I don't want to go to Mam's either. I mean . . . Elliot and Mam's."

Isn't it the same?

She sighed. "I don't know anymore. I'll go with you."

I would be happy to have you.

Sanna stood, arms held out. The end of his tail flopped on top with a heavy thud that nearly slammed her to the ground. She grunted, trapped the tail in her palms, and fought a chuckle.

"Thanks."

He snorted. The crackle of fire on burned branches followed.

"Any idea what part of the day it is?"

No.

"Is the sun out?"

Yes, but the sky is filled with miserable clouds.

"Middle of the day?"

Perhaps.

Sanna scowled. A talking watch would be most welcome. Perhaps a spell existed for such a thing?

A luxury like that would tempt her toward magic . . .

With her fingertips, she followed the curve of Luteis' thickening tail higher. The slippery scales were easy to climb with bare feet. A ridged spine ran up part of his back. She followed the outside edge with her right foot, walking carefully.

Though his wide body easily held her, the musculature and bones lacked permanence. He moved beneath her weight like a restless sea. Her arms wheeled as she stepped. He shifted, bracing his stance for better stability. She sensed movement ahead. Probably his neck swinging around to face her.

Are you well?

"I'm fine."

The ridges stilled near the side of her ankle, no longer shifting. She felt around with her toes, arms held out. Well, maybe this wasn't so bad. Walking on the back of a dragon was, well, the same as it was *with* sight.

She was only slightly more careful and far less certain.

Finally, the ridges ended. She swept her foot over, found a familiar, open juncture near his neck, and plopped onto it with a triumphant grin.

See? She wanted to say, though no one was here to listen. *I can do normal things!*

Luteis coiled his body beneath them, talons digging into the soil. With a grunt, he shoved off the earth. His wings sprawled, opening like wide, black banners. They snapped, pluming to the sides, and pumped.

The ripple of muscle and scale flowed beneath her legs, sending a jolt of power through her. His warmth didn't burn her skin. Though it would have burned any other witch, Deasylva's blessing protected her. His scales heated the backs of her legs in a friendly reminder of who she used to be.

She leaned forward, gripped his neck. The taut scales didn't have much give—thankfully weren't all that sharp, either—but enough she could grab a handful to keep herself seated.

Lean into me, little one.

She ducked.

The sensation of things wheeling over her head followed. Nausea bubbled up from the depths of her gut. The jostling, with no focal point to orient her as it jerked her around, shocked her. Her teeth slammed together, aching through her jaw.

They broke through the canopy.

Sanna's stomach lurched as Luteis straightened, leveling

above the forest. The vast openness felt different than the close confines.

We are through the trees.

The whirling ebbed. Slowly, Sanna released his scales and straightened. The sheer amount of open space sprawling like a globe, so vast and wide and unnerving, made her heart shrink in her stomach.

Fear paralyzed her.

No, she thought desperately. *No, no, no! I love this. This was . . .*

The thought broke away, lost in memories of Luteis twirling, plummeting to the ground, accomplishing crazy feats of flight while she rode his back. The thought of aerial cavorting made her want to scream when it used to delight her.

I trust him, she thought, tightening her hold. *I trust him.*

Sanna forced her fingers to relax, one at a time. With the fresh wind on her face and the unchanging ride, the terror abated slightly. The horrifying sense of being a speck in a vast world where she could fall at any moment still overwhelmed her. Deasylva's magic prevented her from falling, but logic didn't matter. Flying without sight frightened her.

She didn't want to be here.

Even less, though, did she want to be alone in the forest. Less than that? At Mam and Elliot's house. It felt far too much like . . . living with strangers. She might know and love Mam, but Elliot?

Jesse's siblings?

No.

Too much noise, unpredictability, and unknown, without enough Luteis.

This flight was another step forward. Proof that she could exist side-by-side with Luteis. If she flew with him, that negated the need to stand alone . . . forever. They would only part out of sheer necessity.

That was fine.

. . . right?

You are well, little one?

The question startled her. Sanna forced her shoulders back. Wind whipped past, cool and quick, scrubbing the words from her lips.

"I'm well."

Without sight, is it different to fly?

"Yes."

How so?

"It's . . . I don't know." She swallowed hard. "It's hard to explain. Try flying with your eyes closed."

A pause.

Unnerving.

"Yes."

Are you frightened? The register of his voice dropped, a certain indication of stress. She struggled through her reply.

"No, Luteis. I'm not frightened."

But I want this over with as soon as I possibly can, she silently added.

A noise in his throat seemed to indicate that he had something to say, but snuffling interrupted him.

Ah, a mortega. I can smell it from here. Hold on, little one.

Sanna grappled for purchase, gripped his neck—despite the fact that the magic prevented her from falling off of him—and squeezed tight. Her knees squashed his muscles when he plunged down.

They plummeted.

With a cry, Sanna buried her face in her arms, cheek to scales, and hid from the whipping branches. The expansive air disappeared and the obscurity of *things* arose.

A short eternity later, Luteis slammed into the ground with a *thud*. Sanna bit back a cry of pain as her body lurched into his hard neck, not expecting the sudden stop. The dying squawk of the mortega silenced beneath his talons. He shook it with his right paw until the spine cracked in half. The coppery scent of blood filled the air.

Luteis sniffed.

A most lucky night, little one.

Unable to bear the squelching sounds of his meal, Sanna slipped off his neck. Barefoot, hands in front of her, she groped around. Luteis, occupied with his carcass, began to devour the creature.

Sanna found a tree, slid down the trunk, and settled in the roots with a sigh. She curled her knees to her chest, set her chin on top, and waited for the world to stop spinning. She could do the things she used to.

Except now she wasn't sure she wanted to.

SEVENTEEN

MAXIMILLION

The streets of Chatham City were a wild place, filled with witches with filthy faces, chapped hands, dirty clothes. Mud and sludge caked the back streets and alleys, layering the cobblestones with the drudge of humanity.

The more open passages, wide enough for carriages to scuttle through, were slightly cleaner. Witches employed by the Central Network used spells to get rid of refuse. When rain didn't wash the roads, the Head of Highways hired witches to spell buckets of water down the roadways.

Every weekend, witches gathered around parts of the city in ipsum-soaked revelries to burn the accumulated trash in giant bonfires, negating the lurid gathering of garbage.

Max kept a hand on the small of Isadora's back as they strode away from Bella's Dressmaker Shop. He'd sent the nine dresses Isadora selected—five everyday dresses, two elegant pieces for formal events, and two work dresses for cleaning and other chores—back to Wildrose with a spell.

The urge to pull her closer and hex the males that stared at her from the shadows was difficult to ignore.

"Up ahead, we'll take a right. The crowd will thin out there."

She opened her mouth to respond, but the noise from three empty barrels, rolled on their side by a witch running down the road, clattered too loudly. Her lips closed. Max put pressure on her spine as they turned, and she scuttled to keep up.

A quieter street awaited.

As the buildings ribboned back, more elegant shops appeared. Restaurants, a high-end patisserie, and a tea store with plants dripping down each side of a glass window that said *Maude's Herbal Concoctions and Potions*. The farther they moved from downtown Chatham, the more she relaxed.

"Here," he murmured.

He ducked into a building with a sign declaring, *Tremaine's,* across the front. Isadora followed. Sunlight streamed through wide and tall windows, framed by linen drapes. High-backed chairs, crystal settings, and silver utensils filled round tables in the open area ahead. A man with shiny hair slicked to the side acknowledged them with a nod.

"Ambassador." He bowed stiffly at the waist. "Your table awaits."

"Thank you, Phil."

"Your table?"

"I'll explain upstairs."

They ascended winding steps to the left, into a quieter portion of the restaurant. No one lingered on the second floor, as expected during the middle of a weekday. Phil led them to the far corner, behind partitions, where two windows on either side of a corner wall allowed an elevated view of the city.

Sunlight warmed the area. Chatham Castle loomed high in the background, a stoic, stone presence, just in front of

Letum Wood. Max held out a chair and Isadora nodded her thanks as she settled in it.

"The usual, Phil. Thank you. Oh," he added, "a pot of tea, please." He sent Isadora an inquiring glance. "Chamomile?"

"Sounds lovely, thank you."

Phil left again.

"You come here a lot?" she asked with an amused smile.

Max sipped at a cold glass of water that appeared, settled by the cool quench. "I do. My position as Ambassador requires intense negotiations. Tremaine's has always maintained a quiet place for me to do so when needed. You can come here anytime, should you desire it. Phil will remember you."

When the thud of the waiter's retreating shoes echoed down the stairs, Max leaned back into his seat, eager to have this conversation over with already. She lifted her brow in silent question.

"An explanation about Bella," he said.

She nodded.

He set his elbows on the table, folded his hands in front of him, and stared hard at her. The good gods, but he didn't want to tell her about Bella. Bella would lead to Caterina, and there wasn't another witch on the planet he long to utterly forget as much as Caterina.

Like a ghost, she tended to conjure if one even thought her name. Caterina made Bella seem like a sympathetic puppy in comparison.

"Max?"

He swallowed, shook his spiraling thoughts free.

"Forgive me. I'm . . . Isadora, I . . . before you came along, I had a different sort of life. A quintessential bachelor, I suppose you could say. As an Ambassador, there were . . . obligations. A social presence was often required, if you will."

She went oddly still, eyes wide and surprisingly open. Max

spoke faster, his shoulders inching back, as if he had an itch he couldn't reach.

"I courted many women. Most of these relationships were superficial, needed for events where another person was expected to accompany me. Mere acquaintances, really. Often, I requested a specific woman attend social events with me as a strategic social ladder. To discuss political moves, potential border disputes, etc. As often as I could possibly manage it, I went alone. I couldn't always do that."

He paused.

A cup of steaming hot tea, already steeped, appeared in front of her. Next to it, a squat white pot with golden designs swirling from the bottom to the top, like flickering flames.

"Oh, lovely." A sip soothed her parched throat. She had a second sip, then met his gaze. "Of course, Max. None of that surprises me."

He blinked, shook his head. The next words would cost him something. Perhaps such was the price that Isadora truly requested. He had no choice but to say them. If he wanted to keep Isadora, he owed her the truth.

And oh, how he wanted to keep her.

"There have been . . . many lonely years, during which I attempted to satisfy a hollow side of myself with women friends."

Her eyes widened.

"Lovers?"

He shrugged, then stopped and nodded. "If that's the term you want to use, though love never entered into the equation. Never. Not once."

"Mistresses?"

"Not that, exactly. We had a physical relationship when it was convenient, but no commitment."

His emphatic protestations were lost in her shock. For a fleeting moment, he thought she'd laugh. Instead, her gaze dropped to her napkin. Her fingers fiddled with the edges of the plush silk piece, a product of the Southern Network.

"I'm not shocked that you've taken lovers, Max," she said quietly. "You're a very handsome man, kind, and you would take care of any woman under your protection. How many have there been?"

"Countless dates, only two . . . lovers, for lack of a better term."

"Bella?"

He nodded, jaw tight.

"Who was the other one?"

Max fought the urge to wince. "A woman named Caterina."

"Caterina."

The murmur of Isadora's lilting voice, so curious, with a name so caustic, sent a shudder down him. He never wanted that name to grace her lips again. He remained silent, allowing Isadora space to think.

"For how long?"

"Bella? On and off for the last seven years. Caterina and I haven't spoken in as many. We see each other now and then but . . . there is no reconciliation."

Attempts to keep his tone lighthearted clearly failed, for deeper curiosity darkened her questioning gaze. He kept speaking, if only to stop her from asking the inevitable.

"Bella and I were . . . noncommittal. We had agreements and arrangements when we needed someone for a social event or . . . companionship. I haven't reached out to either of them since long before we handfasted."

Since he met her, he realized.

Understanding flooded Isadora's features. "Oh, you were making a stand today, at Bella's. That's why you went with me?"

He nodded distractedly. "Partially, yes. I wanted to be

there with you, but . . . also, yes. A stand. I had already spoken to Bella, informed her of the handfasting. She wanted to meet you and know more about you. I decided it would be better to introduce you, let her ask questions and see you. Otherwise, she would rely on gossip and underground half-truths and perhaps spread the worst. This . . . allayed her for a little bit."

Another odd stillness had overtaken Isadora. She stared at him, eyes fixed, in a look he couldn't hope to read.

"Bella is the center of social life in Chatham City," he continued, in what might sound like a nervous ramble. "I first reached out to her when I worked as the Assistant to the Ambassador, Dahlia, to help me gain greater social presence and understanding of Central Network culture. Particularly in Chatham City."

"I see."

"You don't," he countered, regretting the shadow in his voice. "If I hadn't brought you, Bella would have done her own research. She would have spread the word of our hand-fasting based on lies and assumptions. By the end of the night, the gossip rag out of Ashleigh that posts updates about social events would have been wagging like a wildfire. With you at the center of it. Taking you there today prevented her from doing that. It was an acknowledgment of my former friend-ship with her, in a way. A grudging of respect that she so craves."

A frisson of rage interrupted her pretty expression. He half expected her to slug him in the nose, only the sound of shoes coming back up the stairs prevented it.

"A little warning might have been nice."

"I thought to spare you embarrassment."

"You didn't trust me."

He hesitated. "It's not a question of trust, Isadora. It's a question of introducing you into the cutthroat world in which you have entered as my wife. Scandals, gossipers, witches who have no business in our lives, will always be a force we must reckon with. Sometimes, we must beat them at their own game. You asked to see if our lives could blend together? This will be part of it."

Phil returned. His presence bought them time for silence and contemplation. Max loathed that this conversation must happen at all. Isadora wanted to trust him, and he wanted her to do so.

Which meant all cards must be on the table.

Plates wafted up the stairs behind Phil, settling neatly in front of them. Isadora's cup scooted to the side, rattling softly, moments before her food appeared. Gleaming roast, dripping with hot gravy, coated half the plate. Golden roasted potatoes, crisp on the outside, mealy and warm on the inside, sat next to a pillow of peas and carrots, both slick with butter.

Isadora watched the arrangement with distant fascination, but cogs turned behind her glazed eyes. Max's favorite beef and mushroom pie settled in front of him, drips of gravy dropping down the cast-iron pan in which it baked. The smell sent a heady whirl of hunger through him.

When all settled on the table, and the tangy scents of gravy and crust floated from below, Phil turned to him.

"Anything else?"

"No, thank you, Phil. This looks delicious. My regards to Tremaine, please."

"As always, sir."

Phil departed and silence bloomed between Max and Isadora, filled with all the things he wanted to say, but didn't have the courage to speak. Isadora studied the food, hands in her lap. She peered up at him through sooty eyelashes.

"May I ask you a question or two about your relationship with these women?"

"You may ask me anything."

Her hand came up to rest on the table, fingertips on top of the silverware, but she made no move to pick them up.

"Did you ever care for them?"

"We were acquaintances operating under a mutual agreement."

"Nothing more than basic affection?"

He shrugged. "If one could call it that. Affection is . . . a stronger term than I would apply. We had an understanding."

"Would you consider them friends?"

"No. The relationship was decidedly less . . . jovial . . . than that."

"Purely carnal?"

Max met her gaze in surprise. He hadn't expected such a bold question. The heat of their kiss in the Eastern Network, not to mention a week ago in the forest, testified to some burning passion in her soul.

"I suppose one could call it that," he said.

Isadora rolled her eyes. "You can say the word *lovemaking*, Max. It's not going to bite you either."

Despite her bravado, heat flushed her cheeks.

His jaw tightened. "I never meant to avoid it."

"There is a question for you, though, I would imagine, regarding our own intimate relationship. Isn't there?"

"We are husband and wife, but that doesn't make us intimate. I'm content to let you drive that side of our relationship as you see fit. I'm inclined to believe I have far more experience than you, though I won't make assumptions."

Her lips momentarily twisted, as if holding in a laugh. The gravity in her eyes belied the flash of amusement.

"What if that wasn't true?"

"Then we'll both benefit from our experience."

She paused, thought that over, and sighed. "No, there is no lovemaking experience on my end, you were correct. You are the first witch that I've ever kissed." She hesitated, then added, "I will let you know my expectations around our intimacy, and thank you."

"For?"

Isadora picked up her spoon, studied the flicker of candlelight reflecting out of it. "For allowing me to dictate our progress, and giving me advanced warning of the *gossip rag* as you called it. I believe I know what you're talking about. A newsscroll, isn't it? One with only social updates listed?"

He nodded.

She chuckled. "Pearl waits for the daily updates every evening, you know."

"Well, she'll get an eyeful eventually. Not tonight, I would imagine. It'll take some time to circulate, now that I've satisfied Bella. The longer we can keep you out of Network interest, the better for your safety."

His thoughts circled naturally to Caterina, but he forced those away with a frown.

"Should I expect anything?" she asked.

"No. No one will directly approach you with my name attached, but they will talk behind your back. Some witches might seek out an audience with you. You can do whatever you want with such inquiries."

"What kind of inquiries?"

"One never knows," he said with a wry sigh. "Mostly social events. You'll receive many invitations. Some out of obligation, others out of curiosity. Eventually, when society gets to know you, they may calm."

Isadora picked up a fork and poked at a roasted potato. Grateful to turn the topic, Max reached for his spoon. Gravy leaked onto the flaky, golden crust when he pressed into it with the tip, eager to eat.

"Speaking of social events," she said, a little more brightly now, "do you attend them much?"

He scoffed.

She waited.

Realizing she hadn't meant it as a joke, he cleared his throat. "Not when I can possibly avoid them."

"Why not?"

"The Advocacy required too much of my time. So did Greta, when she was alive and wreaking havoc."

"I see."

He studied her. "You?"

"I would love to participate in social events."

"Even with your powers?"

She nodded. "Yes. The magic has been ebbing since we wrapped up things in the Southern Network. I'm not as affected these days. I love to speak with other witches and don't love the idea of being cooped up at home all day. Will this be a problem for you?"

He paused to consider. "Not if there's balance. If I have more evenings at home, to recover from work, than in society, I can handle it fine."

"That's good to know."

A bite of pie dissolved into scrumptious ecstasy on his tongue. He savored it for a moment—no one imbued flavor like Tremaine—then asked, "Do you have any . . . former love interests I should be concerned about? Anyone that might come out of the forest to fight for you?"

Isadora set down her tea cup with a thoughtful laugh.

"Ah, no."

"I might have been your first kiss," he drawled, amused by the chagrin he saw there, "but that doesn't mean others weren't interested."

"No jealous suitors of which to be concerned. There was someone Mam wanted me to handfast, but . . . no. It would never have worked."

She closed her eyes, inhaled the heavy scent of her food, and plucked her first bite off the fork. How didn't she know her utter perfection? A blush rose on her cheeks when she registered his attention. She cleared her throat, swallowed.

"This is delicious. Thank you, Max. And . . . it's nice to be here with you. I hope we can do it again."

He rubbed his lips together, nodded once, and returned to his food.

No, they wouldn't do this again.

They'd do it over and over and over again.

Eighteen

Isadora

Max breathed so quietly over there.

Isadora lay on her side and stared at their darkness-drenched bedroom. Somewhere in Wildrose, a clock declared the hour with low, droning chimes.

Eleven o'clock.

A shore of glimmering coals illuminated the inside of the hearth with a glowing crimson line that flared and retreated. Snow slushed against the window panes, occasionally sharp and pelting.

She snuggled deeper under her blanket and tried not to glance over her shoulder where Max lay in quiet repose, face relaxed in sleep, skin darkened from stubble. If she let herself, she'd stare all night, unable to tear her gaze from the attractive lines of his face, his strong jaw. When he wasn't scowling at the world, he looked like a little boy.

Remnants of their conversation drifted through her mind in a quiet ebb and flow.

We are husband and wife, but that doesn't make us intimate. I'm content to let you drive that side of our relationship as you see fit.

Heat rose to Isadora's cheeks as she recalled the low burr of his voice, the way his eyes darkened as he said it.

Egads, but he could melt her like butter.

Mam and Daid rarely spoke of physical affection, though they touched often. Gentle things. A hand on the back. A fleeting kiss. Sanna couldn't handle more than seeing a quick kiss before she turned away in disgust. Lucey had given Isadora most of her information about intimacy between a handfasted couple.

The passion of their first kiss, the way he defended her with such self righteous rage in the Southern Network, left no question whether Max felt *something* for her. Ardor, certainly. She held no fear in that regard, only that she didn't want to give that part of herself away until she knew, with certainty, that Max loved her.

Above all, his disinterested relationship with the other women worried her. Could he close her off from his heart so easily? Turn what they had into a business transaction? The clod of a man would surely try.

She wanted to laugh, if only to banish the jealous tones that crept inside her at the thought of Bella and . . . Clarice? No. Caterina. The thought of Max being with or kissing other women wouldn't surprise anyone. He was generous beneath all that prickling austerity, and kind. Overly capable in almost everything he did, and pristinely put together, like today. His dark jacket, white shirt, had echoed the strands of his perfectly-combed hair and swampy eyes.

Isadora curled deeper into the blankets, used a spell to stack more wood on the fire and closed her eyes. Her thoughts ran to the list she'd sent him a week ago.

1. Court me as if we weren't handfasted so we can get to know each other. We should ask lots of questions.

2. Prove whether our lives can merge.

3. Meet Mam and Sanna together.

4. I want you to tell me you love me. In words. Out loud. And mean it.

Well, he certainly struck out to satisfy number one. Though could they ever stop learning about the other? Witches changed daily. He remained a vague figure without edges in her mind, but today had conquered several of the hardest conversations.

Sleepily, she wondered what might come next in their story. For how did one prove whether lives could merge?

Did love grow to fill the cracks that didn't fit?

She fell asleep unable to answer her own questions.

———

The forest, still as a held breath, sent instant reassurance through Isadora several days later.

She stood below the giant trees, closed her eyes, and listened. Snow trickled from high branches, falling in gossamer drapes. A mist brushed past, grazing the tip of her nose. She filled her lungs with a deep inhale and the swirling scents of the forest.

Oak.

Pine.

Cold.

"I've missed you," she whispered and opened her eyes. The trees didn't speak back, but she thought she heard a sigh.

Snow crunched beneath her feet as she stepped over a fallen log, an exposed root, and onto a worn footpath. Petite boot marks filled it, coming and going. They wound around a few trees, then straightened into a rigid trail to a familiar cottage in the woods.

She paused to appreciate Lucey's home, bathed in a circle of light that barely peeked through the upper canopy. Rocks ringed a space around it. Inside the circle of stones, grass hid beneath pockets of wet snow. The wooden, stacked boards, sparkling windows, and a column of fluffy gray smoke painted an idyllic picture.

The door creaked open, admitting a wry smile set in a familiar face.

"Well?" Lucey called. "Are you going to stand out there all day?"

Isadora rushed down the path and threw herself into Lucey's waiting arms. They embraced, held tight for several long moments, before Lucey let her pull away. Eyes bright, she gestured inside.

"Come in, come in. Sonja and I have been waiting for you."

———

Half an hour later, a freshened cup of tea sat in front of Isadora, petaled by biscuits, a silver spoon, and a squat pot of fresh cream. Crumbs littered the table from the cookie she'd already eaten, and the cup of tea she'd already drank.

Lucey and her wife, Sonja, sat across from her, on the other side of a round, uneven table that trembled when touched. The low moan of an animal out the back door startled Isadora, causing Lucey to laugh.

"Believe it or not, we have a cow."

"A cow?"

"Sonja loves animals. And I love being self-sufficient. It's a lovely match, though keeping dragons away from our bovine lady has been interesting."

Isadora laughed. "I can't imagine."

Sitting next to Lucey, their hands clasped together on the table, was Sonja. A witch with a slightly tilted nose, dark eyes, and a kind smile. Her black hair, intricately braided against her scalp and hanging halfway down her back, was at odds with Lucey's mousy blonde bun and pale skin. The contrast created a lovely dichotomy. Sonja smiled at Isadora with a depth of warmth that normally came from years of friendship.

"Well, now I can officially say that the many good things I've heard about you have not been exaggerated," Sonja said brightly. "Particularly for the wife of our very . . . ah . . . charming Ambassador?"

A twinkle filled Sonja's umber gaze.

Isadora laughed. "Already, Max's fame precedes me."

"Get used to that," Lucey quipped with another smile. She gazed adoringly at Sonja, squeezed her hand, and turned back to Isadora. "You've already given us an update on Wildrose and Max—sounds like things are progressing steadily enough. I think you are wise to give him a deadline and a goal. Max does well under pressure."

"Let's hope that carries over outside of politics and Advocacy work."

"And Wildrose? What do you think of his lovely manor?"

"It's . . . big."

Lucey's gaze tapered in thought. "Has he told you yet?"

"Told me what?"

"About the basement."

Isadora blinked several times. In her many tours of the house, mostly by herself, she'd never stumbled across a basement.

"Basement?"

Lucey chuckled. She set a small silver spoon in her teacup and stirred, looking not at all surprised by the question.

"The basement of Wildrose housed Advocacy members for years. In fact, headquarters is hidden at Wildrose."

Isadora's jaw dropped. "No!"

Lucey peered at her over the top of her cup as she sipped. The affirmation in her eyes shocked Isadora further.

"Really?"

Lucey nodded.

How *hadn't* he mentioned such a detail? Isadora struggled to piece it all together.

"So . . . *Wildrose* was headquarters?"

"Well, yes. But also no. None of the Advocacy members went into the higher floors, save a few. Faye, obviously, because she ran Wildrose and the Advocacy. Myself, because Max saved me in Chatham and I lived there for a while. Charlie built the headquarters, after his father died. It was an old cellar that he transformed."

"Faye never mentioned it was at Wildrose! She said that Charlie built it and she helped run it, but . . ."

Pieces of the puzzle assembled together in her mind. Of *course* Wildrose housed the Advocacy. She'd always assumed that headquarters lay underground somewhere, but hadn't given much thought to where. There were no windows and no doors, save one, that led to a hallway she'd never walked.

Isadora leaned back in her chair, weakened by the revelation. She attempted to speak, but words failed her.

"I'm sure he has plans to tell you," Sonja offered hopefully. The question in her words lingered. Isadora brushed a lock of hair out of her eyes. Nausea swelled up in her throat, but she swallowed it back.

How many secrets did Max have?

"Can we talk about something else?"

"Sanna!" Lucey said. "Your message mentioned your sister? Let's discuss her."

Relief ensued, despite the transition from one difficult

topic to another. "Yes, Sanna. Let's talk about my sister who continues to insist she live in the forest with a dragon."

Lucey grimaced. "Oh, no."

"I need your help." Isadora bit her bottom lip. "I don't . . . Sanna won't listen to me or Mam. She insists on . . . being who she used to be. She can't! She can't live alone in Letum Wood. That's madness. I need you to talk to her. Convince her that this isn't a good idea."

Sonja's face softened into a look of compassion. She looked to Lucey, who blinked several times. After a prolonged moment of thought, Lucey set aside her tea cup, settled her free hand on her lap.

"Sanna has a lot of grieving to do, Isadora."

"I know, but—"

"Do you?"

Lucey leaned forward, staring hard. Isadora's immediate rebuttal slowed. She forced herself to think about what Lucey asked.

Hesitation stole over her.

"Well . . ."

"Do you *really* know how much she needs to grieve? Do you comprehend that she's not only lost the future she wanted, but parts of herself? She can't see anymore. Can't run through the trees and swing on vines the same way. Could we possibly comprehend?"

Isadora opened her mouth, then closed it again.

"I . . . I suppose . . . no."

"None of us can understand the true weight of what Sanna bears right now. It's been a little over two weeks since her vision receded fully?"

Isadora nodded, already contrite.

"Two weeks." Lucey leaned back. "That's hardly time to comprehend such a vast loss, not to mention move on with a solid plan that *you* approve of, which is not her obligation.

Sanna needs time, Isadora. Patience. Compassion. She doesn't need you—or your Mam," she added gently, "telling her what to do and how to live her life. Believe it or not, Sanna is an adult. A grieving adult."

Duly chastened, Isadora shrank in the chair. For several heartbeats she could only stare at the tabletop. Tears rose in her eyes, blurring Lucey and Sonja. When Isa lifted her attention again, Sonja's mournful gaze struck a deep chord in her chest.

"I hate this for her," Isadora whispered.

Lucey leaned forward, clasped Isadora's hand in hers. "I know you do. We hate it, too! But you can't take it away."

"I wish I could."

"And deprive her of the chance to learn? To overcome? To adapt and find her new path, her better self?"

Isadora's lip trembled. "No, I guess not."

A distant expression came to Lucey's eyes. "I haven't dealt with something as momentous as losing my sight, like Sanna, but I have been forced to choose between who I wanted to be, and what was given to me. It's not an easy path. Knowing Sanna, I can't imagine she would grieve away from Luteis or the woods. Allow her this time and space."

"But it's not safe!"

"I'm sure she's far more aware of that than you. She has a forest dragon that loves her, Isadora. From my understanding, he doesn't leave her side. It could be far worse. Luteis will help."

"But there's only so much he can do. What if she hurts herself before she figures out that she needs help?"

Lucey released a heavy breath. "The Defender paths make it clear that she could have been hurt many times."

"You've checked?"

"Of course." Lucey smiled demurely. "As I'm sure you have as well?"

With a sheepish chuckle, Isadora nodded. Lucey and Isadora were magical equals in the Watcher and Defender power, but they didn't speak of it all that often.

Lucey continued in a pragmatic tone. "Of course, we want to keep her from harm, but it's ultimately up to her, isn't it?"

"I want to do more for her than just wait!"

"Me too, but it's not our place. We can't experience this loss for her. She has to carry it herself."

Isadora stumbled over that, unwilling to accept. "Then . . . what can I do to help her?"

Lucey squeezed her hand again. "You let her fall and pick herself back up. You cheer her on as she does. You support the efforts she makes, and be there when she truly can't do something. She will find her way again. Sanna is nothing if not determined. Eventually, she'll come to you for help. When *she* is ready. Not when you're ready for her."

Tears dribbled onto Isadora's cheek. "I love Sanna so much. She's my sisterwitch, my twin. Watching her go through so much pain, it's . . . I'm sad for her."

"We all are. But we can't let grief turn to pity. She needs confidence and time."

With a sniffle, Isadora wiped the healing tears away, straightened back up. A leaden weight had lifted off her chest she didn't know was there. Egads, but life had thrown dreary challenges their way.

"You're right, Lucey. I . . . thank you. You've reminded me of who I should be for Sanna. But I do want to ask about the blind witch you know? The one who was also a sighted witch, then lost it?"

Lucey brightened. "Yes! He's the sweetest man. His name is Gilbert. He lost his sight when he was twelve, I think."

"Oh, Gilbert," Sonja murmured with a smile. "A darling man. Very kind."

"How old is he?"

"Forty, I think."

"Would he really be able to teach Sanna how to adapt?"

"As strange as it sounds, yes. Reading special books, using a cane to see ahead of her. Even skills like chopping vegetables, cooking for herself, the sort of things that she might figure out on her own, but would be much easier with guidance."

"And magic?"

"So much magic." Sonja nodded quickly. "Oh, he's a whiz with spells. You wouldn't believe he's blind if you didn't see it, the way he runs his house, walks around Maytown."

Hope swelled up in Isadora on Sanna's behalf. "Would Gilbert be . . . I mean . . . is he . . . understanding?"

Lucey smiled, knowing exactly what Isadora meant. "He would understand Sanna's grieving process and the intense emotions it entails. She could meet with him here, if that would make her feel safer. He has a spot that he transports to in the house when he needs me."

Isadora recoiled. "He can transport?"

"Yes! There are ways for blind witches to transport, believe it or not. Sanna could be a real powerhouse."

"She will be," Isadora said.

Lucey patted Isadora's hand. "I commend you for coming to us first, and not making the decision for your sister, as much as I would imagine you're tempted. Sanna needs to flounder before she understands, and she will."

A clatter of noise outside drew their attention. Isadora turned to find Jesse standing in the doorway, waving. Lucey smiled widely and motioned him inside.

"Jesse! My favorite second-oldest brother."

Isadora scraped the residual tears off her face, sniffled, and straightened. Jesse eyed her with a questioning gaze. "Isa, good to see you. Everything all right?"

She smiled. "You too, Jesse. Yes, fine. Just talking about Sanna."

He sobered as he crossed the room, embraced his sister, then Sonja. Lucey pointed him into the open chair between Isadora and Sonja. He lowered, taking in the table. Sonja spelled a plate in front of him. A cup flew over from the cupboard, settled with a light clink. Biscuits hopped across the top, settling in a flower-like design on his plate.

"Thanks." He leaned back, tea cup in hand. "I'm ravenous. Just returned from one of the forester villages to talk about trade."

Lucey perked up. "A new one?"

He nodded, gulping the tea. "Just wanted to introduce myself there. Found some supplies for Daid, maybe some new jobs I could pick up to earn currency. The family won't make it through the winter like this. Not with Simon and Lenny eating half the house at each meal."

A shadow crossed Lucey's face. "Will Daid accept the supplies?"

"No, but Roxi will."

Mention of Mam's name drew Isadora's attention out of her spiraling thoughts. "Mam?"

He shrugged. "Daid is stubborn and refuses to trade with the forester villages for supplies. Says the family needs to survive on their own, with what he can trap. But your Mam isn't so obsessed with proving herself, not with so many mouths to feed, so I'm trading for supplies and giving them to her."

Lucey softened slightly. "Well, at least Roxi will see sense."

"Roxi might soften Daid for you, too," Jesse said.

Isadora's brow scrunched. "Is something wrong between you and Elliot, Lucey?"

A wry expression crossed Lucey's face. Sonja reached over, squeezed Lucey's shoulder.

"My father isn't very keen about my life choices. Breaking away from the dragons, becoming an Apothecary, working for the Advocacy, and handfasting a woman. It's . . . tenuous between us since Mam died. I think . . . somehow he blames me for her death."

"That makes no sense."

She shrugged. "I agree, but matters of the heart often don't make sense."

"I'm sorry, Lucey."

Forced energy illuminated her expression. "All is well, Isa. I have you, my brother, my love, and the Advocacy. That's all I need. One day, Daid will come around."

Jesse wolfed down his second biscuit, then asked, "How is Sanna?"

"Fine." Isadora sighed ruefully. "Determined to live with Luteis in the forest."

"Can't say that I'm surprised."

"Me either."

"I'll check in on her." He picked up the teacup, which Sonja refilled with a spell. "I've learned to transport. I bet I could find her. If she's not flying all over the Western Network with Luteis anymore, she can't have gone far."

NINETEEN
SANNA

S anna winced when the underside of a tacky leaf tugged at her skin. With a hiss, she delicately peeled it away. The wrinkled skin held despite the speed at which she yanked it off her arm.

With the tips of her fingers, she felt around the edge of the leaf. Firmer than a flower petal—not so willowy and breakable—with tiny spines that jutted off the top. Not much stronger than most foliage. She could easily rip it in half. She pressed the back of the leaf to her pant leg, peeled it away again. Still tacky.

Interesting.

When she had sight, she never paid attention to the little things. The adhesive side of a leaf. The brittle scent it issued. As if losing her sight made her understand other things more clearly. Struck by another thought, she crumpled the leaf into a ball and pitched it to the side.

"Luteis?"

A sleepy voice stirred in the back of her mind.

Yes?

She reached down with her left hand, felt the poky

remnants of a fish spine from dinner. A little flesh remained that she peeled off the bone to eat.

"I've been thinking about a layout for the house. I should have a guest room for visitors like Isadora or Mam."

A thrill darted back through her. Just thinking about a home—all her own—with solid walls, a predictable, known outline, and all the solitude she wanted made her want to dance.

First, however.

A place to put it.

Shoving aside the eagerness that she didn't quite know how to channel into actually *building* the thing, she let her thoughts continue.

We have been searching for a place for more than a week now.

"I know."

You are . . . aware of what you want.

She snorted. "You were going to say picky."

He sniffed and didn't disagree.

"It's not that I'm picky or overly critical," she said with a hint of annoyance, because he might be a *little* right, "it's that we have to construct it in a certain way so that it's actually helpful to me."

True.

"Without a water source, it would be a waste of time."

Unless you could magic water to yourself?

His tone suggested something *else* she didn't want to get into right then. Thoughts of magic stirred up hints of Talis and the tragedy of breaking Dragonian magic on the beaches of the Western Network.

Magic.

Sanna.

Not a great mix so far, but not something she'd rule out entirely. She thought about it more than ever these days.

"Yes, that's an option, but I don't want to rely solely on magic for water. It sounds practical in theory, but the execution could be very different. Magic requires energy, just like everything else. Not having sight requires so much more *focus* than I expected. To have to give more concentration to magic?"

Her nose wrinkled.

Learning magical spells would give you a sense of progression.

"Maybe."

There is another stream not far from here. I'll take you there. If we don't find anything acceptable, we may have to look closer to forester villages. We are already in the depths of the forest. I fear going much deeper might yield . . .

He trailed away. Without being told, she knew exactly what he was thinking. A close encounter with a forest lion three nights ago had set him on edge.

"Closer to forester villages? No, thanks. I'd really rather not be around other witches. It's a matter of . . . security."

Or is it fear?

Sanna growled.

Luteis said nothing. The tips of other leaves brushed along the back of her forearm as she scooted closer to the winter bush. Not unheard of in the forest, where strange magical things thrived. The leaves would fall soon, when the true depths of cold descended.

"Let me toss away this fish, then we can look at the other place you mentioned. For now, I don't think going closer to a village is necessary."

And why not? I have been thinking about this.

"Oh?"

I've concluded that it could be advantageous to your health to stay close to witches. If you refuse to use witch magic.

His unwillingness to drop the topic made her uneasy.

"But I always have you."

Always, he said, with a faint note of something she couldn't read. Though not lacking conviction, it held . . . question.

"It's going to be fine," she said with an ease she didn't quite feel anymore. They would both have moments that the other one might need courage. She could be that for Luteis. He did it for her all the time.

"We'll find a place first. That continues to be our main goal. Once we find it, we'll figure out what's next."

Like how to build it, she added silently.

Luteis huffed a breath, sending steam into the air. The warm mist curled around her face, clinging to the fine hairs along her brow.

Yes. We find you an area, and then we find you a home. Small steps, I believe, are most advantageous.

———

Sanna woke to the hair on the back of her neck standing up.

She pulled her knees to her chest, wrapped her arms around them. Not a sound issued. Only the smell of wet leaves assaulted her. Not a boggy stench, like a belua, or the acidic scent of their foul, purple spittle.

Luteis?

Groggily, he replied. *Yes?*

Do you smell anything?

A pause, then a sniff.

Perhaps.

What could it be?

I'm not sure.

She frowned. Something lived in Letum Wood that he hadn't encountered yet? He was fifty years old!

No idea?

No.

But—

It is a wide forest, he said, clearly anticipating her thoughts. *There is much I don't know yet. Stay here. Allow me to investigate.*

Her heart thumped in her chest. She didn't move, pasted her spine to the roots of the tree at her back. Luteis slipped away, near-silent. Of course something *must* be out there. The forest was noisy otherwise.

She blinked several times. The darkness had a strange tint to it. As if she saw flashes of color, though she really *saw* nothing at all. Tonight was no exception. Her mind played tricks on her, rotating through remembered colors.

A cracking sound overhead made her shove back. Her spine dug into the trunk, arms splayed at her side. Breath held, she waited.

Where are you, Luteis?

Not far. What is wrong? I sense distress in your voice.

She almost said, *I heard a sound,* but that would have been pathetic. Also, ridiculous. Letum Wood was full of sounds. A single crack would be—

Another followed, with a dingy smell similar to fetid water. She recoiled. A clacking, like several large rain drops falling at the same time. Leaves rustled overhead. Sanna scuttled to the side. The musty air dissipated as quickly as it came.

Little one?

I think something is here.

I shall return.

A growl came from not far away, followed by the roar of flames. Luteis threw fire in warning. Overhead, the strange clacks faded, as if something rushed up the tree. Heavy and lumbering and . . .

A bead of moisture fell on her head. She reached up. It was

goopy, thick, like a gelatinous blob. Not the pearly, thin saliva of a forest lion, or the acidic spittle of a belua.

With a shudder, Sanna shoved away from the tree and stumbled into a clearing. Why didn't she have a club or a knife? What fool lived in the forest without a ready weapon? She might not be armed, but she would have to defend herself.

Visions of forest lions whipped through her mind. They were sneaky, devious creatures. If it had been high enough, prowling from the tops of the trees, it might have avoided Luteis' keen sense of smell, then slipped down once he left.

No, they smelled rank, hissed, and attacked in packs. They didn't . . . *crackle*. Besides, they always hovered before they leaped and this had been above *and* in front of her.

Groping with her feet, hands waving in front of her, she stumbled farther away. Would it do any good? Probably not, but it was better than waiting for death.

Breathing hard, she walked without feeling ahead. Rocks scraped her soles. Her hands swung around, haphazardly clearing the way. Bushes and twigs danced around her calves. She ignored them.

Where are you?

Turn to your right.

He roared again, his thudding footsteps drew closer. The ground trembled. Sanna's fingers found a trunk. She felt along it, attempting to gauge its width. *Big* was all she concluded. Certainly wide enough to house another lion, but she pressed her back to it anyway.

Where was she?

At one point, she thought she'd been facing south, but now she had no idea. Did it matter? She had no other sense of direction, nor place to go. No trail to find, no path to trod. The sense of looming branches seemed close, though she felt nothing when she lifted an arm.

Luteis's tail thrashed through undergrowth. She hadn't

gone far—of course, how could she?—but enough she felt marginally better.

He sniffed around, snorting.

I am at the tree where I left you. I agree that there was a creature. It has departed that tree, but I believe it would be wise to sleep elsewhere tonight.

"A lion?"

No. Not a lion. At least, it doesn't smell like the typical forest lions. I am . . . perplexed. This creature eludes me.

She shuddered and stepped away from the tree. His heat drew closer. When she reached out a hand, scales met it. Relief coursed back through her.

"Thank you."

I'm sorry, little one. Distress thickened his voice. *I didn't smell it before. Even now, the scent is vague. I should not have left you alone. The fault is mine. If something happened, I—*

He stopped, sniffed.

What is in your hair?

Duly reminded, she reached up again. The blob had spread its gelatinous texture. "It fell on my head."

His heat encompassed her.

I have never seen this before. It's milky white.

"Really?"

Does it hurt?

"No."

There is no smell to it.

"Not at all?"

None. Had I not observed it, I wouldn't have known.

"That's . . . weird."

Very strange.

His wings rustled as he pulled away. She patted his scales, moving closer to his leg and the security his heat offered.

"It's not your fault, Luteis. You kept me safe by searching, and when you came back it sounds like it scuttled away. If you hadn't screamed . . ."

She didn't want to entertain any idea of what *could* have happened. The grisly details would only frighten her. With those thoughts came questions of whether Luteis could be with her all the time.

What kind of life was that, glued to his side constantly? At first it seemed ideal. Now? Suffocating. Overwhelming.

Almost impossible.

The nauseating effect of flying without vision would make every single hunting trip miserable.

If only she had a house.

A safe place.

Previous conversations rose to the forefront of her mind. Conversations she'd avoided because she didn't want to face the reality of her situation. She needed a way to defend herself, even if she couldn't see. With a weapon she risked harming herself, but she could train to use it while unable to see . . .

. . . somehow.

"Well!" She forced a resolute tone. "Another thing we know for sure about life while blind in Letum Wood is this: I need a weapon."

With a grim tone, he replied, *I'm inclined to agree.*

"We'll put that on the list, I suppose. Right next to *find the perfect place for a house* and *build it.*"

Luteis's bleak response issued with great hesitation. *And so we shall. Let's wash that . . . muck . . . out of your hair, then sleep.*

He nudged her gently with his snout to the left. Eventually, they found water. The shock of the cold stream brought her fully into the moment as she scrubbed the goop from her hair. When they returned, she lowered to the base of a tree. Luteis followed, tucking himself closer to her side. His wing hovered above.

Sleep was a long time coming.

TWENTY
MAXIMILLION

Max found his wife standing on the back porch of Wildrose, arms folded, surveying the grass.

She wore one of her simplest day dresses, meant to be a working dress. Basic linen, embroidered designs, with straight arms that cut off at her elbow and a gathered waistline. Deep pockets lay on either side in hidden rectangles beneath the surface.

"Merry meet."

She didn't startle, but folded her arms across her middle.

"Merry meet."

He approached tentatively. Her tense jaw, pulled-back shoulders, provoked caution. Though they'd been living together, in the South and then here, for over four months now, he still hadn't learned exactly how to read her.

When her hands unfolded to prop on her hips, and her squared jaw opened, he braced himself.

"Where is headquarters?" she cried.

He cursed under his breath. Swallowing a rise of annoyance—who had gotten to her now?—Max paused where he stood. Several paces separated them, which felt wisest.

"To the right, along the side of the house."

Isadora marched over.

He followed.

Snow crunched under their feet as she crossed the paved stones and stepped onto the lawn, dingy and yellow under pockets of snow. A gray sky threatened to burst in a storm that would blanket everything again. Cool drafts blew from the west, heralding the squall.

She paused a few paces away from the edge of the house.

"Here?"

"Yes."

"Not a sign."

"No, there wouldn't be."

The skin between her eyebrows wrinkled.

Max stuck his hands in his pockets and hazarded a guess. "Lucey?"

Isadora turned to face him. "Yes, Lucey told me." Slightly reddened, swollen eyes meant she'd been crying at some point. The thought wrenched his gut. The good gods, but what was he supposed to do when she cried?

Had he caused this?

"Are you all right?" he asked. The tone came out far crisper than he intended. To her credit, she offered no platitudes.

"I'm not sure. I think I'm upset with you, but . . . it doesn't seem quite fair to be angry, either."

"What have I done?"

She eyed him ruefully. "Nothing, I suppose. At least . . . I don't know." She threw her hands in the air. "How many secrets do you have, Max? What else will I discover in the course of our handfasting? The headquarters for the Advocacy was in the basement all this time, and I had no idea. Faye didn't even tell me!"

He sighed, deadened at the question. *How many secrets do you have?* Were the truths he held secrets? Not really. More . . .

untold facts. Things that they hadn't quite got around to yet because why overwhelm her?

He attempted to soften his stiff tone, but failed spectacularly. "I don't intend to hide information from you, Isadora, believe it or not."

"When were you going to tell me?"

"Should that have come during the night you saw Wildrose for the first time, our trip to the dressmakers to obtain you proper clothes, or when you discovered the woman I once courted? Work has been so easy to escape from to give you a tour, hasn't it?"

Sheer willpower kept his tone under control, though a caustic edge riddled it. Isadora clenched, held her breath, then let it all out in one blow.

"You're right."

Astonished, he could only stare.

"I beg your pardon?"

"You're right." She swung a hand over the grass. "I'm not being fair. Lucey sort of . . . put me in my place today. Reminded me that I have to let witches move at their own speed. I'm upset, but I realize it's because . . . well . . . I don't like being in the dark. I'm unfairly expecting you to tell me everything at once, but I think I'd hate that too."

Her gaze lifted, met his. Hints of sheepish apology lined their depths. "Sorry, Max. I came on strong today. I suppose it's a result of us just . . . figuring out where we stand. I'm trying to be open and fair."

He blinked, utterly perplexed. One moment frustrated, the next contrite. She turned away. A protracted silence began, allowing him to sort through the whirlwind of the last few minutes.

Would their life forever be like this?

Swept up in the windstorm of Isadora one moment, then

dropped onto firm ground again the next. He held the thought, arrested by it.

He certainly hoped so. Livened up the boredom that once plagued his evenings.

"Isadora, I know you don't trust me. I understand that what I said in the Southern Network hurt you. And I know that you want me . . . to say the words that will help you feel safe in our handfasting. I'm working on it. But please give me the benefit of the doubt? I'm not your enemy. I didn't ask you into this handfasting to hurt you. On the contrary . . . "

I love you.

The words wouldn't come. They solidified like rock in his throat, clunky and awkward. He wanted to say them, but deeper fears stirred his chest. Haunting terrors, borne of a darker childhood he hadn't yet escaped.

Saying *I love you* meant so much more.

After a held breath, she nodded.

"Thank you, Max."

He held out a hand. "Shall we go inside together? I received an invitation to a little soiree tonight, if you're interested in meeting more witches. I think it would be wise to be seen in more political circles before the gossip columns take off. Later, I'll give you a full tour of the basement and an explanation of how the Advocacy used it, I promise."

Isadora turned, slipped her fingers into his. Electricity crackled up the length of his arm, infusing his bones. She nodded.

"Yes, I'd like that."

"It's not too short of notice?"

"No, I don't mind."

"Impressive," he muttered. He loathed social events on a whim. The eagerness in her smile told him she felt otherwise.

How different could they be?

He pulled her close, arm tucked under his, and led her to the back door.

"Then allow me to preface some of what you'll be walking into tonight. The good gods know that political soirees are rarely a fun time . . ."

Twenty-One
Isadora

The locked doorknob wouldn't give way—not even with an incantation.

Isadora stood at the far end of the third floor, near long windows that sent banners of sunlight into the hallway. The edges of her skirt dusted a forgotten floor. Aside from her own footsteps, it was a floor that clearly hadn't been trod in quite awhile.

At the end of the hallway stood a curious door. Carved with swirling designs, like ocean tides, or stars, or curling clouds wrapped around pegs. The intricate work must have taken ages. She imagined tiny chisels, impressive patience, and great love. The stain alternated from dark to light, expertly shadowed.

She ran her fingers over the closest design, then crouched down. A keyhole peered into a room with soft tones, revealing muted sunlight, a wall, and one side of a window. She straightened.

"Well, what do *you* hide?"

A stroke of inspiration pushed her to reach above the

door. A ledge around the doorframe would make the perfect place for a—

Oh.

A metal something clattered off the top, landed on top of her head, then thunked to the floor. Grimacing, she rubbed the sore spot and bent over to pick it up.

Indeed, a key.

Immeasurably pleased with herself, she inserted it into the knob and turned. The intricate filigree finally moved. With a deep groan and a slow creak, the door swung inside.

Isadora held her breath.

The wispy layout of a nursery appeared. Dust lay thick on the wooden floor, left bare. Two cribs, side by side, stood in the middle of the room. Ruffled fabric around each bed hid firm mattresses. Small, sewn animals lay on the sheets, below dangling banners that stretched over the tops.

A sacred ambience permeated the air as she ventured in. To the left, folded diapers, clothes, wooden toys, and extra blankets filled the shelves. The supplies waited in stoic silence, abandoned who-knew-how-many years ago. She touched each tiny shirt, the rattles, and imagined the quiet cooing sounds of the children. So many gowns, in different colors and sizes, guessed at more than one baby.

Twins?

As she ventured farther, Isadora attempted to remember details about Charlie. Did he have siblings? She didn't think so. Aunts, uncles? He and Max both clung to each other and Wildrose for sheer lack of blood family.

Trails appeared in the dust as she ran her fingers along the edge of the crib top. She hummed, a lullaby Mam used to sing. The sound echoed in the cavernously bare room. Drapes pulled partially over windows bled dim light. She turned, skirt whirling, when a line in the wall caught her attention. The wallpaper split in a strange . . . no. That wasn't a split.

That was a seam.

Intrigued, she ventured closer. Though almost perfectly concealed, a slight discoloration of the wallpaper gave a segment away. When this room was first wallpapered, one might not have noticed it.

The devastating, aging effects of time, however . . .

Isa peered into the hidden seam. Darkness. As she pressed her fingertips to the wall, a groan issued. The sound repeated with more pressure. She pressed twice. The wall trembled in and back out.

A hidden cubby?

Her fingertips traced the seam, testing for weakness. Several colorful panes to the right, the portion of the wall shifted ever-so-slightly. Two panels wide, then. About the length of fingertip to elbow.

For minutes, Isadora attempted to open it. She tapped at the bottom, pressured the sides. Bracing a rattle in the seam to pry it open failed spectacularly. Like Wildrose, the nursery wasn't ready to yield its secrets.

Finally, she issued a spell. Another. A third. Nothing happened. In exasperation, she attempted a final, obscure incantation used to retrieve lost things. Failed. Vexed, she splayed her hand against the paper.

"What do you hide? Might I see it?"

Heat gathered under her palm, illuminating with a whirl. The wall shifted. It moaned apart at the seam. With a gasp, she grabbed the edge, catching it before it slammed closed. The tips of her fingers ached as she slowly eased it open on rusty, interior-facing hinges. It swung toward her, then moved without restraint.

Isadora paused in quiet astonishment.

A bundle of letters lay on a small shelf. Aside from dust, nothing else was there. Twine bound the letters together. She picked them up, studied them. The smell of aged parchment and old ink drifted from inside.

Carefully, she closed the hidden compartment.

A rocking chair squeaked as she lowered into it, letters in her lap, and plucked at the twine. The parchments shuffled apart when the string loosened in her hands. She pulled the top one free.

A letter.

If age and time were any indication—not to mention difficult-to-read handwriting—these letters were from over a hundred years ago.

Darling,

I burn for you. Wish I could see you. How are your babies? Is there any news? Until you return to my side, I will be only half of a man. Never whole without you.

When can you come to me? Will he know?

Yours

Her eyes widened.

"Intrigue!" she murmured. "Who is this man?"

A sound in the hallway drew her gaze higher. Her name rippled from near the stairs.

"Isadora?"

"Here!" she called, quickly closing the letter. "I'm in here, Max."

Hastily, but gently, she stacked the letters together, tied the twine, and looked up just as he appeared in the doorway.

Her heart hiccuped.

He leaned one shoulder against the doorframe, gazing on her with inquiry. He'd undone his top button, removed his jacket, and unbuttoned his vest. As casual as she'd ever seen him, outside his pajamas. Did he realize how handsome he was? Her lips tingled, burning for a kiss.

His gaze darted around the room, then back to her. A blush bloomed across her cheeks. What did he think of his wife lurking in a nursery? Heavens, but she hoped he didn't draw unnecessary conclusions.

Amusement lined his tone.

"What have you found?"

She stood, spelling the letters to an empty drawer in her armoire for later. "Ah, I was exploring. This locked door has had my curiosity for some time, so I decided to find my way inside. I discovered the key and . . .well . . . here we are!"

"Interesting."

"Isn't it? Do you know anything about this nursery?"

"Not a thing. This room has always been locked."

She smirked. "Well, when one knows how to find a key . . ."

"The key?" He frowned. "There is no key to this door."

She gestured to the doorknob.

He studied the wrought-iron key poking out. "Ranulf told me that someone had enchanted it to remain closed. One of the former occupants, I believe. A great-great aunt, or something. I can't remember. Apparently, the spell was of distant and unknown origin. According to Ranulf, the magic hid the key. Said key would only appear to certain people and under very specific circumstances."

"What circumstances?"

He shrugged. "It was never known. We assumed an incantation."

"Well . . . how strange. It lay on top of the door."

"Impossible. Charlie looked there a dozen times."

"What do you want me to say? I reached up, the key was there, I came inside." The flash of heat against her palm when she pressed it to the wall and found the letters renewed. Magic, definitely, but not of her own making.

Max eyed her warily. "What have you done?"

"Nothing, Max. I swear it. I attempted a few simple opening spells, but of course they didn't do anything. Then I asked to see inside, felt above the door frame, and it lay on top."

"Really?"

"As you see."

He appeared both puzzled and troubled.

"Your manor certainly keeps a woman on her toes."

Shaking that off, he straightened. "I suppose I'm glad to hear it. Are you hungry?"

"Ravenous."

"Allow me to fix you something to eat?"

He held out a hand. Startled by the gesture, she accepted. Their warm fingers slid together as if they'd never been apart. The ease in which he increasingly touched her was a delightful sign of things to come.

She hoped.

"Thank you. I would like that very much."

———

Steam luffed off the top of a boiling cauldron, filling the room with a sticky heat. The rhythmic *thunk-thunk-thunk* of Max's knife on the cutting board filled the room. Isadora stood at the fire, a long-handled wooden spoon in hand as she stirred a simmering concoction of spices in a cast-iron pan.

"You know," she drawled with a teasing tone, "you are one of the highest-ranking members of the Central Network political hierarchy."

"I am aware."

"You could always pay someone else to fix your meals and spare yourself the trouble."

"I could. Yet, I do not."

"Why is that?"

He hesitated, mouth half open. He gathered another bunch of wild green onions, likely gathered from the greenhouse she spotted across the way, and rubbed a few clods of dirt off the white bulbs.

"I don't mind cooking."

"Aren't you tired at the end of the day?"

"Yes, and often hungry."

"Are you short on currency?"

He snorted. "Hardly."

"Do you like doing it?"

The green tops of the onions disappeared from their stalks and into thin ribbons under the flash of his knife.

"I like doing something other than meetings, messages, or political discussion. If I'm going to eat food, it would be a waste not to enjoy it. Preparation is part of the process, and I like to see it transform from start to finish."

She paused, thinking that over. In fact, she'd never thought much about it either way. Food had always just been food.

"Wildrose was often quiet," he continued, "even with the Advocacy in full swing downstairs. At the end of the day, I sometimes hated that there wasn't more waiting for me than just . . . the study. The paperwork. More of the same."

"So you began cooking?"

"Yes."

She studied the color of the spices in the pan, waiting for them to turn the gentle golden color he described. She set the wooden spoon on the side, then reached for the fire poker when the oil bubbled too violently. Scattering the logs gradually reduced the boil to a simmer.

This unfettered view into the real Max was most welcome. She leaned into the chance, worried it might flitter away.

"I'm surprised you had time to cook, between your requirements at the castle, the Advocacy and . . . everything else in your life."

With a start, she realized she didn't know what *else* there was.

"I don't always," he admitted. "I'm . . . attempting to enjoy it while I have the time. And someone to enjoy it with. Which may not always be available."

She blinked, arrested. Well, look at that.

Max could be downright pleasant.

"What's your favorite thing to cook?" She slipped the spoon around the bottom of the pan in looping swirls. Two more minutes, then she'd add the greens.

"Anything."

"Do you bake?"

"Sometimes."

"Cake?"

He glanced at her, a hint of a smile on his face. "You like cake?"

Isadora grinned. "It depends. We rarely had sugar at home, so I've only tried cake from my time at Miss Sophia's. I did like it. The flecks of carrots made it sweet and—"

"Wait." He set both hands down. "You've only ever had carrot cake?"

"Yes."

"Chocolate?"

She shook her head.

"Butter yellow with lemon creme?"

Eyes wide, she shook her head again. "No, but that sounds delicious!"

Max returned to his chopping, muttering under his breath about child abuse and heathen parenting. Laughing, she turned back to the pan, tossing several handfuls of greens into the mix. They began to wilt.

"How is it?" he asked.

"Almost done to your specifications, sir."

"Bring it over when you're done."

"Yes, Ambassador."

He muttered in annoyance again.

Minutes later, she stood across from him, hands protected with a thick mitt. She dumped the green, spice-filled concoction on top of the bread and goat cheese he'd pieced together, then warmed on top of the fire. The hot greens and spices began to melt the cheese. He dribbled the green onions on top and nodded once, satisfied.

Suddenly uneasy, he glanced at her. "Ah . . . I don't know what it's called. I sort of . . . made this up."

"Looks delicious."

"It is."

She smiled. "I'm excited to try it."

Her eagerness seemed to soothe whatever concern popped up. He relaxed, slipped a toasty piece of bread onto a plate, then shoved it in her direction. She grabbed a knife, cut off a square, while he did the same.

Her first gooey bite of soft bread, melted goat cheese, and the perfectly-spiced greens-and-other-sundries topping melted in her mouth. The crackling top tasted like heaven. She closed her eyes.

"Delicious."

When they opened again, Max stared at her in unabashed admiration. "You're perfection. You know that, don't you?"

Stunned, she could only stare. He returned to his meal, had a bite. After chewing, he nodded. "You did it perfectly. Well executed, Isa."

She had another bite just to occupy her mouth, ridding

herself of the obligation to speak. What could she possibly say when he looked at her like that?

Nothing.

Isadora finished half of her green-topped bread before she found her voice again.

"The nursery that I found, that . . . admitted me inside . . . it made me wonder what you think about having children."

If the question surprised him, he gave no sign. Max reached for a cloth napkin as he said, "I haven't thought much about it."

"Not at all?"

He snapped the napkin, shaking it out before wiping his fingers on it. "No."

"Oh."

He lifted an eyebrow. "I hazard a guess that you have?"

"I suppose. Not very seriously. Mam wanted me to hand-fast Jesse and I know he would have wanted loads of children. He's the second oldest of six. So I have *thought* about it, but not seriously. One of the Parker girls had her children's names all picked out and plans for how often to have them . . . I never did that."

A definite chill entered his voice. "And who is Jesse?"

"Another Dragonmaster."

"Are you close?"

"No."

He made a noise in his throat.

"Anyway, I thought maybe we should establish expectations around children. You know, if we're going to keep doing this," she added.

To his credit, he displayed no annoyance. "Not a bad idea. Regarding children? If we had one or two, I think I should be fine with that. If we didn't, I would also be fine with that."

"Then we'll just . . . see what happens?"

He shrugged. "The most arduous part of the process is

yours, Isa. I leave the decision to you, as you'll endure the most rigor. Whatever you decide, I will be here to support you."

The unwinding pressure that sat on her chest began to dissipate. Isadora managed a smile, startled by how deeply his response affected her. In the world she grew up in, such expectations were universal. She would have children, because it's what they did.

To have the choice . . .

She set those thoughts aside to consider later, when she had time to chew on them. Food finished, he washed his plate and set it aside on a towel to dry. Isadora nudged the remaining part of her bread toward him, but he waved it off.

"If you don't want it, Ean can have it." Max motioned toward the third bread. "I made that for him, but he'll eat yours as well. The lad would eat Wildrose if I let him, he's so hungry these days," he finished in a mutter.

"I have yet to meet Ean."

"Oh, he'll appear soon enough." He paused, regarded her. "I'm tired and believe I'll retire to bed. You?"

"Yes, that sounds good."

"I found a book that I thought you might be interested in." He held out an empty hand. The next moment, a small tome appeared there. Slightly tattered and well loved, but holding together. "It's filled with silly riddles that you fill in yourself. I don't know why I thought of you, but I did."

A grin crossed her face. "Really? I would love to do them! Will you do them with me?"

"Of course."

His quick, sincere capitulation made her heart flutter. She accepted the book, clasping it to her, and slipped her arm through his.

"Thank you, Max."

He tugged her toward the stairs. "Don't thank me yet. I'm horrendous with fun."

TWENTY-TWO
SANNA

"Luteis, I think you've found it."

How will we know for certain? I'm positive we've traipsed at least half the forest.

"I can tell!"

Sanna spun in a circle. The air didn't hover as close as other parts of the forest. Though she couldn't see the branches, she felt their weight. As if magic loomed more prevalently in some spots than others.

At her feet, a brook bubbled. Sips of the water were clean, not brackish or strange. Smaller undergrowth cluttered the ground, but not too thick. She'd already measured out a square forty paces wide, each corner marked with a cairn of rocks that were too big to be an accident. Despite the house map, more space remained around it.

The ground is fairly flat, he said, as if slowly convinced by what she said.

"Any signs of forest lions?"

Not that I've found.

She thought of the strange creature that almost attacked in the night nearly a week ago, then dismissed it. No other indications had shown themselves. Their days had been quiet and calm as they warbled around, returning every other day to update Mam.

I believe you'll want another sighted witch to confirm that this is a good spot, he said with worry in his voice. *While I can observe and report with my eyes, I am not a witch. They may think differently, understand better. Your sister, perhaps?*

Sanna stopped spinning. The exultation in her blood slowed. She paused, arms at her side. He had a point, but was it a necessary point?

"Maybe."

Your Mam?

"Ah, I'd rather wait on that. Where *are* we again?"

Luteis hesitated, and in the pause, she read a world of uncertainty.

"Luteis?"

We are in the forest, though perhaps not as deep as you might like. I followed the stream, he continued hastily, before she could interrupt. *It led me here. As to where? I have no other landmarks with which to orient you. All is forest.*

True.

Dragons didn't map the world out like witches. Daid used to have an old, curling parchment with a sketched layout of Letum Wood and the basic large structures in the Central Network. Chatham Castle. A city named Ashleigh. Curiosity compelled her to wonder where, in that defined world, she stood.

Luteis wouldn't have been so uncertain if there wasn't something that pushed him to be so.

She paused.

"Are there witches nearby?"

I believe so, but have not confirmed. We're in closer proximity to witches than before, and I fear you won't be pleased with that. It couldn't be helped.

She wasn't thrilled with the prospect, of course, but she wouldn't voice that to him. The anxiety in his tone softened her. He tried so hard.

"You did perfectly, Luteis. Thank you."

Truly?

"Yes. The creek appears healthy. The undergrowth isn't so heavy. We have enough space, on flat ground, to build a house. From what I can feel, admittedly, not much, the trees are a more manageable size here to obtain lumber from."

I would agree. The forest is far more healthy than other places.

"Good. Is it close to hunting?"

I find it acceptable for my use. The water is clean, and the forest not overly dark as in other parts. There are areas of Letum Wood that not even dragons would traverse. We are far from those and the . . . threatening influences they yield.

"Really?"

He shuddered, scales rippling. *Yes, and I would not expose you to it. Here is ideal for a dragon. The trees are spaced far enough apart to allow quick and easy navigation. Most branches are quite high, which decreases the likelihood of a forest lion or belua attack. It seems to be a quiet area. Yes, this shall do nicely.*

"What about the winter? Where will you sleep?"

In the forest, as I always do.

"But there's no cave."

He snorted. *I never hibernated in caves. This is a weakness in the vapid forest dragons that Talis turned into whelps.*

She giggled. Luteis' staunch opinions on the other forest dragons and their lazy, incompetent state hadn't changed in the weeks after the breaking of the Dragonmaster magic. Though many had redeemed themselves by fighting against Prana, such as Junis and Elis, the others that refused to learn to fly received his enormous and near-eternal disdain.

Cara received the most attention, however, as Luteis very much wanted to mate with her.

I stand by my suggestion, he said with a bit more levity. *I think your sister should view it. There may be concerns that I wouldn't be aware of. Aside from that, I believe we have found the place.*

"But how do we get Isadora here? She can't ride you."

A fair question. What of her magical means of moving around?

"Yes, transporting, but Isa says that it's unsafe if you haven't been to the spot where you're transporting first. I don't think she'd just be able to transport to my side."

Hmmm...

Impatient to begin, Sanna waved that off. "Well, let's deal with that later. For now, maybe we can figure out how the house will lay out. Do you think forty paces is wide enough?"

I wouldn't know.

She set her hands on her hip. How big was the house she grew up in? The table where they sat? Exactly how much furniture did she need?

In the back of her mind's eye, she harbored a picture for the house. An idea of how it would lay out in front of her. Now that she tried to conjure it, the details remained elusive. Twenty paces for her bedroom? No.

Ten?

Grr...

Furniture popped into her mind. She hadn't thought of chairs. How would she fashion those to the right height? She could create stools, somehow. Nails and a hammer, which were easily enough found, except...

How would she use them without smashing a thumb?

A plethora of new questions occurred, leading her to the realization that finding the best place had been the easy part.

Sanna swallowed rising panic, born on a wave of questions

such as *how will we cut down trees for lumber?* and *where will I find firewood?*

"Can you smell any fairies in this area? They're nasty neighbors if we build too close. It's the final thing that I can think of to check."

Another wise idea. I would like to check for fairy stumps. Would you be all right here if I climb higher into the trees to sniff around?

"No, I don't mind. Just . . . stay close?"

She tried to keep a nervous tremble out of her voice. Based on the softness of his tone when he responded, she didn't do a very good job.

Forever, little one.

The hard beat of his wings as he soared into the treetops followed. Sanna drew in a deep breath, let it back out. The delighted babble of the wintry brook belied the waiting silence. An entire world stared at her, but she couldn't see it.

In that world, dangers awaited.

Sanna stuffed aside the terrifying curl of fear and focused on circumscribing her new place. While her fingers dug into the soil for rocks—large ones for walls, smaller rocks for furniture, such as a table—her mind kept a loose track of sounds. Within this spot, she would be safe enough.

Attempts to flick dirt off the tip of her fingernails led to questions about soap. How was she supposed to stay clean?

Mam would have some, she imagined. Yet, that was a capitulation. An admittance that she couldn't live her life alone with Luteis.

And yet . . .

The truth lingered somewhere in the background. Why did her life have to be yes or no? Could there be an in-between?

She worked steadily, gratified for purpose, when Luteis

returned. His talons tore through the bark as he slid down, gouging it, before he landed sprightly on his feet.

I am convinced there are no dangers here.

Relieved, Sanna let out a deep breath. "Thank you for checking. I'll map this out, then we'll fly back to Mam's, have a bath, and let her see that I'm still alive."

Something she would appreciate, I believe.

"I loathe relying on her for anything," she ended with a sigh, then sniffed her shirt and recoiled. "But by Drago, I desperately need a hot bath."

The distant sound of laughter bounced through Mam's dining room the next day. Luteis hunted while she waited safely with Mam. The pop and hiss of a fire sent bursts of heat into the room, like having Luteis close by. She shuffled near to it, felt with her toes for the edge of the stone hearth on the floor.

Thanks to a warm bath, the scent of fresh soap in her wet hair filled her nose. She'd scrubbed her scalp with her fingernails, cleaning the amassed grit there, then every inch possible.

Asking for help might be difficult, but worth it.

Mam's knitting needles clicked together, accompanied by an occasional whisper as she counted stitches. Sanna found her way to a rocking chair, leaned back, and rested in the quiet. Four sturdy walls gave her a depth of peace. For the first time in weeks, she fully calmed, eager to create her own place.

"Have you given any thought to letting your sister teach you magic, Sanna?" Mam's musing tone, an inquiry that seemed a little *too* easily asked, startled her.

"A little."

"Really?"

"You think I should learn it, too?"

"I think it's an option for you."

"Some spells might make it easier to adapt, if they existed."

"Hmm."

"Why do you ask?"

"Curiosity."

Mam's tone gave no satisfaction. A seat groaned on the other side of the room, near Mam's voice. Elliot, most likely. He snorted and snuffed enough that she knew he hadn't moved since dinner. An occasional soft breath and snore came from his direction.

For once, she was glad she didn't have sight. She didn't want to see Mam with anyone but Daid, even if she was happy for them.

Sort of.

"Mam, do you . . . that is . . . when you handfasted Daid and left life in the Network, you promised Talis you would stop using magic."

"I did."

"Did you really stop?"

"For the most part. There were a few desperate circumstances when you were babies that I used calming blessings or healing incantations. Largely, however, I kept my word."

"Was it hard?"

"Yes. Magic can be dangerous and used for nefarious purposes, but it has many good things about it, as well."

Rigid Mam, so anti-magic, such a rule-abiding witch, floated through Sanna's mind. The Mam that spoke today stood as a testament to the power of change. The ways life challenged and forged all of them.

"Do you use magic now that Talis is gone?"

Mam hesitated. Shuffles likely meant she had readjusted her yarn. Elliot, his children, and the Parker kids probably produced a sprawling pile of clothes that needed fixing.

Keeping up with the socks had been a challenge in a family with only two children. Sanna couldn't imagine seven.

"I hadn't thought that much about magic before Talis died and the mountain dragons arrived and your daid died. Lately, I have used spells I kept tucked away in memory. It's the kind of thing that's hard to forget, once it's a part of you."

"Do you feel safe using magic?"

The clicking sounds stopped. "Oh, *amo*, of course it's safe. I know it might not feel that way for you because of . . . well . . . what Daid and I taught you. Perhaps that fault is mine, or maybe it belongs to Talis. Either way, the farther from Talis I go, the more I see that when I joined the Dragonmaster families, I swapped one terrible master for another."

"What does that mean?"

Mam sighed. A world of hurt and weariness lingered in the sound.

"It means that I left a world rife with magic and witches that used it to hurt others. I found another restrictive world, but at least it offered security and love. I have never regretted my decision to handfast Rian. Except . . . life with Talis as dragon sire also required much, and . . . I'm not sure what I'm trying to say."

The quick accedence, and the unexpected change in tone, startled Sanna. Indeed, it seemed as if there was *more* to explain, but Mam didn't know how.

"All our life," Sanna said slowly, "you told us that magic was bad. That it was forbidden. Now you want me to use it. It's . . . confusing."

Mam paused, her rigidness obvious in the air. "I'm sorry, Sanna. We were doing the best we could."

"I can't just unlearn years of fear, Mam." A fist pressed to her heart. The thud of her heartbeat beneath her ribs echoed in a dull refrain. "There's a block in my heart. Right here. It's . . . scary."

"I believe it's like anything in this life." Mam's controlled tone meant she tried to hold herself together. Her voice wobbled, rife with emotion. "Anything can be good or bad, depending on how you use and look at it. Magic is a powerful tool, or you could consider it a weapon. Isadora has been using it now with great effect."

Sanna snorted. "I'm not Isadora."

"Nor do I want you to be. Magic is something you might use to navigate your . . . new world."

"You can say it, Mam. You can say that I'm blind."

"I know."

"Why don't you?"

Tears entered Mam's voice. "Because I don't want it to be real for you. I'm sorry, Sanna. I'm trying to honor your life. I'm trying."

Guilt washed through her. She hadn't made this easy on Mam. Not that it was easy on any of them.

"I know. I'm sorry. I just . . . I'm trying to figure it out, too."

"I'm glad you came home," Mam said with a little sniffle. "Really glad. I worry about you out there. It's . . ."

She stopped. The chiding voice didn't resume, like it had weeks ago. Sanna sighed in silent relief.

A step in the right direction.

The click of knitting needles resumed. Stillness drenched the house. Outside, Greata called to Hans. His distant laugh echoed from the back of the house, where the trees gathered in a copse. For long minutes, not another sound stirred, outside Elliot's deep breaths.

Mori, but what was Sanna supposed to do with her time now? Before, she would have prepped her hunting gear, trapped with Daid, sprinted through the forest. At least Luteis and the home search had kept her busy.

Now what?

"Jesse asked about you," Mam said.

Sanna frowned. Not the topic she wanted to broach with Mam again, but she couldn't help her curiosity.

"What's he doing these days?"

"Trading, finding work. Attempting to carve out a new life, I think. He wants to live in the forest, but doesn't want to be a trapper."

"What does he want?"

"He's figuring that out. There's a whole world out there, as you know more than most, that none of you have seen." Her voice dropped. "I think Greata might leave too, as soon as Hans is a bit older."

Sanna's voice lowered. "Elliot is okay with all of that?"

"Ah, no."

The short reply didn't continue. Sensing Mam wouldn't discuss it with Elliot so close, she let the topic go. Her curiosity over the matter continued. Maybe Isadora would know.

If only she had a spell . . .

A voice floated through her mind.

Little one? I have returned.

Sanna shot to her feet. "Luteis is back. Thank you for the bath and dinner, Mam. As soon as we figure out a way to get you to the spot, we will."

"Sanna—"

Sanna edged closer to the door, left hand held out to track the wall. Her fingertips drummed over the rough boards. "It's all right, Mam. We can do this. See you soon, promise."

Mam's farewell cry rang through the air as Sanna fumbled for her coat, then rushed outside.

"I love you!"

The door slammed shut behind her.

Twenty-Three
Maximillion

The descent of calm made the back of Maximillion's neck prickle. His empty office lay in its usual repose. Not unusual, at this time of day, when witches scuttled to the dining hall for lunch.

An edge in the lack of noise lifted his hackles.

He stood.

The tap of approaching feet came from the hallway. Moments later, Wally rapped on the door. At his call, Wally opened it. Though concave and thin-boned and timid in appearance, Wally reminded Max of himself at that age. A sense of pent up ferocity purred beneath the surface.

"Ambassador," Wally said in a resonant voice. "You have someone requesting to speak with you. I don't know who he is. He's from the Central Network, but I couldn't figure out where. When I saw him, he was speaking with Council Member Maren and asking about you. She gave him directions to your office, so I came in advance to give you a warning."

"Thank you, Wally."

"Several scrolls have also arrived that require your attention. Shall I have them ready, just in case?"

Four scrolls popped into sight on his desk. Max glanced at them askance. Rarely did he have to respond to missives since Wally had taken over. The witch had replies down to an art form. *Have them ready* was code for *leave them to deal with if you need a way out of this conversation.*

He didn't pay Wally enough.

Before Max could respond, a body appeared in the doorway. A light-haired man with striking blue eyes, a prominent cleft in a stubborn chin, and hair swept to the side of his head. His barrel chest took up all the space. Wally retreated to the right with a surreptitious nod in Max's direction.

Indeed, Max didn't know this witch at all.

Rare enough.

After a quick pause to gain his bearings, the witch stepped forward. "Ambassador Sinclair?"

"That is me."

The man smiled. A quick thing, without much depth. "My name is Ronald Torkelson. I came without a prior meeting arranged, and for that I apologize. I'm passing through the castle and wondered if I could steal a moment of your time?"

Max hesitated. Definitely unusual. Later, he'd have a conversation with Council Member Maren about boundaries and the importance of his time. Ronald's relationship with Maren meant Ronald could be politically important in some fashion. He suspected business dealings, based on Ronald's pristine appearance and expensively tailored clothes.

Curiosity compelled his response.

"You have five minutes."

Ronald nodded once, reached into a pocket, and pulled out a faceted watch. He spun a dial, pressed it, and set it back into his breast pocket with a grin.

"Five minutes."

He stepped just inside the doorway, hands folded behind

his back. The stance drew his hefty shoulders out. Instinct told Max to be wary, and he staved off the urge to slide into the paths and see what appeared.

"We haven't had the honor of meeting yet," Ronald said. "I am a close friend of several Council Members, mostly through business dealings. I am well-known for my extensive real estate holdings throughout Chatham City."

A bell rang in the back of Max's head.

Ah.

Indeed.

He hadn't met the witch, but he'd heard the name. Ronald Torkelson had more than *extensive real estate holdings*. The man owned almost half of Chatham City, and not the ramshackle half, either. Many merchants rented space from him to sell their wares.

"Yes, I've heard of you before."

Ronald beamed. "Delightful. I'm always happy to hear that. Well, I've had some interest in a political career for some time, but haven't really made any strides forward with it, due to . . ." he cleared his throat. "Well, Greta was an interesting witch, wasn't she?"

Max said nothing.

Ronald continued, nonplussed over the silence.

"Now that Charles has taken over, I'm hopeful for a far more prosperous reign. As such, I've taken to creating and supporting several volunteer agencies that work throughout Chatham City. You may have heard of some of them. Shelters for the Guardians that need a place to get back on their feet. Education initiatives. That sort of thing."

Ronald paused. His intentional wait, filled with an expectant look, burdened the air.

Max said nothing.

A moment before the aggravating silence would have exploded, Ronald cleared his throat. His shoulders tightened, but he didn't give up eye contact. Witches like Ronald—so self-assured, driven, and ready to change the world to his own liking—were easily dealt with.

"One of these agencies," Ronald continued, "is an investigative team that looks into the backgrounds of those holding office in the Network."

A sliver of ice shot down Max's back. He held no guilt. Torkelson could investigate whatever he liked in Max's background, but his heart raced as he thought of Charlie, Isadora, even Faye.

Ronald cut a quick glance. Seeing no change in Max's expression, he spoke again.

"This team was kept quite busy by Greta, of course. We worked in partnership with the *Chatterer* from time to time, even with Charles, when it was required. A few times, the elusive Advocate reached out to us for information, which we were happy to share. Before, ahem, we knew more of what lay behind the scenes there."

Max filed that away later to verify with Charlie. It didn't sound too far outside the realm of possibility, as Charlie maintained relationships with all kinds of informants. The words that caused the hair on the back of his neck to stand up, however, replayed through his mind.

Before, ahem, we knew more of what lay behind the scenes there.

Now what did *that* mean?

Max paused, sensing that Ronald would move quickly now. To hurry this along, he glanced at the clock.

Ronald complied.

"My investigative team has come up with some rather interesting information lately. Some clues, I suppose you could call them, about what happened in the Southern Network to support the creation of the Mansfeld Pact."

A definitive chill entered Torkelson's voice.

Max forced a bored expression, eyebrow lifted. "Your team has read all the articles that have been and are currently being published about it, you mean?"

"Well, of course." Torkelson smiled, but it didn't quite meet his eyes. "As elusive and vague as they were. We've begun to branch out to other sources closer to the action. Regardless, I'm speaking rather to the witch you handfasted. Miss Spence."

"Mrs. Sinclair."

"Forgive me, yes. Yes. You are still together." A hand lifted, pressing to his lips. "You see, we've learned that some believe she swayed the outcome of the Mansfeld Pact with her abilities as a reputed Watcher."

Suspicion rose like a noxious cloud in Max's gut.

"We feel this is of utmost importance, and we're working to prove this assertion, as we do for all facts, naturally." Ronald cleared his throat. "Which brings me here."

A parchment at Max's fingertips rolled up, tapped his fingernail, then straightened back down. He cast a quick glance at it.

Wally's handwriting filled the inside.

Has associations with the League of Free Borders. Might have founded it.

The good gods.

The League of Free Borders was a group of radical, frustrated witches that popped up minutes after the Mansfeld Pact finalized and had been harassing Network officials ever since. They were firmly against the closing of borders and isolationism.

Several members had shown hostilities toward Watchers in the past weeks. Their top three leaders held high positions on the Advocacy watch list. Big Leo had interacted with them personally in his attempts to infiltrate the Central Network and pull Watchers to Carcere.

Suddenly, Torkelson's comment made sense.

Before, ahem, we knew more of what lay behind the scenes there.

Torkelson helped the Advocacy until he realized the aim. He didn't want to support Watchers.

Torkelson's appearance was a veiled threat, not a surprise visit. His ability to navigate to Max's office, smooth his way into a five minute conversation, and the disrespect of speaking about Isadora as if she didn't still hold Max's name.

Rage ignited in his blood like flames.

Max's stomach twisted as he returned his gaze to Torkelson. "You have one minute, Mr. Torkelson, to get to the point."

Ronald smiled and gestured to his pocket. "Yes, of course. Time is ticking, indeed. I want only to ask about Mrs. Sinclair and her magical powers."

"You may not."

"Well, forgive me, but I *may*. It's not your place to stop me from inquiring. I figured I would give you a chance to give me the information, instead of others. Until we have discovered more of the facts, I don't want to speak with her. Bias, and all that. We work for clean debate and acquittal."

"To what end?"

"The truth. I firmly believe that the Mansfeld Pact will lead to the downfall of Alkarra. Such extreme isolationism may serve to quell the wars that a poor leadership structure started, but given time—five, ten years maybe—we'll see a dissolution of our economy, of resources. The lack of free trade will breed greater black markets, criminality. I love my Network, Ambassador, and don't wish to see it fall apart."

"My wife has what place in those bleak assumptions?"

Ronald's blonde eyebrows lifted, as if in surprise. "Why, everything. What if we prove that she does have such great magical power, and she used it to influence a political decision? Imagine if the Central Network allowed her free reign? We suspect she holds great power, a secondary issue that should have been addressed with greater restrictions on her freedom, but that's a topic for another day. It was Isadora Sinclair that brought a powerful, future-seeing magic into a political equation in order to influence the sequence of events into a position that would better serve her."

Ronald leaned forward, gaze tapered.

"The question that I *will* answer, Ambassador, is why? What aim does she have? What motivations does she chase? For it wouldn't surprise me if we were to see her attempt to find a job in the Network. Using her powers, to weasel her way into a position—perhaps one such as yours?—that would allow her an unparalleled position to influence witches that Alkarra has ever seen."

An amplification of Max's burning indignation fanned to relentless zeal. He forced it back with a controlled breath, drew himself to greater height, and strode across the room. Ronald didn't cower, nor move, but his frown deepened.

The pocket watch cheeped a sound.

"It's a topic I shall not entertain at all, Mr. Torkelson. Your five minutes are up. If you return to my office with another veiled threat, I will have you placed in the dungeons until it's clear that you may not bully a Network official."

"I never—"

"Silence!" Max roared.

Ronald drew in a sharp breath. His features hardened as he slipped back a step, into the hallway.

"You have made your position clear, Ambassador."

"I certainly hope so. Any further threats against myself or my wife will be met with a force the likes of which will make your head spin. Challenge me, Mr. Torkelson, and you and your businesses shall never recover."

The door slammed shut in his face.

———

Isadora's hair gleamed in the firelight.

Entranced, Max watched from where he stood on the other side of the master suite, near the door. She sat in front of the fire, a comb in her hand. The teeth sank into her drying locks of hair, pulled down. The velvety strands slipped through like silk, neat and orderly. Once she finished one section of hair, she moved to the next, humming a calmer version of a bawdy tavern song. Probably learned it from the odd friend of hers, Baylee.

Every now and then, she giggled.

A simple white nightgown covered her shoulders, dropped to her elbows. The shift moved restlessly around her knees when she wiggled on the ottoman where she sat, near the fire. The buttery light cast on her features made his throat thick.

He swallowed hard, swamped by thoughts of Ronald Torkelson and Isadora and the muck of such threats. The good gods, but not another witch would touch her while he drew breath.

He advanced into the room, careful to make noise as the door closed behind him. It latched with a firm click. She whirled around, brightened with a smile. His chest clenched as he set aside his jacket and a sheaf of papers he would deal with later.

There would be no escaping this innocent siren.

"Merry meet," she said.

He approached from behind. She tilted her head back, hair gleaming in waterfalls of dark blonde strands. An impish smile appeared. He couldn't stop himself from leaning down, pressing his lips to hers. Her smile faded into surprise.

Before he lost himself, he pulled away.

"Let me?"

"S-sure," she whispered.

He grasped the comb from her hand and sank it into her hair. She pulled her knees to her chest, bit her bottom lip. The comb pulled through her knot-free hair. The soothing motion calmed him, but not as much as the reassurance of touching her.

She was fine.

Ronald Torkelson had no power over her.

All the same, he silently brought a piece of paper and a pencil. With a spell, he commanded the pencil to write.

We need to talk.

It disappeared, on its way to Charlie.

Only then did he notice the books splayed on the floor. Journals. Well, sort of. Leather-bound tomes filled with thick pages. Paintings decorated each one. The books didn't close all the way. They canted open at strange angles, unable to shut due to the crackling paint.

Most of them revealed still life objects. Fruit. Tables. A chair. The front of Wildrose, an open cellar door. He'd seen them once, as a teenager, but hadn't been able to figure out which occupant of Wildrose painted them. They were expertly done.

"Treasures from your explorations of Wildrose?"

"Yes." She chuckled softly. "I found them this afternoon. They're . . . interesting."

A pause. He let the hair sift through his fingers as he pulled the comb down her scalp. Fascinating, that anything could be so soft. The smell of rosewater came with each stroke.

"Are you all right, Max?"

"Yes."

She blinked up at him with a curious gaze. "Will you tell me about your day?" Her breath hitched at the end, as if waiting for something.

A rejection?

A denial?

He'd certainly done so before . . . but that had been before they decided to remain handfasted. When his feelings for her were so dangerous and volatile and powerful. Not that much had changed.

Torkelson flashed through his mind, and he couldn't help but wonder if one ever really settled into love.

"Yes, I will tell you about my day. Thank you."

He continued to brush her hair with methodical precision. While he combed, he mentioned a few interesting points. Witches she knew, political situations she vaguely tracked. The more he spoke, the easier the words came.

Then he stopped.

Torkelson had been the last productive moment of his day. The rest dissolved into fits of rage and distress.

"And then a few interruptions came. I was late dealing with the work I didn't get done because I had a hard time focusing."

The repetitive motion of comb against scalp seemed to have soothed her. She'd only interrupted his flow to make a witty remark or two.

Eager to turn his thoughts, and not wanting their time to end, he set the comb aside, walked around the ottoman, and settled next to her. Tendrils of warmth from the fire reached out.

Isadora scooted to his side, leaned her cheek on his shoulder.

"Nothing too exciting happened to me today." Her hand fluttered around them to motion to Wildrose. "I checked on Mam, found these books in the library. They're . . . fascinating, aren't they? Such delicate detail work in something that isn't all that exciting."

"Vibrant forms of still life art."

Her arm slid through his. He yearned to hold her, but stopped. Could he slow this progression? Could he promise to let her have the lead in their intimacy when she felt so good?

By sheer willpower, he held back.

"Sanna used to brush my hair," she murmured, groggy. "We would sit in front of the fire at night and brush each other's hair. She hated it—grew bored after a few minutes— but she knew that I loved it, so she'd brush it until I told her to stop. Well, until she was ten or so. Then she refused."

He opened his mouth, but wasn't sure what to say. She turned her face to him, chin on his shoulder.

"Do you have any good memories of your childhood, Max?"

The startling question gave him a moment of pause. "Depends on what you would consider my childhood."

"When you were little, before you met Charlie."

The instinct to scoff and say, "Absolutely not," was a hard one to overcome. He paused, thinking, and finally said, "There was a witch named Abbi. She would shelter me, as best she could, from Antonio's wrath. She also taught me to read. Most of her teeth were missing, and she smelled like sweat and urine because she couldn't move around very well, but she was kind to me. The first time I read a letter all by myself, I was . . ."

He faded into the memory for a moment, whisked back to the sultry heat of his Eastern Network home. Abbi, her gummy grin, cackling voice. Imperfect, but perfectly so. She'd been the only reason he survived once Mere died.

". . . proud, I suppose. That is a good memory."

Her arm tightened around his. She offered no condolences and allowed a moment of connection to swell.

"Have you seen Abbi lately?"

"She died."

"I'm sorry."

"She was in pain and . . . well, I don't know if anything exists after this life, but even oblivion would have been better than living in that wretched swamp."

He heard the bitterness in his own tone, but didn't know how to get rid of it. Isadora tilted her head against his shoulder. He watched her from the corner of her eye. Her lashes fluttered closed.

He tangled their fingers together because he had to touch her. *Could* touch her. She squeezed, a yawn peeping out of her.

"You're tired," he whispered.

She nodded, eyes still closed. Unable to resist any longer, Max wrapped his arm around her, pulled her into his lap. She obeyed like a missing piece. Her body curled around him as if she'd always been there.

Max stood, carrying her across the room. The air cooled by degrees as he stepped around the splayed books and toward the bed. She reached for him as he lay her down in the giant four-poster.

Her eyes fluttered open.

"Stay with me, Max?"

He hesitated. Unable to say no to her soulful gaze, and with Ronald bright in his mind, Max lay on the bed next to her. She scooted into his arms, spine to his chest, and snuggled in. He squeezed her tight. Roses filled his head. He'd never forget their dulcet scent.

Not a soul will harm you, he silently promised.

She drifted to sleep, blissfully unaware.

Max stared at the wall and tried not to hold so desperately onto hope.

Twenty-Four

Isadora

A veritable hothouse of plants awaited.

She stood at the top of a longhouse made of glass. Moisture slaked the walls, dripping in tumbling beads. Plants populated gardens both in the ground and above. Planters, hanging pots, shelves of starts barely peeking out of rich black soil. A permeating, earthy smell filled the air. She braced her hands on her hips, breathed deep.

"Well," she drawled. "What have we here?"

A squeak of a voice came from behind her. "It's a bloody greenhouse. Haven't you ever seen one before?"

Isadora whirled with a shout. A muddied little boy stood back there. He had rickety, thin legs, arms almost too long for his lanky frame, and gangly teeth at odd angles. His wide eyes were bright, however, and dark as night. The black hair tousled on top of his head stood almost straight up. Dirt streaks marred his wrists, neck, and cheeks.

"Well, merry meet," she said, hand to her fluttering heart. "Who are you?"

"Ean."

Her eyes widened. "Ean? Oh, Max has told me about you."

The lad's suspicious gaze tapered. "You Miss Isadora?"

"I am."

"So he *did* handfast someone?"

She hid a smile. "He did."

"Huh. Thought it was a rumor."

She motioned to the manor with a lift of her hands. "I've been here for almost three weeks. How have we not met yet?"

"I don't go in the manor much. Just for food."

"Why not?"

"Ghosts," he said solemnly. "The place is haunted. Can't you feel them?"

Isadora schooled back a laugh. "Ah, no. I haven't observed that yet, though it certainly is an interesting place."

He shuddered. "Many ghosts. I sleep in the stable. Ghosts don't like horses. Sometimes, we have goats and they don't like goats neither."

"I haven't seen inside the stable yet."

He eyed her. "How long did you say you've been here?"

"Obviously not long enough. Tell me about this greenhouse, Ean. You take care of it? Clearly run by magic, if you're growing starts in the dead of winter."

He picked up a water pail at his feet. His other hand clutched soiled trowels and a rake. "Yes, to the magic. But only environmental magic, and it doesn't work for every plant."

"What does that mean?"

An exasperated eye roll followed. "Environmental magic!" he cried. "We heat rocks to keep it warm, and pour water on them to create steam for the plants. In the winter, we only plant tubers, because there's not enough light for stuff like peas. Spells to deflect the cold. You know, environmental."

"Right."

"Mr. Maximillion lets me stay, so I keep the greenhouse.

He likes to cook with fresh vegetables and spices. He works with some of the Network school teachers, too. So students come here to learn and test new spells and read grimoires for planting and herbology."

"How very kind."

"Not really. We want to know the good stuff, too."

"Ah, yes. I've noticed he does love to cook. Do you want to sleep in the house? There are so many rooms."

Ean shrugged. "Better than an orphanage, and I told ya. No. Too many ghosts."

"Right."

He motioned with a tilt of his head. "Down here are some flower starts, if you want to see them. Just tried 'em out with Mr. Chen's School for Boys. Two of the older blokes want to be gardeners, apparently. Supposed to be winter flowers that make your heart stronger, or something."

"Sure."

For the next twenty minutes, Ean trudged around the dirt-packed greenhouse, rattling off explanations and vexed sighs that deeply amused her. Roped off areas, fenced with meager wooden stakes and cut by even rows of hoed lines, filled the area. An impressive system of maintenance existed, not to mention organization.

One tall shelf above rows of vegetable starts held a book. She pulled it down. Brittle pages filled with small envelopes, glued with their backs to the paper, lay inside.

"Seed diary," Ean said. "Miss Faye put it together a few years ago. We harvest the seeds from the previous year and keep them in there for the next year. Sometimes, at markets, she finds new seeds. We try to grow and replant those too."

"Very self-sufficient."

"Wildrose is a big manor. Gotta feed everyone somehow. Though, there used to be a lot more witches here than there are today."

Isadora riffled through each page. The envelopes were neatly marked with what appeared to be a woman's handwriting. Faye's probably.

Caramine seeds.

Falfalla spice.

Watermelon salt.

Gourds, variety.

Isadora eyed Ean as she re-shelved the book. "Do you go to school, Ean?"

"Yes."

"Max requires it?"

He shot her a piercing, annoyed stare that almost made her laugh. "Yes."

"How did you find each other?"

Ean shrugged. "Dunno." The way his fingers clenched until the knuckles turned white told a different story. She let the question go, curious about other things as well. Did Max often save other witches, or was it Wildrose? He said the manor existed as a sort of haven.

The Advocacy certainly asserted that.

"Hullo in there?"

Ean and Isadora looked up at the same time. A familiar head of bright red hair appeared at the door of the greenhouse. Charlie waved, stepped inside, and drew in a lungful of air.

"Earthy as ever," he called, laughing. "Ean, you've done some impressive work, my boy."

Ean beamed, illuminated like a candle.

Ah, how interesting.

Charlie gazed around, rattling off questions. Ean answered all of them, asked a litany of his own. Charlie answered each, carefully touched a few plants, cast several spells, taught Ean a few tricks, then looked at Isadora with an equally wide smile.

The lack of a stuttering, bumbling High Priest startled

her. This self-possessed man ran their Network, thank the good gods, and remained an ever-elusive enigma.

He held out an arm. "Isadora, always so wonderful to see you. I came to see if you would be interested in going on a short stroll with me?"

Startled, she could only nod, accept his arm, and follow him out.

———

Snow crunched beneath Charlie's feet as they walked across the grounds, toward the stable. Horses stood at a fence of thick timbers, their dark eyes curious and ears high. Charlie steered their direction.

"And?" he asked, breath fogging in front of him. "What do you think of our manor?"

"It's lovely."

"Odd, too." His nose, tipped red at the end, wrinkled. "So many strange parts. Max mentioned you were diving deep to Wildrose's secrets. You opened the nursery?"

"Yes."

He chuckled. "I'm quite jealous. Tried for years to finagle my way in that room. My father never saw it, nor my grandfather. I believe a distant cousin of my father claimed to have opened it once, but no one ever proved it. She was half-mad with grief over losing a stillborn child, as family legends go."

Her thoughts rushed to the sheaf of letters tucked in her armoire. "Do you know when the nursery was last used?"

"I don't. Max knows Wildrose best. He's read through all the stories and genealogies kept through the years. If he doesn't know, it's lost to history. Though, one might be able to piece it together, given time."

"I don't know how it allowed me—"

Charlie waved her explanation off. "It's better not to ask,

as Wildrose never explains. I'm happy that the magic of the manor approves of you, though I'm not surprised."

The magic of the manor rang through her head.

Fascinating.

A bay horse trotted closer, giant breaths pluming free. She reached out a hand, caressed the soft velvet of its nose. It nickered, shaking its mane. Charlie laughed.

"Are you able to stay busy at Wildrose?" he asked.

"Yes, so far."

"Do you have any plans for a job?" His head tilted to the side. "Working somehow?"

"Eventually, yes."

He made a thoughtful noise in his throat she couldn't quite interpret. For a long pause, neither said a word. The silence wasn't awkward, nor warm. Conjecture over the High Priest rose within her constantly.

Who was he *really*?

Did he throw the wool over her eyes even now? If he did, how would she ever know or prove it?

"Have you seen the cemetery yet?" he asked.

The macabre question broke through her thoughts.

"Uh, no."

"Come. I'll show you the Dauphins. It's a far lovelier place in the summer, I assure you."

They crossed the lackluster grounds, crunching through frozen grasses and patches of snow. A leaden sky threatened to burst with moisture at any moment, and a warm fire with a cup of tea and a book sounded delicious.

Curiosity over Max's closest confidante kept her pressing around a patch of forest at Charlie's side.

Silently, they approached a fenced-off area, tucked into a tree line. The icy top of a pond darkened the ground nearby. Charlie led her to a creaky iron gate, which he opened. Stones and uneven pockets of earth and graves filled the ground.

There must have been hundreds spread over a rather small area for so many.

He stopped, waved his free arm.

"The Dauphins."

"So many?"

"Well, lost souls have always been drawn to Wildrose, some in their final breaths. A few witches they had to bury on top of others, just because there's not much space. One day, Max'll have someone expand the fence, I'd wager, but it would take quite a bit of work. When Mother died in childbirth with me, she slowed the usual expansiveness of the Dauphin name." His eyes twinkled when he looked at her. "Dauphins typically had a lot of children."

She smiled.

A dark feeling stole over her as she imagined, decades from now, her and Max lying side by side with gravestones of their own. Sickness filled her at the thought. She forced lightness into her tone, eager to escape the suffocating, cold place.

"Might we stroll to the road?"

Charlie leaped back to attention. "Certainly!"

As they headed toward the cobblestone path lined with dead rose bushes, Charlie's arm tightened ever-so-slightly.

"How are things, Isadora?"

"They're fine, Your—"

"Please, please." He grimaced. "Not that. Not my title. When I come to Wildrose, I'm Charlie. Just Charlie."

Smiling an apology, she nodded. "Charlie."

"Thank you."

"Ah . . . I'm still orienting myself to Wildrose, to the affairs of my family in Letum Wood."

"To Max."

Gently, she said, "To Max."

He paused at the gravel path and released her arm as he turned to face her. She tucked her hand into her pocket, grateful to see him eye-to-eye. His freckled face and coppery hair proved a stark contrast to the day.

"And how is Max handling marriage, would you say?"

"Fine, I suppose."

"Isadora." A tone of chiding filled his voice. "There isn't a soul in Alkarra that knows Max better than myself, a designation which I assume I'll hand to you as time goes on. He's a hardhearted menace, and those are his good days. How is it *really* going?"

Shocked, she could only stare at first. Eventually, that wore away. She sighed.

"He's been accommodating and kind and thoughtful."

"But?"

"But . . . I think he's afraid to touch me. A kiss is rare. There are gestures of affection but . . . I want to know that he loves me before we decide whether we should remain hand-fasted. With words. Yet . . ."

"He won't say the words."

"No."

"He never has, you know."

She lifted a dubious eyebrow. "Never?"

Charlie's lips turned down in a thoughtful purse. "Not that I can ever recall. Nor do I think he's heard them."

"That doesn't make it impossible for him to speak them."

"Not at all."

Her irritation ebbed. "But it does make it unlikely." She gazed past Charlie, to the strangely motionless ribbon of forest ringing Wildrose. The manor stood stalwart behind them, the ever-present flames issuing from the gargoyles on the top floor again. What started and stopped such snarling creatures?

"Unlikely doesn't mean never," he said. "Max might need a bit more time than others."

Isadora chuckled ruefully. "I have been known to hurry witches along my own schedule."

"Same," he remarked with a cheerful smile. He sobered. "I came today to offer my help, should you ever need it. Someone to talk to when Max is too irritating to endure. I've felt that way before, sometimes. It helps to have another witch that loves him to . . . vent to, I suppose."

She laughed. "Thank you. I'm sure I'll take you up on it."

"He loves you, Isadora. Let me reassure you on that count, as his brother. I commend you for taking the time to figure out whether or not you would work as a couple, and ask you to be patient with him."

Isadora met his steady gaze. Love filled his eyes. She may not know if she understood Charlie, but she did *like* him.

"I will."

He held out his arm a final time. Snow spit from the clouds, falling in hard spurts. "Then let me escort you back inside before it grows too cold out here. One never knows what lingers in the forest."

TWENTY-FIVE
SANNA

S anna growled under her breath.

The front of her dress tugged in a weird way, and it wasn't until she felt the seams along the inside that she realized she'd slipped it on backward. The annoyance might not have been so great, had she not smelled the char of something burning at the same time.

With a shout, she reached for her stick. A hunk of mortega lay on it, carefully pierced through the thickest part of the meat, which had taken her far longer to manage than she wanted. It rotated over a small, crackling fire.

She overreached, knocked it off the spit, and heard a sizzle as it landed in the coals. The tips of her fingers touched superheated soot as she searched for the end with another cry.

"By Drago!" she cried, sputtering. "Just . . . just . . ."

No amount of righteous indignation brought the meat back to her hand. By the time she found the end, three of her fingers smarted and the char of blackening meat filled her nostrils even more.

A summoning spell or two, like the ones that Isadora described, would be helpful right about now.

In fact, she'd give her breakfast to have them.

Sanna felt for a flat rock next to her, set the retrieved meat on top, and gently probed it. Groping around the edges of the makeshift plate, she eventually found the sharp rock she'd kept and sliced into the top of the meat.

Of course.

Black and crispy on the outside.

Cool and raw on the inside.

Suddenly not hungry, she turned away with a huff.

You are having a difficult morning, little one.

"Tell me about it."

Her toes dug into the ground as she reached a hand over the fire, uncertain whether or not to add firewood. The radiant heat turned mostly to coals at this point. Since her meat needed longer to cook, she groped for a few more sticks.

A ring of rocks around the outside of the fire kept the flames in one area. Luteis had started it, which helped dampen her frustration. Still, maintaining a fire in an open forest was a frustrating endeavor.

Where is your other foot guard?

"My shoe?"

Yes.

"I don't know."

She ran a hand through her hair, realized she still had soot all over it, and let out an aggravated raspberry. Today had just begun and already it needed to end. Ignoring what her hair must look like, she shoved it out of her eyes. Later, she'd braid it. For now, her stomach grumbled. She just wanted to eat.

Carefully feeling around the edge of the thin rock where the hunk of mortega lay, she lifted the rock and set the whole thing on the coals.

Let it cook *that* way.

Minutes later, a satisfying sizzle, and the smell of roasting meat, filled the air. Sanna idly searched around her for her shoe, thankfully finding it within reach.

"We have a busy day today, Luteis."

Doing what?

"Well, we've mapped out trails from the house structure to the stream, you've created a basic path that leads to bushes that will likely have berries in the summer, and I just finished lining two of them with rocks yesterday, which helps."

You do seem more confident walking around.

"And you started to gather lumber."

She leaned back. A pile of wooden logs rested behind her, forming the eastern wall. The logs would need to be scraped and branches removed, but it was a start.

I don't desire more searching for perfectly-straight trees that have fallen to the ground, aren't rotted, and will withhold through decades of weather. Your demands are quite specific.

"I know! I know, it's boring. But I'm thinking this: what if we have everything ready, then we can ask for help?"

Are you willing to ask for help?

She threw up her hands. "Yes! If we're ready to go and there's a way for us to also work on the house."

Whom will you ask?

"Jesse and Elliot, I suppose? I don't know anyone else."

This makes sense. Perhaps we could involve Junis and Cara and Elis in our search for lumber?

Yearning filled her. Oh, sweet Cara! She missed her dragon friend. Rosy, too. Young Junis would be growing so fast . . .

"Would they?"

I'm not sure. Things are . . . strained . . . amongst the dragons.

"Well, it certainly wouldn't hurt our timeline if they could help. That way, we can see if Jesse and Elis would help us shimmy the walls together. Shouldn't be too hard, right?"

A dubious pause followed.

Is it truly that easy to build a witch-place?

She shrugged. "I don't know. If we have all the tools and supplies, it doesn't *seem* too complicated. Mam says that Jesse is out in the villages more, trading. He can search for the tools so we don't have to go into the Network."

Why would he do this?

"Because he's my friend."

Hmm. I have studied the construction of the witch-place that your Mam resides in. It doesn't appear as if logs have been shimmied together.

His verbatim quoting made her teeth grit.

"Well, *obviously* we might have to do something a little differently, but if we're going to ask for help—" she forced the words out, mentally accepting their necessity, "—then the least we can do is to be prepared. It's etiquette."

At this, his voice perked up. His strange obsession with witch etiquette and the formation of societal rules around certain behaviors had no explanation. She secretly thought he just liked predictable organization.

I understand, and this seems appropriate to me. For one to ask a favor, one should make it as easy on the helper as possible.

"Exactly!"

I am here to help you always, even as boring and dull as your requests have become.

She ignored the little jab to check on her breakfast.

Wincing, she peeled the pieces of meat off the heated rock. After blowing on one, she bit into it. Juice and blood squelched free, but the inner meat had warmed. Quickly as possible—charred mortega wasn't all that appealing—she ate the hunks and made her way to the stream. Juice coated her hands, her chin. Her trail led the way, over which she felt quite smug.

Soon, she'd need to bathe in the stream. The last of the

soap she'd filched from Mam on their last visit hid in a cubby in a nearby tree.

Once she had a house, she'd figure out soap. And utensils. Maybe a broom, too? Oh, but she'd want a porch.

How to do that?

Shaking aside the compounding needs and questions, Sanna washed her hands and face at the stream. The slick hurry of water past her fingertips soothed as it tinkled by. Ice cold and refreshing.

Carefully, she returned to the fire, not far from the house structure.

"All right! Let's get back to work. Now, when we left last night, we had the rocks outlining the general layout of the house."

A pause.

Little one?

She tensed, uncertain how to read the sudden confusion in his voice.

"Yes?"

I have just noticed now, but . . . the rocks. They are . . .

"What?"

Not present in the same fashion.

"What do you mean?"

They're different. Instead of the rectangular shape of your house, they've been . . . knocked aside. As if someone trampled through.

"Impossible," she whispered. "We were both here all night."

I agree.

"Tell me what you see in greater detail. Are the lines . . . gone?"

All of them.

Her heart sank into her stomach.

"Really?"

They'd worked so hard to place the rock walls in straight lines. Gathering the stones required days. Painstaking, slow work without magic or sight.

I cannot be certain. The rock lines are gone, yes. Scattered. The evenness is lost. Rocks are . . . everywhere. Now that I look there are . . . strange marks in the ground. Little holes, like miniature feet.

The swish of his tail along the dirt followed. Sanna stood. A crackle of the fire popping startled her.

"Luteis?"

A moment, please.

He sniffed, snorted. His tail no longer swished along the ground. The previously delightful, safe space held a sinister tint.

She counted to thirty before tentatively asking, "What do you see?"

Rage filled his tone. *Dots in the ground. Markers, even. They have shifted the rocks. The rocky outline you set out before has been eradicated. I believe half of the stones are missing entirely. But how?*

Tentatively, she slipped her boot off and felt ahead with her toes. When her big toe hit a rock, she crouched down. Others scattered around that one, arms length apart. Tossed at random, perhaps. Yesterday, they'd marched in a line.

"Everywhere?"

I'm sorry, little one.

He snuffled again, sending gritty dirt into the air around her feet. She stuffed her foot back into her boot with deepening disheartenment.

I smell nothing unusual, just like last time.

"When?"

When the unknown creature was near. It left the gelatinous blob on you. There were similar prints in the ground.

"There were?" she squeaked. "Why didn't you say something?"

I thought they were unrelated. Now that I see them again, they hold a great deal more significance.

Sanna shuddered. Monsters and creepy creatures and all manner of who-knew-what lurked. Letum Wood's nefarious, angry side was nothing to tempt.

"You think that whatever made those marks is here?"

I'm not sure what to think, only that I've seen these before. The lack of smell is almost as suspicious . . .

She straightened, eager to be away from the dirt. She recalled the disgusting drip and ooze of tacky substance on her scalp all too well.

"Why would it destroy our house plan?"

I cannot imagine why.

"What about the lumber?"

Still there.

"Why?"

His silence responded. She hadn't meant for him to answer, anyway. How could they possibly interpret what this meant?

"The creature might have some intelligence, is what you mean. It wants to be rid of us. Trying to eradicate our plans?"

Yes.

"Like a warning?"

Poorly constructed, but yes.

"What if it's just a coincidence?"

Seems unlikely.

The creature would have followed them here from their previous spot, which might explain why so many days had passed since it acted. The realization only deepened her uneasiness. Luteis' lack of ideas or counterpoints likely meant he didn't want to frighten her.

A horrifying thought occurred.

"How close did they come to you last night?"

Strain filled his voice. *Close enough to touch.*

She let out a long breath. What kind of creature could wreak such havoc without waking a dragon, slip by close enough to touch, not carry a scent, and track them through the forest? Gnomes made too much racket. Mortegas would be too frightened of Luteis. Fairies? No, they'd be more ruthless.

Her entire body felt heavy, like it might puddle at her feet. A scream built up in her throat, but she didn't give it freedom.

Just when they were making progress . . .

Sanna crouched back down, pulled the rocks together that she could reach. She attempted to force resolution to her tone, though it sounded limp as an old breeze. "This means we must . . . start again. Pull it back together. It's our home. We'll stand up for it. Right?"

Little one, I . . .

She paused, hand above a rock. If he said they should go, she'd listen. She'd tear herself away from the dream.

Somehow.

Part of her yearned for him to challenge her. One of them had to break this determination to prove herself, didn't they? Deep down, she *hoped* he stopped her and told her to cease this madness and get help, already.

She couldn't do that on her own. This was the Sanna she had been before, and she clung to that Sanna in all her ferocity. Concerns hung in the air between them while she waited. Time stalled on the edge of a breath.

I will continue to explore and learn. It will not take us by surprise again.

With a sigh, Sanna set her hand on a rock.

Decided.

Time to get back to work.

TWENTY-SIX
MAXIMILLION

A thick scroll landed on Charlie's desk with an unceremonious *thunk*. Max stopped pacing to stare at the High Priest, who accepted the scroll with a raised eyebrow. His solemn expression gave Max pause.

"I have a feeling I know what caused the livid brow on your face."

Max said nothing while Charlie perused the scroll, then set it aside.

"Confirmed."

"If Ronald Torkelson makes one move toward Isadora, Charlie, you will not be able to stop me. That scroll details exactly what he said to me a week ago. I took the notes immediately after our discussion."

"To what end?"

"Evidence. We haven't had a chance to meet in private until now, and I didn't want anything missed."

Charlie stood, set his hands on the back of his chair. His gaze tapered on the scroll for an assessing moment. Instead of the ridiculous outfits he used to wear as Charles, the idiot

High Priest, he'd phased into normal attire. A vest, long-sleeved shirt, and plum jacket covered him today.

"It's too late, Max."

"Excuse me?"

Three pieces of parchment popped off the table, wheeled closer. Max scrutinized them, frowning.

"What is this?"

"The League of Free Borders has announced an official inquest into the happenings in the Southern Network before the formation of the Mansfeld Pact. What you are reading now is your official document. There's one for me, Felicity, and yourself."

"Felicity? He involved the new High Priestess?"

"As Moderator of the Discussion."

A growing pit of dread formed in Max's stomach as he read.

The League of Free Borders is announcing a formal inquiry involving and regarding the Network-compensated witches present at the meetings in the Southern Network that initially led to the formation of the Mansfeld Pact.

Such inquisition shall eventually be presented first before the moderator and those involved, then before the Council, as agreed upon under ESMELDA LAW Article 4, subsection 19, point a.

Initial assignment shall begin within seven days.

"Network-compensated witches?" he breathed.

"You and me. Not Isadora."

"Why not?"

"The Network didn't pay her to be there, so he can't force an inquest on her."

Max flung the official declaration of inquest into the fire and began to pace. "If they truly dive into that night and discover how powerful Isadora is, she won't be safe."

"I know."

"If word spreads about her abilities, and Torkelson is able to incite enough fear into witches, *none* of us will be safe."

Charlie sighed. "I know."

Max halted. "So what are you going to do about it, *Advocate*?"

A warning glare slowed Max's ire.

"Ronald has the right to inquest it, and the League of Free Borders grows in popularity every day. There are witches who want to be heard, and they demand answers. They're turning to the League of Free Borders because it's the first organized place for them to do so. I think the witches deserve both a place to be heard and answers, so I'm going to let the inquest happen without opposition. We'll take this one step at a time."

"That's not enough."

"Isadora will be safe. I swear it, Max. You know that I won't let it go that far."

"You may not be able to stop it. Witches are frightened after what happened in the South. There are unknowns around isolationism that we are still puzzling through. Pressure has been rising. This might be the outlet that the populace needs in order to act. I don't want Isadora to become the figure the Network blames for this political decision. That's *exactly* what Ronald is setting her up to be. A social sacrifice."

Charlie leaned against his desk, legs crossed at the ankles, but tension tightened his features.

"It might be his motivation, it might not. He might be that concerned about the Network and economy. As a business witch, it's not outside his realm of concern. Max, think logically, not with your heart."

"I'm not," he snapped.

Charlie rolled his eyes. "Sure you aren't. Rash, angry decisions are purely born of fact all the time. Think of it this way: maybe the results of this inquest will eventually usher in a new period of peace for Watchers and Defenders?"

"Impossible."

"We don't know, Max. You can search the paths all you want."

"I already have."

"And?"

Max scowled. "Inconclusive."

Wisely, Charlie let that go. "Our official interview will come next—I'm not sure when. Under the Esmelda scrolls, Ronald must request the inquest first by scroll, then in person, with the moderator and those to be questioned upfront. These can take years to really study, Max. It's bureaucratic. Ronald will probably try to speak to witches in other Networks, and that will take ages to confirm and approve under the Mansfeld Pact. As Ambassador, you'll be part of it!"

"Fine. But he can't appeal to Isadora."

"Not yet, as she wasn't compensated by the Network. Eventually, he can. I'm doubtful the Southern and Eastern Networks will even reply to his appeals."

With a final glower, Max turned to the door. Charlie called to him halfway there.

"Oh, and Max?"

He paused, hand on the doorknob.

"As a command from the High Priest, don't tell Isadora just yet. No reason to concern her, nor put the pressure of silence on her. Until we have reason for this inquest to be in the *Chatterer*, I don't want it known. This could take awhile."

Twenty-Seven

Isadora

I sadora had expected Wally to be surprised when she showed up unannounced at Max's office, but his too-wide smile made him appear . . . nervous. She stood next to Max's desk, a linen bag of lunch goodies in hand, utterly perplexed.

Oh, please, she thought. *Make space for me, Max. Show me that you'll make space for me in your busy life.*

How else would they test the third point on her list? *Prove whether our lives can merge.* Was work more important than relationships? Could he handle unexpected turbulence or shows of love?

Wally's eyes darted to the door, then back to Max's desk, then her. Too much time in that circuit and he'd pass out.

"Max isn't here, you say?" she asked, just to fracture the weird air.

"No, Mrs. Sinclair."

Egads, but would that title ever feel normal? "All right. That's fine. I brought a book and can read while I wait for a while. Do you know when he'll be back?"

"I don't."

"*Can* I wait here?"

Wally hesitated. "Ah . . ."

Conflicting emotions contorted his features. Clearly, he didn't want to deny her the chance to wait for Max. Perhaps he didn't have that ability. But he also didn't want her to stay.

"Wally, forgive me for being straightforward, but is something wrong? Is me being here a problem?"

"Wrong?" he squeaked. "Ah, no, Mrs. Sinclair. N-nothing is wrong."

"Please, call me Isadora."

"I-I-Isadora. I, uh . . . it's fine. Surprises are fine at inopportune times. This is fine."

No further explanation followed. Deflated, Isadora set the bag down. She should have arranged to have lunch with Max instead of surprising him, though the test was more in the surprise and how he handled it than anything else.

Several hours of shopping in Chatham City—though she bought only food for lunch—lay behind her. She was bored at Wildrose, but wouldn't admit that. Isadora lifted the linen bag onto his desk.

"Well, I suppose I will leave this here for him, then. It's his favorite . . . I think."

The door blew open. Max, speaking as he strode, entered the room with all the force of a hurricane.

"Wally, Ronald is headed here for the inquest announcement. I need you to—"

He stopped, drew up short. Tendrils of hair on his forehead skewed to the side, shuffling. He wore his usual white shirt and vest, this time emerald, which brought out light tones in his eyes. His sleeves were buttoned tight with cufflinks instead of rolled to his elbows, which meant he must have come from a meeting.

"Oh."

She managed a wan smile. "Merry meet, Max. I was . . .
dropping off lunch for you. I hope we might eat together?"

Max's gaze darted to Wally, who gave a wide-eyed
response, then back to her. Confirmation that *something* was
afoot.

"Thank you, Wally, you may go. I'll take it from here.
Please, work at your desk outside." In a firmer tone, he said,
"Admit no one."

Wally nodded, slipped past. Isadora, overjoyed that Max
would nudge aside his day even a little, dropped the mystery to
consider later. Max had passed a most important test without
even realizing it.

One step closer to confirmation.

"Really?"

Max nodded distractedly as he shuffled behind his desk. "I
can spare a few minutes to have lunch with you."

"I brought a fresh loaf of fig bread that Pearl left at home,
then some cold cuts from a place on the edge of Chatham
City. There's lemonade to wash it all down, in the jar."

His expression brightened a tad. "Sounds delicious."

"I thought so!"

He peered into the bag. A chair clattered across the floor
and stopped next to his with a spell. She slipped around the
desk, heart pounding in her throat. Moments like this left no
doubt in her mind. Of course they'd handfast and last forever!
He made impressive progress toward being the sweet man she
knew was in there. Loving Max felt so easy sometimes.

If only he would *touch* her.

When she stepped up to his side, he lifted her onto the
edge of his desk. The lingering heat of his hand left her breathless. While Max extracted lunch from the bag, she chatted
about window shopping. They pieced together sandwiches.
He asked questions, she parried. His attention never wholly
arrived, but she *had* interrupted him at work.

This whole situation thrilled her.

By the time Max downed the last of the lemonade, twenty minutes had passed. He cracked a slice of chocolate cake in half, passed the larger piece to her. She sank her teeth into it, reveling in the rich taste of raspberry creme in the middle.

"Now," he drawled, "you have had chocolate cake."

Laughing, she swallowed her bite. "You know, I forgot that I hadn't. It's divine."

"Mine is better. So is my lemon creme."

"You'll have to prove it."

"I plan to. You've had a busy day?"

A hint of raspberry sauce at the corner of his lips was a tempting invitation. Before logic and insecurity paralyzed better sense, she leaned forward and captured the remnants of his dessert with a kiss.

Max stiffened.

A shot of panic bolted through her. Isadora leaned back, eyes wide. She didn't go far. Max clamped a hand around her neck and reeled her in with a little growl. She set aside the rest of her cake, dropped into his arms, and surrendered to his touch.

The sugary treat sweetened his lips. He tilted his head, deepening the kiss. She sucked in a breath, looped her arms around his neck. Breathing hard, Max pulled away.

Eyes closed, he pressed his forehead to hers. Isadora's hands rested on his shoulders. She blinked through a passionate haze, startled to see his office around them. Hadn't she taken to the sky and flown away?

Her trembling hand came to her lips. "I—"

A knock came to the door.

"Ambassador?" Wally cried, unnaturally high. "The High Priest is here to discuss the League of Free Borders."

Max's hands tightened around her arms.

"Max?"

"You must go."

"But—"

"Thank you for lunch." A spell swept away the remnants of food. The cake disappeared, the linen bag. He stood, setting her away from him as he straightened his clothes. "Thank you for coming. I'll see you at home."

"Max—"

"Go!" he hissed.

Hurt, confused, and utterly at a loss, Isadora attempted to protest. A flicker of annoyance in his eyes only deepened the shock, stopping her reply. How could . . .

Was it . . .

The door latch rattled. Outside, Charlie called out.

"Ambassador?"

"Now!" he cried.

Isadora swallowed back rising pain. Without another word, she transported away.

Twenty-Eight

Sanna

I *can find no further hints of . . . whatever the creature might be.*

Sanna grunted and dropped a log on the ground. It clattered against several others in a pile as tall as her waist. With the back of her arm, she wiped the sweat off her forehead and sat down.

"That's good news, right?"

Is it?

The dark edge of his question had her uncertain of anything these days.

"Maybe it moved on."

Maybe. His heat slipped by her to the left. *That seems far too simple of a solution for a place like Letum Wood.*

"True. In the meantime, I think we're almost there. It's all put back together, and more logs obtained, anyway."

Sanna felt along the ground, satisfied when the log that she followed bisected another log at a 90 degree angle. Rocks lay in piles on either side. The northwest corner of the house. At least thirty logs gathered at that corner, ready for . . . whatever came next.

Stripping the bark?

Another bundle of trees they had scavenged, approximately forty paces away, held an equal number of logs. Basic guesstimations—assuming each log was about the same width, then stacked end-over-end—meant she'd need at least ten more logs to have enough to build her little house.

Maybe.

All was conjecture.

Will you put in windows?

"Yes, I'll need fresh air. And if people come to visit me, they'll need to be able to see, even if I don't. We could have it totally closed in for me and it wouldn't matter regarding light, but air flow would be an issue."

He made a noise in his throat, seeming not to notice her amusement over it.

"Anyway, about gathering more logs. I know you—"

A sensation of passing air, then a meaty plop, landed at her feet. Sanna leaped back with a cry.

"What is that?"

Something that fell from the treetops.

"What?"

Astonishment filled his voice. *I'm not certain, but I'm inclined to think it's a . . . carcass. No . . . an egg?*

She recoiled, sniffed. No smell came with it. The urge to reach down and touch it followed, but she didn't give in.

"A carcass?" She smelled again. "But I can't smell anything."

Indeed, it's not a carcass. The flesh is not wasted away or shriveled or dark. It's . . . large, I suppose. About the height of your knee.

"Can you describe it any better than that?"

It's a round ball with white, flesh-like areas. Tissue, it would appear. There are six holes on either side of what might be a body. Joint entrances perhaps?

"Like legs?"

No legs visible.

"Weird."

There is no smell, at least not an overpowering one. A light scent, perhaps, but . . .

He snorted, clearly frustrated.

"Do you think *this* is the creature that might be stalking us?"

No. Something has eaten this one. It is not a whole creature. The skin is stripped off, blood is gone. Parts of it are missing, whatever they are.

At that ominous thought, she fell silent. Questions plagued her. So many she couldn't narrow it down. Had the creature come in the night last night, eaten this, and left it to fall on them?

Or did it *put* that here as another warning?

Little one, I believe we should choose a different spot. We are not safe here anymore.

The thought sent a shot of pain through her belly. Leave? After all their hard work? It had taken weeks to find a suitable spot, and she'd slaved for days getting it organized and laid out and . . .

She already knew the answer in her heart. Luteis was right. At least in one regard.

"I understand, but . . . it just . . . it followed us from our last spot, right? Maybe if we leave it will stalk us again?"

Then we go farther away, or closer to your family, where you'll be safer when I hunt.

The thought of being near Mam and Elliot sent equal shots of relief and dread through her. Yes, the four walls would feel marvelous compared to her frightened jitters now.

But . . . no, she could do this. She *had* to do this. How else could she prove to herself and her family that she was capable of living in the forest?

"We don't have any idea what this or the predator is," she said, a bit desperately. "It could have been killed by a forest lion, for all that we know."

What if it remains? What if we've moved into its habitat?

"What if it's stalking us and it doesn't matter where we go?"

He paused.

It's possible, he admitted reluctantly.

The thought of starting over again, finding more logs, mapping out a different location, a new stream plot, getting used to the area, learning her way around by forming new rock trails in the cold ground, depressed her. Not as much as the fear of being stalked, however. They had two giant problems.

A troubled silence brewed.

"Let's take a break from this area," she said shakily. "We'll go to Mam's. You can hunt and I'll talk to Elliot and all the witches there. Maybe they will know what it is. Then we'll decide if we need to move, or fight. I think . . . I think we need more information. Hopefully, while we're gone, it will ignore the house supplies."

The hot flow of his breath brushed her hair out of her eyes.

Yes, it is a sound plan. But if we don't answer the question of what this is, then I will not bring us back here ever again, little one. I require your safety in Letum Wood above all else.

———

The blissful quiet of Elliot's house was a surprising reprieve. Sanna paused halfway across the dining room, hands held out. The stillness was almost disorienting. No creaks to indicate where witches kept themselves busy, or background laughter to help her figure out who was present.

"Where are all of the children?" she asked.

Mam chuckled. "Several are trapping with Trey. The rest are foraging for more firewood and kindling. They've picked this area clean and need to branch farther out. Greata is doing an herbology lesson while they're searching. Isa, I'm glad you were able to come as well. Are you hungry for lunch?"

Strain tightened Isadora's voice. "No, I just ate with Max, thank you."

"How is Wildrose?" Sanna asked as she found a chair and settled. Given Isadora's previous descriptions, Sanna wanted to prowl Wildrose Manor and . . . well . . . *feel* what was there. The gargoyle-protected grandfather clock in the main hallway that she spoke about, the trinkets in a square closet filled entirely with small drawers.

"Wildrose is interesting. I've been exploring it more lately." Some of the grit left Isa's voice. "There are always fascinating things to find. Sanna, you should come. There's much to feel."

Sanna tried to inspire conviction in her tone. "Sounds great."

The *thunk* of a lunch plate sounded on the table. Sanna palpated a slice of bread, several greens, at the tips of her fingers.

"Sounds like a lovely place, Isa," Mam said brightly. "Elliot and I hope to see it one day."

"We want you for dinner, if you'll come."

"We would love that."

"You too, Sanna. Max needs to meet the family before . . . well, before I agree to remain his wife."

The frost had returned to her voice.

"What if you bring Max here next week?" Mam asked. "Elliot would like to meet him. If all goes well, we'll be happy to visit you at your new place."

What if it doesn't go well? Sanna almost asked, but sealed her lips. Isadora could fight her own battles.

"That should be fine," Isa said, with a remarkably neutral voice. "I'll ask Maximillion and send a note to confirm."

Sanna occupied herself with the bread, thinly spread with the last of the butter Jesse had traded for.

"And how is living as a vagabond in the forest going?" Isa inquired.

Thoughts of her unknown predator, the mussed rocks, strange indentations in the ground, ran through her mind. She forced a cheery voice.

"Very well."

"You like living as a nomad, then?"

"With a dragon, it's not so bad. Without Luteis, it would be far more frightening. Impossible, probably."

"I'm pleased to hear you're aware of that," Isadora said primly. Then, in a far gentler tone, "And I'm so grateful for Luteis. Where are you staying now?"

"Not too far from here. An hour's flight, if you follow the stream from overhead. Luteis found us a place where I'm considering building a house."

"Didn't you used to play there?"

"Maybe?" Sanna shrugged. "I haven't seen it, so I wouldn't know." She set down her slice of bread, rushed with nerves now that the moment had arrived. "In fact, the house is why I'm here. I wanted to see if Elliot and Jesse might be able to help us."

Mam's voice perked up. "Build a house?"

Sanna swallowed a rising ball of emotion. Panic, perhaps. Melancholy, too. A painful mixture of both.

"We've found an almost perfect spot. Stream access, younger tree growth, no signs of lion packs or beluas."

"*Almost* perfect?" Mam inquired.

"Well, there's something that's followed us there. A creature of sorts. I was hoping Isadora or you or Jesse could help us find out more about it before we ask for help building."

Stillness descended. Before their cacophony of questions could follow, Sanna pressed on. They remained utterly silent as she explained, with what details she remembered, each event. When she finished, she sat back in the chair, shocked by how much better she felt. Holding it in felt like cuddling fire.

"I promised Luteis we'd ask Elliot and other witches to see if they know what sort of creature it could be. We think it followed us, but we aren't sure."

"Probably some horrid animal from the bowels of Letum Wood," Mam said, shrill. "My goodness, Sanna! I'm shocked you haven't been eaten. You can't go back there!"

"Mam, whatever it is, it avoids Luteis. I think it doesn't like dragons. It might have gone *close* to him but it didn't bother him. I'm safe."

"For now!"

Isadora must have put a hand on Mam's arm or sent her a quelling look, because a stretch of silence followed. Sanna hung her head in her hands.

Don't take this away from me, she silently pleaded. *Please don't.*

"Sanna," Isa said, "I'm glad you told us. I'll go to the Great Library of Burke and ask the librarians for books on creatures in the forest. Maybe there's notation of an animal we aren't yet aware of."

"Really?"

"Yes, of course. You've worked hard. We can help you figure this out. But maybe, in the meantime—"

"We'll stay somewhere else, I promise. But I'm not giving that spot up!"

Isa's voice remained steady.

"Thank you."

Eating resumed with the quiet shuffle of sleeves over table-cloth, the clack of fork on plate. Sanna finished her bread, and contemplated requesting another slice, when Mam asked,

"You mentioned wanting to build. Who is going to help you do that?"

"I was going to see if Elliot and Jesse knew anything about it."

"Doubtful," Mam said, then hurried to say, "but only because they inherited the houses they've lived in. We can certainly ask."

Sanna deflated, shocked to realize she'd hung all her hopes on their help. What if they *didn't* know what to do next? She didn't know anyone else. The feeling of bees in her chest made her want to leap up and skitter away.

Mori, how had she not thought of that?

"It's a sensible plan, Sanna," Isa said. "I think it's impressive that you're finding a way to make it happen. I—"

"I'm blind, not an idiot," she snapped.

"No one ever suggested otherwise," Isadora said coolly. "You are defensive though. We're not against you."

Sanna let out a long breath, forced herself to relax. Isa was right. That hadn't been fair of her to say.

"Sorry."

She hated that she couldn't see their exchange of glances. So much communication was lost without eyes. The lift of a brow, twitch of lips. Worlds of understanding could pass through sheer motion, all of it lost to eternal darkness.

Everything felt as if it slipped out from beneath her, like quicksand at her feet. If Elliot and Jesse couldn't help her build, what would she do? She couldn't build on her own, no matter how much she tried.

Acceptance hurt.

Unable to bear it another moment, she blurted out, "How do you make soap?"

The question caused another stillness. Sanna turned toward them, her curiosity piqued, before Isadora asked, "Why do you want to know?"

"Because I'd like to make soap."

Mam finally said, "There are many ways to make soap, depending on what you like. You want hard soap to wash with, I assume?"

"Yes."

"I have some extra, if you'd like," Isadora said. "We have a whole cupboard full at Wildrose. Just found it yesterday, actually. It's all gold colored, if you can believe that. Who uses gold soap, and for what purpose?"

"I'd rather make it."

The long pause that followed suggested Mam and Isadora stared at each other. Irritated, Sanna let out a breath.

"You can just say it, you know. Instead of being polite or looking at each other, I'd rather you tell me what's on your mind. I may not be able to see your expressions, but your voices do enough work."

Mam sighed. "Sorry, Sanna. I just . . . why do you want to make soap? Can't you just take what we've offered as a gift because we love you? Everything we do to try to help is met with defensiveness and frustration."

Her spine stiffened. "You're hardly overflowing with soap yourself, Mam."

To that, no answer came.

Isadora broke in again. "I'm happy to send you soap, Sanna, whenever you want it, but I have a feeling that's not what you really want. If you want to be self-sufficient and make it yourself, I can find books on soap making, but you won't be able to read them."

Relief stirred in Sanna with Isa's comment. At least her twin understood, on some level, what she wanted to do.

"I appreciate it. I just . . . I want to make my own soap."

"What if we do it together?" Isa suggested. "I know Babs used to make it for the Anguis community. Mam, you must have helped at one point?"

"Yes." She hesitated. "I suppose what I don't remember, Skye will. She helped her mother often enough. Can we try it next week? We might have to gather supplies that I'm positive we don't have."

"Can I help?" Sanna asked.

"Yes."

"Then I'll be here."

"Anything else you need?" Isa asked. "I found some old clothes in the basement of Wildrose when Max and I toured through it. They're out of fashion, but the fabric is sturdy and could easily be repurposed into new gowns."

"I'll take them," Sanna said quickly.

"But how—" Mam started, then stopped. "Never mind," she said as hastily.

Sanna scowled. "Just like everything else," she muttered. "I'll figure it out."

"I'll bring them when we put the soap together," Isadora promised with a brightness she used when dispeling tension. "I'll try to find rose petals, too. I believe we might even have lavender, if you want scented soap."

"Sounds lovely," Mam said.

Sanna stood up, felt her way along the edge of the table, and carefully crossed the room. A chair that hadn't been there before banged her shin. She rolled her lips to suppress a curse, scooted it out of the way, and continued into the kitchen. Finding the far table, she set the empty plate there.

"Thank you, Sanna," Mam called.

Little one, Luteis said from without. *I have returned.*

She could have cried with relief. "Thanks for having me for lunch, Mam. Luteis is back. Isa, it was good to hear your voice again. I'm glad we can communicate more than we did when you were in the Advocacy."

"If you'd let me teach you magic, it would be even easier!"

"Soon!" Sanna called.

And it was the best she could do, though the scorched, frightened part of Sanna curled away at the thought. Magic, dragons, Letum Wood, Daid's death. All of it had been life-shifting enough. She couldn't take on more now.

"Can you ask Elliot about the creature, Mam?"

"I will tonight."

"And I'll find out what I can," Isadora called, but Sanna was already headed toward the back door.

Twenty-Nine
Maximillion

C harlie, Ronald, and Felicity entered Max's office a breath after Isadora left. Charlie led the way, sent Max a solemn look of warning, and headed for a chair.

Suspicion climbed Max's spine like a spider. Most unusual for them to congregate in Max's office, of all places. The League of Free Borders was a Network affair, not an inter-Network affair, which should have shoved it firmly off his lap.

Nevertheless.

The High Priestess, Felicity, was a spirited woman. Unlike Greta, she knew when to reign her opinions and words in. She had burnished skin, ebony hair, and full lips that often pressed into a thoughtful line. Her eyelashes curled so high they nearly touched the underside of her eyebrow. Even *she* carried a sober shroud.

Only Ronald smiled, and a bit too widely at that. With a silent nod, Max motioned the three of them into chairs across from his desk. He lowered into his.

"Ronald," Charlie said with a wave. "The floor is yours, as

you requested. You have ten minutes to make your official announcement."

Max fought not to clench.

"Thank you, High Priest. High Priestess. Ambassador. I won't take up too much of anyone's time today, as the Ambassador and I have already spoken about this at some minimal length."

With considerable willpower, Max suppressed the urge to correct him. In their previous discussion, Ronald made veiled threats, but said nothing of an inquest.

Now, all made sense.

"All of you have received the written announcement of inquest, so I'm here to fulfill the obligatory in-person declaration, in which the High Priest and Ambassador shall be involved. The High Priestess, in her good graces, will moderate after all interviews have been conducted. I represent the League of Free Borders as I present this to you today."

Three scrolls drifted around the room, issuing to Charlie, Felicity, and Max. Max commanded his open with a spell, but already knew what to expect. The same easy-to-read, slanted handwriting filled the interior.

Max licked his lips and let his thoughts spin for several moments. They hurried to Isadora and the pained look when she departed. Ronald had all the ill timing on his side.

Ronald turned to Charlie. "Any questions, High Priest?"

"No. It appears straightforward enough."

A silent inquiry to Max.

"I accept," he said.

Ronald's study lingered for a moment before he turned to Felicity, who nodded.

"I accept the position as moderator."

Ronald bowed slightly at the waist. "Thank you all for your cooperation as we begin this journey to the truth. The League of Free Borders is interested in the preservation of the

Central Network. We will be here for as long as we need to be, and will follow bureaucratic channels as is required. We will not be swayed."

The undertone of promise wasn't lost.

"Glad to hear that!" Charlie called brightly. "Felicity shall record this beginning today and your team can get started with their investigation, pending continued checks with Felicity through the length of their study, of course."

Torkelson nodded.

Max wanted to claw his face off.

Torkelson had every right to fund and drive a formal investigation into the Network dealings, but he didn't like it. The uncertain parallels to Isadora only made Max more irritated than ever.

Torkelson had an agenda.

What did he gain by the inquest? Not known, yet. He sought to prove a point, perhaps. Earn a following, undoubtedly, and set himself up as a desirable Council Member. The insecure motivations stymied Max.

Charlie rose. "Thank you, Ronald. I trust your investigators will be in touch. Felicity, you shall take over from here."

Ronald bowed at the waist. "My deepest gratitude, Your Highnesses, Ambassador. Thank you for your time."

Charlie and Felicity waited for Torkelson to leave. After he exited the round office, Max commanded the door to close with a spell. Before he could issue it himself, Wally sent a silencing incantation around the doorframe from outside.

Max leaned his hands onto the desk. "I don't want Isadora anywhere near this."

"You can hardly stop it, Max," Charlie said. "Once they finalize their investigation—which could take months to years —they'll present it before Felicity, ask us questions, and then take it to the Council. Isadora must go before the Council at some point."

"To what end?"

Charlie let out a long breath, shaking his head.

"I don't know."

Felicity regarded the inquest letter, brow furrowed. Max didn't know her well. He approved of her political work—she was thorough, decisive, and far less emotional than Greta—but still hadn't proven herself entirely worthy. Charlie trusted her, though, and that meant something.

"I can buy you time," Felicity said. "I'll announce it to the Council tonight so we maintain diplomatic fairness and he can't say that we showed any favoritism toward the two of you, but it could be longer than expected before the inquest is scheduled with the Council. Sometimes, inquests die out of sheer time or lack of interest."

Max hesitated, then nodded. "Thank you."

"At that point, we'll have a better idea of what's happening with the Mansfeld Pact and all of this will have died down," she suggested.

A little too optimistic for his blood, but he appreciated the sentiment.

Charlie tapped Max's desk. "It's not you he wants, my friend. It's something bigger than that. He wants the Mansfeld Pact stripped away, or political power of his own, and you're the path he's using to make it happen."

The silent affirmation of Max's gut instinct calmed him.

"Thank you both."

Charlie headed toward the door, but paused.

"Oh, and Max?"

"Hmm?"

"Don't be a fool. This isn't about Isadora yet—don't make it so out of fear."

Max returned to Wildrose carefully.

Very carefully.

No lights burned in the manor, no food waited in the kitchen. The stone cold hallways devoid of life were testament enough. His lovely wife was not pleased with him for commanding her to leave after their enchanting luncheon together.

He could hardly blame her.

He climbed the stairs to find the door to the master suite ajar. Light spilled onto the ground. He slowed, peering through the slit. Isadora lounged on the divan. Her shoulder moved as she pulled a blanket higher, then turned a page in a book.

Well, she hadn't packed up and left Wildrose.

A positive sign.

The door creaked as he swung it open. She didn't glance up, but her shoulders tensed. He tossed his greatcoat toward a hanger that sped from the armoire. The hanger slipped underneath the lapels, then swung the garment closer to the fire. There, it hovered close to the heat. Moisture dripped, evaporating off the hot stones.

"Merry meet," he said.

She did not deign to reply.

Max ground his teeth together as he removed his shoes, coat, vest. He unbuttoned his cufflinks and rolled his shirt over his forearms. Loosening his garb cut the choking feeling. Able to bear it no longer, he sat across from her. She didn't peek out from behind the book titled *Hidden Creatures in Letum Wood.*

"I would like to explain and apologize for the way we parted earlier today."

A chilly set of differently-colored eyes appeared over the top of the book. As quickly, they disappeared.

She yawned.

"Your surprise was appreciated. Very appreciated. I was happy to have you, but you came at a . . . most inconvenient time. When I asked you to leave, a man had come to my office for a meeting. He's . . . not a safe man."

Slowly, the book lowered. Her brow appeared first, then her lashes, finally tapered eyes.

Hopeful, he pressed on. "I didn't want him to know you were there because I couldn't be certain how he would act." Max leaned his forearms onto his bent knees. "I didn't have time to explain the situation. Frankly, I didn't want you to know that you could be in harm's way. Perhaps I should have."

He held his breath, waited for her to speak, move, indicate life existed in that marble-like body. When his head whirled for want of air, she spoke.

"Yes, you should have let me know. If I'm in peril, I deserve to be part of the solution."

Up shot the book.

Down went her eyes.

Max tightened his jaw, forced his teeth together. "I presume," he said slowly, "that you're angry with me."

"Oh," she drawled, languidly turning a page. "You are observant, Ambassador."

Further irritated, he rubbed a hand over his face. "Please, accept my apologies. It was circumstantial and had nothing to do with our kiss."

She froze.

Her fingers clutched the book so hard the knuckles turned white. His belly filled with slush and ice and the gnawing terror of fear. Ah, so he'd landed on the real issue. It hadn't been the dismissal.

It had been the *timing*.

Now would be the opportune moment to say those words she most wanted to hear. To secure her wavering trust. *I seek to protect you,* he wanted to say, *because I love you with depths previously unknown.*

He couldn't.

The words stuck in his throat, too tight to release. Her glacial, cutting gaze would tear his soul in half, should he give her the power. Power she didn't know that she possessed.

All at once, Isadora sat up. The book dropped to her lap and so did the blanket. She glared at him, hair mussed charmingly around her neck. Her eyes snapped with the force of a thousand suns.

"You were an ogre, Max. Such a delightful meal, and that kiss, and then . . ."

"I know."

She shoved the book aside, pressed her fists into the cushions, and leaned forward. Tears swam in her eyes.

"I love you, you cad! I love you more than I ever thought possible to love another witch. There are moments when I'm convinced that we will last forever. That you and I were always meant to be. That *something* bigger drew our hearts to each other against all odds. And then . . ."

Her chin wobbled. Words dropped as she gazed away. "Then I wonder if you really understand me at all. I can't help but think I'm only a fool in love, convincing myself that you will one day feel this too . . ."

Agony rushed through him. The words sat on the tip of his tongue, ready for recall. *I love you. I adore you. You are the force behind my spinning world, my surviving heart. I stay in this fight for you.*

The truth prevented him.

I cannot give, he thought, *what I have never received. I am not lovable, and one day you might see it. Watching you fall out of love would destroy me.*

Could a man who had never known love actually give it?

Not in the ways she deserved.

Helpless, she stared at him. Her brow scrunched in word-less fear. Panic illuminated her eyes, her drooping lips.

"What do you have to say to that, Max? Say something! I've put my heart on the line again. I'm willing to be vulner-able and scared *for you*. Can you give me the same? Will you? Or do you really not love me?"

Max staggered back, as if struck.

"You think I don't love you?"

Hesitantly, she nodded. Tears glittered on her cheeks, each speck a burden against him. He'd give all of Wildrose to step up, touch her, wipe them away. To never see such agony in her expression, and certainly not because of him.

Wasn't *this* exactly what he tried to avoid?

Her voice was a broken whisper.

"Can we actually do this, Max?"

Max stared at her, heart in his throat. He turned away, unable to bear the agony in her question.

"I don't know, Isadora."

"All I need is assurance that you love me, too. One thread of hope that I haven't wasted my time, my heart, my . . . soul . . . on a man who chooses not to care for me!"

He whirled around, thunderstruck.

"What did you say?"

"It's a choice, Max!" she cried, fist pressed to her breast-bone. "Love is a choice. I'm convinced of it. We choose the way we want to feel and you never choose . . ."

A strangled sob stopped her.

"You never choose me."

His shoulders heaved up and down. He opened and closed his fingers, feeling the tension thrum all the way to the very tips. Terror clutched him in her white-cold hands. He couldn't breathe. The room pressed down from all points, leaning right into his chest. He stood, ran a hand through his hair.

"It's not so difficult for everyone else," he growled.

"I refuse to believe you're incapable of love. I refuse to let you victimize yourself that way. You can say the words, Max. They're just words. Unless you don't mean them, in which case . . ."

"What do you know?" he snapped, whirling on her. "You who grew up in a loving home with two parents that never abandoned nor beat you bloody nor left you to starve. Did you scavenge through the garbage in search of dinner? Did you stand at your mother's graveside and wonder if she never said the words because something inside of you was utterly unlovable? You who heard the words every day and never thought about it are free to judge me? Not all of us had such luxuries, Isadora. You don't know what you ask."

She reared back, as if slapped. All color left her face. Max stalked to the door, ripped it open, and hesitated. Regret already filled him, swimming below the inky memories that threatened to surface.

"I'll sleep in my office."

The door slammed behind him.

THIRTY

SANNA

The icy cold stream froze Sanna's knuckles. She crouched near the bank, closed a fist. The tight joint had no feeling.

How odd.

Totally numb.

Could she manage that with her feelings? With the paralyzed sensation in her chest? Doubtful.

Sanna leaned back on her haunches and withdrew her hand from the stream. Her palms pressed into the dirt with sharp prickles of ice. Her breath billowed in front of her as she tried to recall the lacy designs the smoke used to make.

Did Luteis seethe in this penetrating cold? Did fog whisper off his scales on chilly days? Dragons were bottled fire, so it stood to reason. But she couldn't remember. A cracking stick brought her attention around. She jerked back to the moment.

"Just me," Jesse called. "I came to check on you."

Sanna stood, spun around to face him. She shook her fingers, flicking the last of the water droplets off their tips, and shoved them into her coat pocket. The crunch of his boots over frosty ground approached.

"How did you know where to find me?"

"A hunch. You always liked this spot. We're not all that far from Anguis, really."

Heat bloomed across the back of her neck. When was the last time she stood alone with Jesse? She couldn't remember. Definitely before she lost her sight. Since then . . . well . . . all swirled in a miasma that made it hard to recall.

"I asked Luteis to bring me here because it feels safe."

He stopped within arms length. She could feel his closeness and resisted the urge to reach out and confirm.

"How are you, Sanna? Roxi says you stopped by yesterday, had some questions about building a house."

"Oh! Yes. I have . . . yes. So many. Do you know how to build a house?"

He chortled. "Definitely not."

"Oh."

"Daid knows a little. Enough that we could probably figure something out, but there's a lot we'd need to learn and a lot we'd do wrong."

"I see."

Her throat tightened. Tears came so easily, sometimes without warning. She pushed those back. While she had Jesse, she could get answers. Besides, it was nice to have someone else break up the daily monotony.

His voice moved, as if his head twisted around when he said, "Is this where you want to stay?"

"No, we're just here while Isadora looks into something for us."

"The creature?"

"Did she tell you about it?"

"Roxi did. Daid's never seen or heard anything like it, though. Me either."

"Nothing?"

"No. Weird that it has no smell. Not even for Luteis?"

Her shoulders slumped. "He says there's a vague something, but nothing strong and identifiable. We can't understand it either. Isadora is going to a library to find a book on creatures in the forest."

"The Great Library of Burke?"

"Sure? That sounds right."

He kicked at a rock. The hollow *thunk* of it hitting the tree reverberated around them. "I'm jealous. I've heard a lot about it, now that I'm speaking with villagers a bit more. Wish I could see it."

"I'm sure she'd take you."

"There'd probably be books on building houses there."

Suddenly, the library sounded a lot more interesting.

"Really?"

"Sure."

"But . . ."

Her elation died. How would she read the books? Someone else would have to read it to her, and didn't that defeat the purpose of living independently? No matter how she looked at it, she needed help. Isadora *had* mentioned special books that she could feel . . .

His tone changed undeniably, dropping register. "Hey, what are those?"

"What do you mean?

"Those . . . things . . . on the trees? Did Luteis tell you about them?"

"What things?"

The rasp of shoes moving over snow came again. His voice was a little farther away when he said, "They're white, kind of bulbous. Giant sacs, maybe? They're sticking out of the tree trunk just behind this one. Probably thirty of them."

Cold fear struck Sanna in the chest.

"White?" she whispered.

"Yes. Almost like . . . I don't know . . . like giant spider eggs? Except they're attached to the side of the trees."

Sanna froze.

"What?"

Another twig cracked under his feet as he shifted away. His voice rang from even farther back, but she didn't have to strain to hear.

"There are several. All of them are higher up, spread across several trees."

"Luteis never mentioned them."

"Huh. Well, you can't miss them. They're . . . pretty huge. They make the trees look misshapen and strange."

Luteis? she inquired.

A beat of quiet passed before he replied. *Yes, little one?*

Where are you?

Not far. Do you need me?

Yes, please.

A distant dragon cry followed, not far to her right.

"Luteis is on his way back. We'll ask him, just to be sure, but I don't think they were there before. I'm sure he would have mentioned them."

Wouldn't he?

Sanna curled her fingers into her palm, grateful that her gloves hid the nervous gesture. Despite attempts to push Mam's voice away, she couldn't stop thinking about her suggestion that Jesse and Sanna court each other.

Just . . . weird.

Gratitude that he was here followed in a rush. What if the white things were going to attack her? Did his presence stop them?

"What is Luteis doing, by the way?" he asked.

"Just stalking some rodents for me to eat later."

"You stay here alone?"

"He didn't go far. There was a rabbit he scented not far away. Otherwise, I go everywhere with him. Just in case."

"Oh."

"He doesn't leave me unless I go to Mam's. He's really good to me. Always taking care of me and keeping me safe."

Somehow, the words rang hollow. They were true, but perhaps not something to be so proud of. Really, her dependence on Luteis had only increased as they ventured into the challenge of developing her independence.

Without him, the forest was so . . .

. . . terrifying.

No matter how much she tried to convince herself otherwise. Admitting it came with a heavy weight of grief.

"How are you, Jesse?" she asked, eager to hear more of his voice. It changed the forest in a friendly way. "Mam says you're busy in forester villages."

He huffed a laugh. A budding excitement thrummed underneath. "Yes, very busy. A blacksmith just asked me to apprentice with him. He said I'm strong as an ox and promised a steady stream of supplies if I wanted them."

"Are you going to accept?"

"Already did."

"Oh!"

"Daid isn't too happy." He let out a quick breath. "But that's Daid and it's my life. He's having a hard time admitting that the time of the Dragonmasters is over. I'm not the only one leaving the families, you know? Lucey already built her own life. Greata will leave as soon as Hans is a bit older. Trey will probably stay and trap, at least for awhile. Build up some trading power. I think he wants to see if it will work out for me first, then he'll give life in the villages a try."

The dissolution of their former life came without much fear in his voice. Didn't the thought of so much change frighten him? Unseat what he always knew?

"Daid is . . . struggling," he continued. "He wants to hold onto the old ways and hide in the forest. That might have worked when we had three families to support each other, but now?"

He blew a raspberry.

Sanna sucked in a breath. By Drago, she understood Elliot's response better than Jesse's, and what did that mean about her?

"You don't want the old life?"

"No," he exclaimed. "Noooo. There's so much more out there! Magic and witches and supplies and . . . did you know that there are spells to fetch water and do laundry?" His fingers snapped. "It's that easy!"

She startled.

A short-lived yearning bolted through her, then back out. Indeed, it sounded fantastic. Life without sight would be much easier, but magic always came at a cost.

"Maybe Elliot is afraid of using magic," she said, bristling. The ground trembled as Luteis approached. "Elliot has been told all his life that it's wrong, and bad. It's hard to just . . . just turn that off and do something previously forbidden!"

"But it's *not* wrong. We're here to do magic, Sanna. It's part of what witches *are*. Talis deprived us of a fundamental facet of our existence, and I say good riddance to him. I'm living my life."

"Well maybe Elliot doesn't truly realize that yet!"

The shrill note in her voice startled her. She paused, breath held, and waited. Jesse seemed to do the same. Finally, her emotion ebbed. The de-escalation of panic left her shaky.

"I'm sorry," she whispered.

"No, it's my fault. I shouldn't ask you to talk about things you're not ready to talk about. I'm . . . sad, Sanna. For Daid, my siblings, and for you, too. Talis tried to convince us that using everyday magic would harm the dragons, when really he just wanted to control us. In the end, we lost. Your situation is different, anyway."

She reared back. "What?"

"Well, you *tried* magic. You engaged with it, then you lost everything. You commandeered a powerful magical system, became High Dragonmaster, and set all dragon races free from bondage. *Mori,* but your unwillingness to use magic probably has more to do with all that it cost you, not just fear of Talis."

He said the last like a toss away comment. Something he'd observed, but maybe hadn't proven yet. She felt like he'd reached into her soul and plucked a chord. Her body trembled, as if she dipped into a cool bath, then a hot one.

Probably has more to do with all it cost you.

By Drago, that was it!

She didn't actually fear long-dead Talis, nor the vengeance of a hidden god. Drago had long dissolved in her mind. She feared the *magic.* Meddling with such powers had introduced her to all manner of dragons, different parts of Alkarra, and a grand scale of ability previously improbable. In the end, she walked away without her sight, a life she didn't ask for, and no connection to the dragons she saved.

All because of magic.

Rising emotions surged like a tide too great to battle. Tears sprang to her eyes. Only Luteis saved her from an epic emotional breakdown.

I'm here, little one.

He nudged her from behind. She reached back, touched him. The moment her palm hit scales, she calmed. The tears evaporated to deal with later.

"Merry meet, Luteis," Jesse said. "Good to see you again."

Luteis snorted an amiable greeting. *He is quite pleasant, as far as witches are concerned.*

Sanna cleared her throat, removing the final vestiges of emotion. "Show him, Jesse?"

It didn't take long for Luteis to comprehend what Jesse pointed out. Shock filled his serpentine voice.

Those were not there when I left, little one. Only a short while ago.

"That's what I thought you'd say," she whispered darkly. "Luteis says that they weren't there earlier. He's only been gone twenty minutes, maybe."

"Huh."

"You didn't see anything?"

"No."

Little one, I will not allow you to stay. We must leave. The forest isn't safe. Whatever this creature is, or isn't, it stalks us.

It'll just follow us! We can't lead it back to Mam and Elliot's. We're going to have to get rid of it in a different way.

He growled.

"What are you going to do?" Jesse asked.

"We're going to find somewhere else to sleep tonight," she announced. "We'll keep moving until we figure out what it is. Will you do me a favor?"

"Anything."

"Send Isadora a message? Tell her we're going to follow the stream north. Luteis will leave burn marks along the way. She can find us along the stream, or back at Mam's. I'll check in there everyday around dawn. Until we know what we're fighting, we need to evade."

"Sure. Right away."

"Thank you."

Sanna put her hand on Luteis's flank, comforted by his warmth. Whatever stalked them wasn't about to leave, and she wouldn't bring it to Mam's doorstep. It would harm Elliot's children, perhaps destroy their home.

"I'll come check on you," Jesse said with unusual gravity. "Sanna, please be safe."

"We will. I promise."

He left with a mere whisper. The quiet rang until Sanna broke it with a steely declaration.

"We're not going to run from it, Luteis. We're going to face it down. Blind or not, this is my forest, my home. I will not be bullied away."

THIRTY-ONE
ISADORA

A pen-and-ink image of a grotesque, horrifying spider filled the page in Isadora's new book. Hairy, bumpy joints on too many legs framed a fat body protruding with jointed tentacles. Dripping fangs, wide as a human mouth, spanned half the body. At least twenty eyes reflected a terrifying maw of rage.

Petrifying, but still not worse than how she felt inside. Isadora set thoughts of Max and their horrendous argument to the back of her mind.

"Well, after several days perusing books, talking to librarians," *and avoiding home like the plague*, she silently added, "I think I've found our winner."

She lay the book on Mam's table in front of Sanna. Jesse, Elliot, and Mam circled behind Sanna in curiosity. As one, they recoiled on various cringes and groans. Mam gasped.

"Hideous."

"Ugly beast."

"*That* is stalking Sanna?" Jesse cried.

"What?" Sanna asked. "What is it?"

"That," Isadora declared, "is a presumed creature in

Letum Wood that others have called the *Reine dux arachnae.* Queen of the spiders. Though it hasn't been officially studied by scholars, and only a handful of first-hand reports are recorded for the last two or three centuries, many witches believe it exists."

"What does it look like?"

Isadora smiled. "Oh ho! Just you wait. I learned a spell so you can feel it yourself."

With a murmur of magic, the darkest lines in the image rose out of the parchment. The lesser gray lines rose with less height, and anything without ink remained flat. Delighted, Isadora clapped.

"Feel it, Sanna!"

Tentatively, Sanna reached out. She pulled in a sharp breath, ran her fingers around the edges. Clustered at the bottom of the page were small, round balls, similar to what Jesse described seeing on the tree trunks around Sanna. She felt those, too.

"I can . . . I can understand," she breathed. "This is a leg?"

"Yes!"

"And the body?"

"Mm hmm . . ."

Sanna squealed. "Oh, it's . . . I can understand!"

"Magic," Isadora whispered in her ear, then straightened. "The *Reine dux arachnae* is the mistress of an estimated hundreds of thousands of spiders that live throughout Letum Wood, in varying sizes. None, of course, larger than her, though some might be adjacent. Scholars haven't confirmed anything, but feel certain that she feeds on the legs of the spider underlings beneath her and is aided in her exorbitant growth by magic. Some assume she's very territorial, and coils anyone encroaching into her territory in her web, to later be fed to her babies."

Jesse recoiled. "How utterly terrifying."

"How big is it?" Mam asked with a gulp.

"Accounts report twice the size of a human male, from foreleg to hindleg, though it can't be certain. Very big is all that's believed."

Sanna paled. Her searching fingers paused right over the spider's gaping maw.

"Really?"

"Well, most is conjecture. The only consistent account that I found for this little darling is her utter lack of warning. Horses, dragons, donkeys. Anything carrying a witch was almost always taken by surprise, if anyone lived to tell the tale. One account said that they observed spider sacs, such as you saw, in the trees above them when they had awoken. A minute later, all sacs broke forth and thousands of spiders attacked."

Sanna whispered, "Thousands?"

Pleased that Sanna appeared to understand the gravity of the situation, Isadora pressed harder into it.

"Thousands. I believe Jesse thwarted an attempted attack the other day, while Luteis smelled a rabbit. There's one more parallel to your situation, too. The only sign that the *Reine dux arachnae* has been present is a gelatinous-like fluid that drips from her fangs. Sanna? Are you all right?"

Sanna leaned her body forward, head on the book. She wilted there, as if her bones had melted.

"Fine. I'm fine."

Mam and Elliot exchanged concerned looks. Isadora put her hand on Sanna's shoulder. Sanna shoved her off, slowly straightened.

"I believe this could be what you're facing, Sanna. Other accounts indicate that once the *Reine dux arachnae* finds a victim, she stalks it until she has it or it dies. Why she hasn't killed you already, I'm not sure. Though some suggestions have been made that dragons are their greatest natural enemy."

"It's her." Sanna nodded, still peaked. "She found me and

she wants me. All the signs are there. The question is: how do I get rid of her?"

"Well, there have been stories about foresters she stalked until they died, so the only certainty is to leave the forest and never come back. Or kill her, but few accounts of such a thing exist."

Color entered Sanna's cheeks again, perfusing them with a flood of color. "This is my home! I won't be run out by a spider."

"Then you have to kill her."

Sanna gritted her teeth. "Fine. Tell me how."

Isadora hesitated, looking back to the book. "The only thing I could find occurred about a century ago, when a witch was able to stab her with the antler of a mortega. She bled pink, then shriveled into a ball and burst into a thousand baby spiders, all of which seeped into the ground. Seems an odd weapon, but it killed the current *Reine dux arachnae.* He survived enough to give his account, and I read the original, thanks to a very excited librarian who hadn't seen another witch in days."

"A mortega antler?" Sanna echoed. "That's . . . odd."

"Doesn't make sense, but it worked one time."

"Let's not be insane!" Mam cried. "Sanna is not going back into the forest, certainly not with a mortega antler as her only defense against . . ." Mam jabbed at the book with both hands. "Against that!"

"I agree."

Sanna frowned, her lips drawing down. "Mam is right. Luteis and I will have to come up with a different plan."

Mam slumped in silent relief. "Yes, yes. You have a dragon. Let's put him to use here."

"But mark my words!" Sanna muttered, fist slamming the table. "We *will* make a plan. I won't capitulate my forest to that spider. Do you hear me?"

"I hear you," Isadora said. She peered at her sister, with her roving eyes, determined jaw, and heavy frown. A tingle of suspicion swept over her. That capitulation came a bit *too* quickly. She'd anticipated a bit more of a struggle. The line across Jesse's brow seemed to indicate he felt the same way.

"Sanna—"

Sanna held up a hand. "She's a worthy foe and I'll take it seriously. Thank you, Isadora, for all this information. Seeing it with my fingers helps me understand. I'm going to relay it to Luteis tonight. Mam, can I stay at our old house, in the attic?"

"Yes, of course. It's still empty."

"Thank you." Sanna leaned back in her chair. "Now that we know what we're fighting, we just have to figure out how to get rid of it."

Thirty-Two
Maximillion

Max paced across his office, then back again. The circular turret left little area for maniacal responses, something he'd never appreciated until Isadora entered his world.

A fire snapped in the grate. Somewhere in the bowels of Chatham Castle, a staircase creaked. He started to initiate a transportation spell to find Isa, then stopped himself halfway.

Hands clenched at his side, he whirled back around to pace again.

No.

She needed space. Time, too, though it had been days since their argument. Or, rather, his snapping defensiveness in the face of her boundaries.

He toyed with the fact that he'd gone from *giving her space* to *avoiding her wholeheartedly*. At the time, she'd sprung on him excellent points for which he'd had no refute.

I refuse to believe you're incapable of love. I refuse to let you victimize yourself that way.

Well, that showed how little she knew. Literally, because he'd never told her the extent of his gory, abuse-littered past.

His usual businesslike approach to a problem dissolved to shreds when it involved his wife. Isadora had a way of turning his capable coping mechanisms into dust. Not to mention how the introduction of emotion into his decision-making process created a foggy glass between logic and reality. He comprehended the situation at large, but details eluded him.

The good gods, he'd never felt such fear.

A rap on his office door sent a shock through Max. He paused.

"Yes?"

Charlie called through the wood. "Max?"

He grumbled, but admitted him inside. Trust Charlie to show up when he desired utter solitude. Charlie stepped inside with a quizzical expression. He wore a casual shirt over plain breeches, and his hair lay askew.

He stacked his hands on his hips. "Well, what is it?"

"How did you know?" Max barked.

"Call it a brother's second sense."

"Who told you?"

Charlie lifted both hands. "No one. Max, I swear I had a feeling something was wrong. I tend to follow my intuition."

The possibility that Charlie spoke the truth made his throat thick. Max lowered into a chair, propped his head in his hands.

"I've made a demmed mess of my life," Max muttered.

"Well, I expect you to do such a thing every few years. What happened this time?"

Max would have shot him a glare for the hidden laughter in his tone, but didn't have the energy. He spent most of his concentration trying to breathe, stop himself from tracking Isadora down, and beg her not to leave him.

"Isadora."

"Also not a surprise." Charlie sat across from him. A glass of wine appeared in his hand. A shot of dark ipsum in front of Max. Grateful, Max tossed it back, swallowing the hellfire burn. A spiral of courage wound through his chest in a bolstering flash.

"Your wife is a breath of fresh air, isn't she? Totally turned your life upside down, that's for sure. Let's hear it."

With rote precision, Max relayed their conversations in full. Charlie listened without interruption until Max straightened up, inhaled deeply, and stared hard at his friend.

"Is my marriage over?"

Charlie ran his tongue over teeth and met his gaze.

"No."

Max frowned.

Hope, he didn't want. Truth, he did. Hope was a precious, foolish commodity. Something that one invested in when no other options existed, and even then only as a means to gain the end.

Well.

Maybe it *was* time for hope.

"You don't know that," Max muttered half-heartedly.

Charlie shrugged. "You're right. Isadora could make any decision after tonight and you'd probably respect whatever she requested. But I know her, and I know you, and neither of you have ever been quitters."

"Hardly seems wise to keep a relationship alive for the sake of not losing."

"I never suggested that either. There is a quick fix, Max. You know it already. You don't need me to tell you what to do."

"What?"

"Nice try," Charlie drawled. "You're going to have to say the words, like it or not. Why is it so difficult? I love you, Max. You know that. I tell you all the time. Father loved you. Faye . . . well, she *likes* you."

The droll tone would have amused him any other day, but his rising discomfort prevented softer emotions.

"They are words that hold too much power. When one says it, one gives that power away. You can't take it back."

"I know."

"And you're fine with that?"

Charlie laughed. "Yes! It's true that love is power. What you gain by giving it away is returned."

Max thought of Mere.

"Not always," he whispered.

Charlie sighed. "Perhaps not immediately, no. But the giving of love is a precious, powerful process. It refines *you*, makes *you* better. When you give it, regardless of what the other witch does with your love, a better life awaits on the other side. By the good gods, can you imagine me without Faye?"

He snorted inelegantly into his glass.

Guilt plagued Max. "I'm not always that kind to you, Charlie. I'm a poor excuse for an adopted brother, and I'm grumpy most of the time. What do you receive from our friendship? I've always wondered why you kept me."

Such a question flung a lasting fear into the void. Bits of his soul flew with it. Slivers of dread that he'd always kept tight in his hands, to make sure they couldn't get away. Charlie leaned forward, elbows propped on his knees.

"First of all, you toad, you're not my adopted brother. You are my *brother*. Second of all, you're grumpy, but that's you. I've learned to love you despite your attitude, which is something Isadora has *also* done.

"Love doesn't require conformity, Max. You don't have to exist a certain way in order to earn it. Love is present despite your grumpiness, which is how I know Isadora isn't going anywhere. She fell in love with you over the course of two years, under the grumpiest conditions I've ever seen you in *and she chose to stay.* But if you want her to remain, you have to earn it, and you earn it with honesty."

Max's jaw tightened. The moment to yield had finally arrived. For all his work in staving off the truth, it rushed forward with unnatural speed. His throat was annoyingly tight when he whispered, "I do love her, Charlie. I daresay I love her more than anything I've ever known in this life."

No surprise registered in Charlie's expression.

"I know."

"If I tell her and she leaves?"

"If you don't and she leaves?"

The thought flogged Max's chest like the bite of a whip. He swam in what that horrific regret might feel like. The drowning sensation. The sense of not giving, and having lost. He couldn't abide the thought of disappointing Isadora again.

"You must weigh what you could lose against what you feel now," Charlie said. "Which is more frightening?"

Charlie leaned back, crossed an ankle over his knee. He sank farther into the cushions, the picture of red-headed ease.

"Max, if you decide not to say the words and lose Isadora, I'll be here for you. Know that. I'm not going anywhere. If you say the words and you still lose her, I'll be here. Through whatever you experience, I'll be here.

"But don't be a goat about it, all right? She's the best thing that ever happened to you. If there's one place your heart is absolutely safe, it's with your wife. Not Wildrose, not even me, because I'd choose Faye over you in a second. But with Isadora."

A note of teasing entered his tone that Max understood. Charlie loved him—he did. Max had no doubts about that. But Faye had always been his soulmate, and he'd do anything for her.

As Charlie should, for he felt the same regarding Isa.

Images of his pere and his mere washed through his

memory. The silence of Wildrose, pitted against the dazzle of Isadora's laugh. If all she needed was to hear the words, why couldn't he say them?

Because she could break me with them, came the thought, and he loathed himself for it.

Charlie perked up. "So you'll tell her?"

"I'll . . . I'll try."

Charlie beamed. "I tell you, that's the best decision you've made so far. Even above supporting the Advocacy in our heyday." He stood. The dying fire gave a lackluster glow, heralding nighttime in the distance. Cold crackled from the windows, driving Max to thoughts of home.

"I have something else to tell you while I'm here and you're not going to like it for many reasons. Nevertheless, I'm going to tell you about it and then I'm going to ask you to do something that you won't like either."

Max glared up at Charlie through a heavy brow.

"What?"

Charlie smiled. Two tickets popped into the air between them. Triangular, with a black background and golden, lacy reticulation. On seeing them, Max's stomach sank.

"No."

"Yes."

Charlie sent them to Max with a spell. They settled on his desk. He glowered at them, a metallic taste in his mouth at the sight.

"It's just an opera, Max. You've been several times and I happen to know you enjoyed at least two of them."

Max flicked the tickets away, turned back to his scroll. "I'm not in the mood. Tomorrow is a busy day. I certainly don't want to end it with a social event."

"You will be in the mood when you learn who is going to be there."

"I doubt that."

"Zander and Griffin."

Max paused. The quill halted, spilling a blot of ink that spread in an ever-widening circle. Wary now, he returned his gaze to Charlie. All traces of levity had been erased.

"You know what that means. Max."

Max set the quill aside and used a spell to clear the stain. Indeed, he knew *exactly* what it meant. Business witches Zander and Griffin would want to talk about growing discontent around the political ramifications of the Mansfeld Pact. They were firmly in favor of isolationism and directly opposed to witches like Ronald Torkelson.

In other words—very strong potential allies.

Implications lurked.

"This isn't an Ambassador issue, Charlie."

"No, it's a Watcher one."

"You want me to attend as an Ambassador or an Advocacy member?"

"I want you to attend as Maximillion Sinclair."

"Am I supposed to assuage Zander and Griffin with promises that Ronald won't get any power to reverse our position with the Mansfeld Pact?"

Charlie held his gaze. "No."

"Then what?"

"I want you to be their friend."

Max scoffed, straightening. "I don't have time for friendship, and Lucey has taken over management of the Advocacy. Send her."

"She doesn't know them."

"That's never stopped her before."

"They're potential allies for you later, Max. Particularly if things escalate with Ronald. I'm trying to set you and Isadora up for success down the road, should we need it."

Though tempting, the crossing of political and home life was precisely why Max never wanted to be handfasted in the first place. Entirely too messy. For his part, he understood exactly why the first High Priestess of the Central Network, Esmelda, supported a tradition that advocated against high-ranking officials having a family.

"This puts me into an awkward position, Charlie."

"Doesn't have to be. You're going to the opera where there are no political ties. Griffin is a not-very-powerful Watcher and frightened. He knows of your position in the Advocacy and would be gratefully willing to make connections. Zander harbors growing concerns over the League of Free Borders, and both seek stabilization through friendship. This has nothing to do with work, yet it has everything to do with it at the same time."

Buried amidst all these other reasons lay the real heart of the issue. Yes, he *could* go to the opera as a front for establishing a relationship with Griffin, a secretive and fellow Watcher. They would be wise political ties to make with prominent business witches that, one day, might be able to help him protect Isadora.

After several moments of contemplation, Max capitulated. Maybe Charlie was right. This could be a trust-building step.

Charlie yawned, arms stretched overhead. He shook his head to clear the fatigue.

"If you refuse to go, I'll figure something out. Really, I gave it to you first, before Lucey, because it's an opportunity for you to create protections for Isadora later. I wouldn't relinquish that chance, should you have it."

"I'll go."

Charlie sighed with dramatic gusto as he backed toward the door. "Well spoken, my friend. Well spoken. Oh, and good luck, eh? I have a feeling you're going to need it."

Max walked to the door, tailing Charlie, with parts of their conversation swirling through his head. The burning ipsum loosened his mental strings a bit, allowing Charlie's ideas to settle into a strange in-between. The urge to speak with Isadora fairly consumed him now.

"Thank you. For listening to your brother-sense. I . . . I love you too, Charlie."

Charlie's eyes twinkled as he reached for the doorknob. "You dodgy old fart, I already know that. Save the words for someone who needs them, eh? Oh, and just be honest. That's all she wants."

Thirty-Three
Sanna

Only the gentle scratch of branches over scales could be heard. Sanna, who slumped half out of the attic window, perked up. According to the chiming clock from downstairs—a gift from Jesse—it was an hour to midnight.

Ideal.

Little one?

Here, at the window.

Yes, I see you.

The warmth of his snout appeared. Carefully, Sanna climbed on top, scooted to his neck. He flattened it out as best he could while she slowly made her way down, to the juncture of his wings and back, and settled.

Where are we going? he asked.

Back to our camping spot.

Several strides away from Mam's house, he hesitated. His neck swung to the right in a glance back.

What is it? she asked.

Are you certain regarding your plan?

I'm sure that I won't bring such a horrendous creature to my family. We can't stay here for another minute.

But—

We must, Luteis. She set her hand on the side of his neck. *It's followed us everywhere, it'll do the same here. We know what we need to do, and what we're fighting. If it's true that dragons are their natural enemy, it's a simple matter of drawing the Reine dux arachnae close and getting rid of her. Did you find a mortega antler?*

As many as you asked for.

Did you accomplish the rest?

He hesitated, then said, *Yes. Everything is set up as you requested.*

A long breath rippled through her, draining away the anxiety of bringing harm to her family. She didn't know what they faced out there, but she knew she wouldn't bring it this close to those she loved. Mam had found stability. Isadora loved Max, regardless of whether he said all the right things in her way or not, and Jesse had just started his adventure.

No, her chance to prove herself capable had fully arrived. She could fight for her forest—the way the *old* Sanna would have—and claim her home again.

Blindness be damned.

"Then let's go," she whispered. "If everything is ready, we only have to show up and wait. Tonight, we have a queen to kill."

———

The silence rang through Sanna's ears.

She gripped a club-like branch in her tight fist, knees tucked into her chest. The root well where she crouched stood taller than her head. As far as protection went, it was the best she could find while still laying herself bare.

Fog crawled over the ground, unusually cold, or perhaps Luteis had spoiled her with his natural heat. Her ears hurt at the tip and her nose dripped. She sniffled, hoping to make sound and draw their problem to its inevitable end.

C'mon, she thought. *Let's get this over with.*

Luteis' concerned tone filtered through her mind. *Little one?*

Yes?

You're well?

Yes.

Any signs?

She paused to listen. The same unnatural calm as before. *No, not yet.*

The restless frustration in his voice amplified the quiet. He didn't like standing away from her. He *really* didn't like her plan, though he agreed it was their most likely path out of this mess.

Sanna readjusted her feet and wiggled her toes. Too much of this waiting in the frigid night and they'd—

A *scritch* of sound came from overhead. Forest lions wouldn't make such a light noise. Their talons dug deep into the wood when they slid down. Beluas didn't have a subtle bone in their body. They couldn't move without grunting or noise.

She tensed.

Held her breath.

The clatter of a piece of falling bark came next. Her stomach turned to water. She tightened her hold on her weapon.

Luteis?

Yes.

I heard something.

I shall investigate.

Logic might dictate that forest dragons were hardly

subtle creatures with their gigantic, hot bodies, but their black scales camouflaged them spectacularly. Magic, or just the forest, stopped the trees from making sound whenever they moved by. But not even a dragon could sneak up on a spider.

A string of clacking noises, like talons tapping in a sequence, sounded to the right. Sanna twitched, scooted to the left on instinct. Her heart hammered in a wild song.

I can almost confirm it myself, she said. *Something has arrived. Whether it's the Reine dux arachnae or not, I'm not sure.*

I see only shadows, little one. I'm coming.

Another familiar *scritch*, like the tip of something dragging along the tree trunk, sounded from nearby. She sniffed, smelled nothing unusual. Certainly not a belua, a troll, or a forest lion.

Do you smell anything? she asked.

No.

Me either, which is another confirmation. I think there's more than one.

Undoubtedly.

The thought made her shudder. All the little holes in the ground the other day suddenly made greater sense. Spider legs, all of them. The only thing that had likely saved her was Luteis' heat.

Her mind spun back to the raised bumps of the picture that Isadora conjured with magic. She didn't need eyes to recall the fangs, the legs. The sheer size of such an atrocious monster.

Her hands shook as she silently brought the club in front of her. The tip dragged in the dirt. She waited for the telltale prickle on her neck that arose when something moved nearby, as if instinct could see.

Another *scritch*, this louder. Others came from farther

away, as if from different trees. Spiders collecting and descending as one.

This is my home, she thought in a looped refrain. *My home, my home, my home. This is my home, my forest, my trees. If there's a queen here, it's me. Mori, but I'm Sanna of the forest!*

The pep talk didn't help as the scratching sounds closed in, directly overhead now.

Get into position, she said.

I already am, he growled. *There are many shadows now. Little one, I will not stay away.*

Hold! she cried. *We have to kill her and the only way to do that is to bring her close enough to strike. I'll whack her, you spray flames on the rest. It's our only shot. We just have to hope the two of us are enough.*

A clicking, like teeth tapping together, chattered above. If she had to guess, she'd say ten paces.

Just a little longer, Luteis.

Her legs trembled. She slowly moved them beneath her into a crouch, lifted her club until it rested on her shoulder. With her palm, she felt for the prickly antlers. Luteis had gathered seven spiky antlers. She'd bound them to a heavy stick with a sash so all seven pointed out.

A mortega mace.

The *scritch* stopped.

What she wouldn't give for the Dragonmaster totem over the mountain dragons again. They could transport here, devour whatever threatened her. Talk about meeting the enemy right on! Sanna shoved that thought away. That totem had been a symbol of dragon slaves. It didn't serve anyone.

Another click-clack answered the first. Six paces away. The mace could reach about three paces in front.

Wait, she drawled.

Little one . . .

A dark pit of uncertainty unfurled in Sanna's stomach. From a distant part of her mind, she drudged up a memory of Daid. A rare, but flashing, smile. The way his hair stuck out near his temple. Despite being dead for over a year now, she remembered him so clearly. The result of living on the edge of life and death?

A gift from Deasylva?

She drew strength from his powerful remembrance.

The shuffle and sigh of movements, like legs tapping on dirt, scuttled around her. The hair on the back of her neck rose. Something cold and bristly brushed her cheek. She froze.

LITTLE ONE!

Legs.

Lots and lots of legs.

Hissing, clicking, clacking made a rising cacophony. Dozens of new fears asserted themselves. What if the spiders bit her? Did spiders carry poison? What if they didn't fear fire?

I'm fine, she said. *I'm fine. I'm fine. I'm fine.*

Little one! he growled.

His growing agitation fueled her own.

Sanna's breath sped up.

Then she felt them.

Eyes.

Dozens of eyes. They plunged into her like ice cold tentacles. Frozen promises of a darker underbelly. A world apart. The depths of Letum Wood were the only home for a fetid creature such as this.

And here Sanna waited for the queen of the night.

She gritted her teeth.

"I am not your prey!" she shouted. "I am *your* queen! Luteis, now!"

She swung the club with a scream.

The sheer force of her terror gave might to her arms. She wheeled her body with the swing, throwing it as hard as she could into the air in front of her. It landed against something firm, but softer than a tree. The impact reverberated through her arms, into her teeth. Her entire body jarred.

A high-pitched screech split the silent air. The clacking pierced her ears with a shriek, so fast that all became a blur.

Luteis roared.

Heat built in spurts as he swooped down. The ground trembled from his heavy-footed run. Spiders scrambled away with scuttling noises. His burst of fire came from not far away —but not close enough, either.

Sanna vaulted herself out of the hole, club in hand, and swung a second time. The *Reine dux arachnae* had already moved. Sanna stepped in a cold, tacky liquid. Blood, hopefully. With her fingers, quickly as possible, Sanna counted. Six antlers left. With any luck, one of them was embedded in the queen.

Something stabbed her leg as she swiveled in a circle, club held out. The thud-thud-thud of darting feet followed, and something tried to trip her from behind. She kept her balance, screamed.

"Get back!"

A blanket of fire crackled in the crisp air.

They run from my secundum, Luteis said breathlessly. *Little one, there are so many.*

Screeches surrounded her. Legs. Grabbing pincers. Hard things in her hair. Sanna whirled to the right and left, swinging with fury. The club connected with each toss. A sticky substance coated her shoulder with a viscous plop. She launched out of the protective well just as something *thudded* to the ground, scraping her back. She twirled, pirouetting.

The club hit another spider, then another. A third, sixth, tenth. They amassed on her, overhead. Waves of heat closed in. Luteis's chilling growl, his reverberating thuds, lent a tinge of terror to the air.

A heavy wad of moisture hit Sanna on the back, sending her to her knees. She popped back up, but something hit the club out of her hands.

"No!"

She scrambled to find it, but her palms touched only earth, snow, roots.

Silence fell.

Luteis?

She panted. Her wrist ached from the fall. The strange fluid seeped down her back and scalp, toward her ears. She didn't dare touch it. Instead, she held her breath, listened.

No shuffle of movement.

Little one? Where are you?

On the ground. My club is gone, I can't find it!

The rustle of dried leaves moving preceded a rope snagging her waist, her left ankle. A third grabbed her wrist. Slivers peeled out of the rope, embedding into her skin. Like razor-sharp twine bound together.

She screamed.

They consume me, little one, he cried. *I'm trying! I'm trying.*

The sounds of crackling fire, desperate growls, followed. Tears filled her eyes, jarring loose as another rope twined her right wrist. It jerked her off the ground, then dropped her. She slammed to the floor, smacking her nose. Noise rang in her head like an echoing bell, driving a headache all the way back into her skull.

A sob tore out of her.

"Luteis!"

What had she been thinking?

She *couldn't* do this. She wasn't the old Sanna anymore, and no amount of determination would make it so. Now she'd endangered her life, and Luteis, and for what?

The night morphed into hundreds of click-clack-chattering voices. All of them similar to the chatter of teeth or dancing bones. They surrounded her in a broad circle. The tensile, sharp cord bound her limbs and wrapped her arms and legs tight. She couldn't flail, budge, move.

A giant, rounded body slipped underneath her back, jarring her to the side. A *giant* body. She could hear the other ones teeming like ants.

"Get off me!" she screeched.

The weblike-ropes elevated her off the ground. The harder she fought, the tighter they pulled. Blood oozed around her wrists. Sanna shrieked.

"Let go of me!"

If I had magic, came the thought, *I could break these, could fight them. I'd be more capable.*

She didn't have magic.

Because she'd been too frightened.

The terror. The betrayal. This was *her* forest. Why would it allow such foul creatures—whatever they were—to harm her?

Little one! Hold on!

More clatters followed. She rose farther in the air, hairy tentacles along her arms now. Tears jarred out of her eyes, dripped down her cheeks. Above all the others came a menacing, nefarious hiss in her left ear.

The *Reine dux Arachnae.*

Luteis, she whispered, *I'm so sorry.*

LITTLE ONE!

Up the ropes pulled her. Higher. Gaping air existed beneath. She sensed growing space and distance and . . . death. She captured another sob, utterly paralyzed. Sickness welled up in her body. Rope continued to spin around her, slicing with micro cuts into her skin. The *Reine dux arachnae* had her.

A roar broke the night.

Flames followed.

Such flames. They plumed above her, sizzling and devastating. The *Reine dux Arachnae* squealed, a low, guttural thing of panic. Sanna turned her face away with a grimace. The cords that bound her legs broke. She dropped, feet slamming into the loamy earth. Her arms remained suspended above.

One of her feet hit a creature that chittered in response. Sanna could only kick out with a heel. The spider scurried away, tall as her knee.

Elis has arrived! Another roar of fire. *We are not alone, little one!*

"Sanna?" Jesse called. "SANNA?"

Another bust of fire.

"Here!" she shrieked. Blood slaked down her arms, still bound by whatever rope the queen gripped her with. "Jesse! Please, help me! Help!"

Belches of fire, frantic retreats, sounded as Jesse approached with a guttural shout. The rope around her left hand broke. She collapsed, slamming to the earth. Hands caught her shoulders before her face smacked the ground a second time.

"Sanna!"

His strong hand grabbed her arm. She fell into him, sobbing. "Get it off me! Get it off me!"

The wounds around her wrists burned like fire as the ropes disappeared. He put an arm around her shoulders. She held onto him, shuddering.

"It's all right. It's all right. Elis is killing them. Luteis is attacking a . . . *mori,* a giant spider. I think it's the queen. He just leapt out of a tree and on top of her. Definitely the *Reine dux arachnae.* She's fighting back. Oh, he bit off one of her legs. And another. She's not going to make it, Sanna. He's so fierce."

The vicious sound of a horrible battle followed. Gnashing

teeth, deafening screams, and so much fire. Elis roared a terrible bass, sending spiders into the night. Their bodies squelched under his legs as he stomped around.

"We need to get you somewhere safe," Jesse called over the sounds of battle. "We're right below Luteis and the queen."

Arm around her shoulder, he led them away. Sanna clamped her arms around his waist. A third dragon descended with heat and a terrible roar.

"Junis!" Jesse cried, laughing. "Sanna, Junis has come to your aid. And is that . . . is that? It's Cara!"

The ground trembled as a fourth ran from the trees. Her cry, so familiar, swept through Sanna like a shock. Tears filled her eyes.

"They came?"

"They came for their Dragonmaster." He tightened his hold on her. They slowed. "By Drago, Sanna, they're demolishing those monsters. Another dragon has come! Sellis. He's so big these days, and his fire is scorching. You saved him from that belua, remember? He's here to fight for you. Oh, an entire horde of spiders is running away. They're . . . they're huge. They had you completely surrounded. Cara is keeping herself between the spiders and us. Junis is a glory to behold. He's flying with such skill."

The crepitus of slaughtered spiders and dying screams filled the air. Fire. So much glorious, destructive heat. The cold night banished under near constant flames, the creeping power of a long-lasting secundum, or second fire.

I'm safe, she said to Luteis, frantic. *I'm safe!*

He gave no response.

She squeezed Jesse's arm. "Luteis? What's happening?"

"He's got the queen on the ground now. He's cut all her ropes. She's missing several legs. I think she's wounded pretty badly, but she's still fighting. She's trying to bind his wings . . . oh."

"Oh what?"

Luteis screamed. The ground shook with a *thud* that nearly sent Sanna to her knees. Another gurgling sound of death followed. The thunder of so many legs disappeared, skittering into the tree trunks.

Calm followed.

"She's . . . she's dead."

"How?"

"Luteis landed on her and literally squashed her. Now he's covering her with his secundum. She's torched. Elis and Junis and Sellis are setting all the other spiders on fire. The bigger ones have retreated. It's an utter massacre, Sanna. They've destroyed so many. Thousands, if I had to guess it."

She collapsed.

All the fragile skeins holding her together snapped. Unable to move, she slid down. Something didn't feel right. A coldness in her body. Her muscles didn't respond to her commands. Jesse carefully lowered her to the ground. His grip on her shoulders tightened.

"Sanna, your wrists and ankles are bleeding. You're shaking, and so cold. We need to get you to Lucey. I think there's something in the ropes, like a paralytic. *Mori*, you have so many cuts on you."

Mention of Lucey broke Sanna from her shock. Her teeth chattered. Her entire body felt as if she'd fallen into a frozen lake.

Little one? Luteis cried.

I'm f-f-fine.

Her thoughts were stuttered, coated with disbelief. She allowed Jesse to lift her up.

"I'm going to transport us both to Lucey. She taught me. It might be uncomfortable, but you're safe. Just focus on holding your breath. It helps, all right?"

She shuddered, oddly fragmented now. *Lucey,* she said to Luteis. *Going to Lucey.*

"Sanna?"

"Don't . . . don't tell Isa," she pled.

Before he could reply, a pressure came upon them that threatened to press her out of Alkarra. The pain around her wrists and ankles intensified. A scream faded from her lips as she plunged into magic, whisked away from Letum Wood.

Thirty-Four

Isadora

A gleaming cherry wood bookcase loomed over Isadora. The closely-stacked shelves were thinly spaced, some of them so close together only one book lay horizontal, or scrolls marched in a single row. Most of the books had sturdy leather bound covers, worn on the bottom with gentle frays and tears. Some were bound with thick parchment or tied with twine.

Below those, drawers.

Isadora peeked into one small drawer, no wider than her fist. Velvet lined the interior. In it, small toys, about the length of her finger. Marching Guardians, were they? They had once been painted. Flecks of a hat existed on one. Bits of a face on the other.

She closed it, flipped through scrolls.

Old weather reports.

A scroll on architectural design for above-ground garden plots.

A cleverly concealed false front of book spines was actually a retractable wall. Inside, a box decorated with gems awaited. She extracted the treasure, ran her fingers over the bumpy top, and down the side. A small latch near the bottom gave way, opening it.

She jumped with a squeal.

A sordid, aged doll lay inside, features twisted in what must have been a smile. Paint had rubbed off the face, revealing old wood beneath. Strings made up the hair. An old dress, painstakingly sewed with the tiniest of stitches, had worn away into holes with time.

She slammed the lid shut, shoved it back in the hiding spot.

Grotesque.

Well, that's what she got for snooping.

Shoving off the ground, Isadora stepped back. The bookshelf occupied a small portion of a large wall, accented on either side by thin stained-glass windows that bled the growing light of day. Other knick knacks littered each shelf. Some of them shoved in between tomes, others stacked in front.

Half a globe. A carving of a gargoyle like those that perched on the rooftop, only this one gave birth. An old stack of cards—clearly missing half the deck—with pictures of deathly plants and how to administer them for fastest expiration. Dice with strange runes that she didn't recognize. Isadora unfolded a map of a land that wasn't Alkarra, written with a language that she'd never seen before. A small cup brimmed full with nails and . . . screws? All of them twisted into strange shapes.

She shook her head, thought of Sanna and what fun she'd have here. She should check on her sister. See if—

A call down the hallway caught her attention.

"Isadora?"

Her stomach jolted. Egads, but she and Max hadn't truly spoken since their encounter days ago. Shame and horror filled her at the thought. She hadn't been wrong in her response, of course not. Max had acted rudely and without giving her all the information.

When she recalled her discussion with Charlie, she wondered if perhaps she *did* ask too much of him, too fast.

He concealed so much of his past that would give her the needed context, though. Or she could just be more patient. On and on spiraled her internal arguments, which led her to distract herself here, in this odd room.

"Isadora?"

She shoved a child's prayer book back onto the shelf. The wooden thing wasn't a book at all, but cleverly designed to look like one. Instead, it was a hidden case with an old bottle of ipsum that, when she sniffed, nearly sent her into a fit.

"In here!" she called.

Smacking her hands together to get rid of the dust, she stood up, righted her skirt, and twirled around just as Max peeked his head inside. He studied her, then the room.

"You found the room of curiosities."

"Is that what this is?"

"That's what Charlie always called it."

Isadora glanced at the shelf she'd just combed through. "More like atrocities."

He snorted, half grimaced. "I'd counter you on that in honor of Wildrose's reputation, but you're right. Some of it is horrifying."

Cordiality had returned, as if that night never happened. They'd need to talk about it, of course, but she'd lean into the formality over silence.

For now.

"Where did all of this come from?" she asked.

Max leaned farther in, gaze lingering on a painting propped against the far bookshelf. A rolling hillside, littered with flowers that, when one looked closer, were actually birds.

The grass blades were all triangles, and the cottage home in the very middle a carefully-hidden coffin.

"The witches that roll through here, no doubt. Charlie found many such oddities through the years, and took great delight in hiding them in various places in this room. If you have a keen eye, you'll find an entire cat skeleton, disassembled, throughout each shelf."

"That's disgusting."

"That," he muttered, "is generations of Dauphins at work. Curious family, when you dive into their past."

Isadora's nose wrinkled. Before she could make further comments, he opened the door wider.

"May I pose a question to you?"

Over a month since they left the Southern Network and he still spoke to her like a . . . friend. The thought occurred to her then that this might just be *Max*. He carried so much formality in that attractive figure he couldn't help himself.

She lifted her hands in silent permission.

A moment of indecision crossed his face. Finally, he said, "There's an opera this evening and Charlie has given us tickets. He requested that both you and I attend. For the Advocacy and other purposes that I will explain later, as we'll be late if we don't prepare to go soon."

"Who are these witches?"

"Business witches, mostly. A pair that I have some reason and motivation to remain . . . acquaintances with."

"I see."

"You can say no."

"Oh, I wouldn't do that. Of course I'll go and support you."

He blinked, still studying her. Ghosts of questions lingered in the air.

"Can we talk about the other night after the opera?" she

asked quietly. "I think we need to better understand each other."

He opened his mouth again, hesitated, and finally nodded. "Of course. Let's get this over with first and I will give you all my time. Your attendance is most appreciated. We leave in half an hour. Is that sufficient?"

"Yes, thank you."

Max hesitated, gaze darting around the strange room. "Make sure you lock the door behind you. Never know what will walk out of it."

———

The Opera House in Ashleigh Covens sprawled like a glittering jewel across the interior of Ashleigh City. Torches led the way down gleaming cobblestone streets, over to the curved building that housed singers and support witches. Crowds streamed closer, gentle chatter abounding in the air.

Max kept Isadora's arm tucked close. She held her breath as they scurried across the street ahead of a carriage, an elegant red dress with a black lace overlay swishing around her legs.

"The opera house is so . . . bright."

Max set his jaw and said nothing.

As they approached the front doors, he handed a waiting porter two tickets. Isadora tilted her head back as they passed through soaring doorways, beyond elegant columns sculpted with scrolls. Max carefully led her into a carpeted room lined with candles and the stuffy smell of torch oil.

"We have a box on the third floor." He guided them to the right. "It's a shared box given to the Network leadership."

"A box?"

"A private space that contains several seats and is less . . . busy. Typically, more quiet as well."

"Oh." She eyed a passing female with a flaring skirt twice

the size of hers, dripping velvet and gems. "Is the opera expensive?"

"Egregiously."

He swept them toward a wide set of stairs, where candle-light, chandeliers, and cleverly placed mirrors illuminated the open space. Distant strains of a warming orchestra flowed from several doors, set close together, against the far wall. Hints of brocade curtains and soaring space were just visible.

Max steered her up the staircases. A black-clad woman stood in front of the stairs with a serene smile. Few witches made it past her to go higher. She saw Max, smiled, and stepped aside. As Isadora followed him up the stairs, the woman moved back into position.

"Is this area protected?"

"Box patrons only."

The higher they climbed, the more the gentle ruckus below quieted. For so many witches packed into a small area, there wasn't a lot of sound. A general hush hummed in the air, waiting for something to happen. More black-clad workers populated spots here and there with serene smiles. The stuffy air carried heady perfumes.

Max stopped at a doorway with a locked handle. He reached into his pocket, extracted a wrought-iron key, and slipped it inside. The door opened, and Isadora caught a gasp.

Mesmerized, she advanced.

A literal box hung off the side of the wall, filled with thick, padded chairs. To her right and left were more boxes—all clinging to the wall—with other milling patrons. The lack of candlelight and torches lent a sense of calm.

She stepped delicately around the empty chairs in their box and to the far end. Several stories below, chairs lined the floor, clustered around the stage. An orchestra pit separated the stage from the crowd. The conductor stood at the top, frowning. Papers whirled around him, settling into a specific order. A violinist played scales, and several voices trilled with laughter.

"It's so lovely," she breathed.

Max came up behind her. Instead of his usual distance, his hand pressed into the small of her back. Her stomach fluttered, heart taking off. The glittering candle-light reflected in his dark eyes as he surveyed the scene below.

"How high is this?" she asked.

"The opera house itself is at least five stories." He gestured to the stage. "We're on the third floor, which is the dead center. Supposedly, this box is the best. It was gifted to the Network for the year by the owner, a woman named Caroline House. We take turns attending performances. Faye likes it, in particular."

"Who wouldn't?"

Max eyed her, then stepped back. Isadora tore her hungry gaze away from the magnificent stage and curtains and energy —she wouldn't stop watching all evening, she'd wager—and turned around. The door to the box lay open a sliver, admitting light from the hall.

Max cleared his throat, tugged at his collar. "Er, I should let you know that we're expecting other witches tonight."

"You mentioned that."

"One of them is Zander. An interesting witch in his own right. He wants to be a Council Member, but hasn't yet managed to procure Charlie's trust. He's attempting to be my friend to help his cause, I think."

The thought made Isadora unaccountably sad.

"Does that always happen?"

"What?"

"Witches try to be your friend because of what you can do for them?"

He blinked, frowned, then said, "Well, yes. Of course."

"Isn't anyone your friend just because they're a friend? Aside from Charlie, of course."

Again he met her with that perplexed expression, as if *she* were the one missing something. Isadora wrangled back a sigh.

Oh, Max.

He had so much to learn.

With a wave of her hand, she indicated for him to continue. He shifted, clearing his throat. A thousand-pace stare came to his eyes, as if he were far away. In the paths, most likely, to try to see who would come. A habit of his, she'd noticed. He used the paths to anticipate meetings, but mostly social events.

He blinked out of it, pale. His fingers clenched into fists at his side.

"Demmet!"

Before she could ask what his sudden, heavy frown meant, voices sounded at the door. It swung open, admitting a quartet of witches all at the same time. A woman and three males entered.

"Maximillion Sinclair," boomed one of the males. A rotund man with a portly belly, bright cheeks, and fast smile. "Always so good to see you. Glad you could make it tonight and half an hour before this production starts! Unprecedented. You normally scuttle in as the curtain rises. Where's the wine?"

"Griffin, good to see you again."

The two males in front held out arms to Max. He accepted, stiff as ever. Griffin motioned to the slighter, taller, and a droopy through the face man next to him.

"You've met Zander before, I believe?"

"Always good to see you again, Zander."

Max's fingers curled around Isadora's waist, pulling her to his side. It felt like standing next to a cold stone wall.

"Zander and Griffin, this is my wife, Isadora."

"Pleasure!" Zander boomed. "Such a pleasure. Heard lovely things."

The other couple, male and female, stepped out of the shadows. The woman studied Isadora with a curious mien and a glaze of shock. Max glowered at the male. Ever-so-subtly, he tugged Isadora behind his left shoulder. His hand found hers and squeezed. She took it as a silent command.

A nefarious spark filled the air.

"Ronald," Max intoned.

The other man, a stocky witch with a full beard, blonde hair, and light eyes, smiled. The cloying nature of it set her teeth on edge. He didn't look at her.

"Ambassador, so good to see you again so soon. You've met my date, I believe, Caterina?"

A cold bath washed through Isadora.

Caterina.

Max's former lover. The one he would barely regard in thought, and shuddered over whenever he said her name. If his history with Bella embarrassed him, Caterina seemed to terrify him.

Max nodded, but didn't look at Caterina.

Zander broke in, saving the moment. "Well, Ronald Torkelson! What a pleasant surprise. Didn't realize you procured the fifth and sixth tickets. The founder of the League of Free Borders is here tonight with us at the opera." Zander's too-tight smile lingered at the edges. "Who would have thought such a strange coincidence might occur?"

Max tightened his hold on Isadora. She almost stood behind him now. Griffin cleared his throat and slipped away, calling for a porter from the doorway.

Ronald smiled at Zander, but it didn't reach his eyes. "Always a delight to have a chance to discuss business with the other side, isn't it? The opera is such a . . ." he drew in a deep breath, swirling a hand in thought, ". . . pleasant experience."

Zander returned the smile, his own almost feral. Calculation lay somewhere in those dark folds of thought.

Tension tripled through the box.

"The porter is bringing some wine and comestibles," Griffin said as he returned. "Should only be a few minutes."

"How is business?" Max asked Zander. His voice was smooth as silk, dropping into the easy tones of enterprise she'd learned to listen for. The Max that presented at home, mostly rough-spoken, quiet, contemplative, was an entirely different version of the man presented in front of other witches.

A fascinating dichotomy.

While Griffin rattled off an explanation about company expansions, and Zander inserted jokes about existing Council Members, the tautness held. Ronald edged his way into the conversation. His obligatory laughter did nothing to soften his features.

Meanwhile, Caterina stared at her.

Doubts swirled in her chest. Should Isadora introduce herself? No. Something in Caterina's intensity turned her away. Bored with the business discussion and their posturing, Isa extracted herself from Max's firm grip to regard the crowd below. Seeing she wouldn't go far, he relaxed.

Patrons swelled in ever-growing numbers near the orchestra pit. More bodies filled the chairs at the bottom. Heat billowed through the room. Why hadn't she brought a fan? Isadora closed her eyes, listened.

What would Sanna experience here? No sight, just sounds. Smells. Could she sense the cavernous openness? Or the headiness of the velvety dark, the energy lingering in the air? A body appeared on her right side, followed by a melodious voice.

"My name is Caterina."

A fan snapped open, filled with pearlescent lace and swirling designs that looked like sand dunes blowing in the wind. By the good gods, no wonder he'd hidden Caterina. Her languid voice, beguiling eyes, and folds of shiny hair painted a striking picture. Caterina was loveliness personified. A veritable goddess of beauty.

A cold feeling curled around Isadora's neck like a claw.

She faced Caterina with a radiant smile.

"Isadora."

Caterina returned it with a hooded nod, then faced the stage. Air stirred as she lazily moved her fan back and forth. A porter entered the box behind them. The smell of cheese and wine drifted by.

"You are handfasted to Max?"

"Yes."

Astonishment filled her voice. "Truly?"

Isadora bit back a cold smile. "Yes. We've been handfasted for several months now."

"I'm very surprised."

"I can see that."

Caterina blinked long, thick lashes. Were they real? Had she used magic to enhance them? Some of the girls at Miss Sophia's School for Girls had attempted such a spell. Burned off half their lashes and most of their eyebrows attempting it.

"Max is not the . . . stable relationship type." Caterina's gaze flickered to him, then back to Isadora. "I'm beside myself with surprise over this news."

"He told me about you."

Isadora blurted it out too quickly. Instead of suave and calm, it felt like an admission of guilt. Caterina's lips lifted and fell.

"I'm surprised at that as well," she murmured. "I thought he would try to hide what we had."

"That's not Max."

"No," she said after a short pause. "I suppose not. Forgive me some curiosity, but I must ask: how did you do it? How did you snag a witch like Max? He is so black and white. All or nothing. Max is the sort of witch who would either marry for business or for love. Nothing else. And he doesn't believe he's capable of love."

Isadora fought her rising sense of competition. Wily girl. Caterina was probing, attempting to find out whether or not their handfasting was a sham. Caterina must wonder if Max handfasted Isadora because she benefited him somehow, or did he actually care? Like a circling predator, Caterina hunted for answers.

Jealousy compelled her, Isadora would guess.

With such revelation came a swelling sense of hopelessness. In fact, Caterina was correct. Maximillion had originally handfasted her out of sheer business and obligation to the Network. At one point, he did claim to want her and care for her. But the words she so longed to hear hadn't come.

Maybe they never would.

I haven't, she thought. *I haven't snagged him at all.*

Not really.

Because if she had truly *snagged* him, as Caterina said, then he wouldn't have hidden Caterina. He would have said *I love you*.

Wouldn't he?

Was there more than one way to say the same thing?

Isadora swallowed the rising apprehension, recalling the pain etched in his features evenings ago. The hints of agony and warring dissonance. It didn't add up. She had something wrong here.

Realizing that Caterina waited for her response, she said, "I didn't snag him. He came to me."

The neutral tone was a feat of triumph.

Caterina tilted her head to the side, raking Isadora's profile. Isadora stared ahead, lost in the layers of brocade sweeping the stage.

"You are Isadora Spence? The Watcher that helped with negotiations in the Southern Network, are you not?"

"I am."

"Ah. Well, that explains so much!"

Caterina laughed, as if relieved. "Max has always been a work-oriented man. He appreciates deadlines, efficiency, and clockwork. Emotional dealings with witches have never been a forte of his. I assume that your work with Max in the South is what brought you together? Nothing like a united purpose . . ."

Caterina trailed away, scoffing.

Isadora curled her fingertips into her palm when Caterina chuckled, as if laughing over this whole affair and its absurdity. Rage slipped through her. It wasn't absurd—it was her life. And it was high time someone stood up for Max, believed in Max, fought for Max, trusted Max.

In fact, it was time *she* did.

"Well, best of luck for however long it lasts," Caterina said with an airy giggle. "I understand how it feels to be slighted by a man like him. Please let me know if you ever need to talk once the inevitable happens."

"You sound quite certain about a handfasting you know nothing about," Isadora said coolly. "Pardon my assumption, but is it jealousy that I hear in your voice?"

Caterina had begun to turn away, but stopped. Her lips parted, eyes widened. Fueled by building ire, Isadora faced her more fully. She set one hand on the banister.

"If you're trying to figure out whether Max married me out of love or not, let me assure you; he did. Maximillion Sinclair has loved me from the moment we met. He is kind, compassionate, and understanding. He devotes time and attention to me in ways you might never comprehend.

"Do I love him? With all the ferocious love my heart is capable of. If you're planning on outlasting me and *snagging* him later, I hope you have a long wait in mind. I will never stop loving him, trusting him, or working my hardest to keep him."

Caterina pulled in a breath through her nose.

A hand came to Isadora's waist, warm and heavy. Max pulled her close. "Isa," he murmured, tension thick in his tone. "I see you met Caterina."

Caterina straightened, a bland smile fixed on her face. "Maximillion, a pleasure."

He ignored her.

Isadora tried to take some air, but it lay in a muggy carpet on the world. A wine glass appeared in Max's hand. He passed it to her. She sipped, then gulped. The stuff always gave her a roaring headache, but that's just what she needed right then. A different outlet for the rapidly accumulating astonishment. In fact, she'd just answered her own tenacious question.

How hadn't she seen it all along?

Max *did* love her.

The way he unpacked her bags the first morning after she arrived at Wildrose, or made dinner with her at the end of a long day. The book of silly riddles he brought home, the careful tour of Wildrose. The kisses.

By Drago, the kisses.

Which didn't mention his protective side, his loving side. He made space for her during a busy day and attempted to protect her from unrealized dangers. She'd made him a list that he tackled very seriously.

She wanted to laugh, then cry. Elation bubbled inside. Max *loved* her! There was no need for a trial period or the words to come from his lips. She felt it all the way in her burning bones.

Maximillion Sinclair, the haughty Ambassador in the Central Network, loved her, Isadora Spence.

Love was enough.

They could do this.

Zander's booming laugh echoed through the air, startling her. United strains rose from the orchestra in a warning trill. A cascade of quiet rippled through the opera house. Caterina faded back to her date that glowered from the shadows.

Max passed her a glass of water that he conjured.

"Here."

She gulped half the drink, dizzy from the heat and the realization and the depths of love in her heart.

Did Max hear her refutation of Caterina?

The sweating condensation against her palm, and the clink of ice against the glass, reoriented her. She let out a long breath, sipped again, then pressed her forehead to the cool edge. The sweltering heat of the opera house heightened.

"I'll explain everything later," he murmured. "I promise, Isadora. I'm sorry she got to you before I noticed. Whatever she said, don't let it poison you. Don't let it send you into anxiety. She's a viper and—"

She laughed, squeezed his hand. "No, Max. Don't fear, don't worry. Quite the contrary."

His face dropped into a maze of questions as she reached up, touched his cheek. She pressed a kiss to his lips, then pulled away with a broad smile.

"I love you," she whispered. "And I know that you love me. I'm sorry it took me so long to see it, Max. Burn my list. I am satisfied. I want to be with you forever."

He blinked.

"What—"

"Later," she whispered, giggling. Dazed, he reared back, but not far. She motioned him into a chair. He complied, woodenly. Torches along the sides of the chairs extinguished, one at a time, dropping the opera house into a pervasive darkness. The chatter of voices calmed, leaving a tepid silence.

Zander and Griffin sat next to each other on the front row

of the box, fingers entwined. They were slightly below the chairs in the back, where Caterina and Ronald stewed in silence. Caterina deftly avoided Isadora's gaze.

Max pressed a kiss to her temple.

"Later," he promised.

THIRTY-FIVE
SANNA

Lucey's soothing touch pressed on Sanna's shoulder.

"Sanna? Are you awake?"

Sanna sucked in a deep breath, let it out. She straightened out of a tangle of blankets, and tried to wake up.

"Yes. I'm fine."

A chuckle followed.

Sanna rubbed her eyes, blinking awake. Memory served in fractals. The transportation magic. Jesse carrying her . . . somewhere. Vaguely, she recalled Lucey's voice, a slippery, loose feeling sliding through her limbs. Then warmth, and a relief from the pain, and blessed sleep.

Sanna pushed to sitting. Fresh sheets crinkled under her fingertips. A light smell lingered in the air. Lemongrass? Every few seconds, the ground trembled.

"Where am I?"

"At my house in Letum Wood."

"Oh."

"It's late morning. Your dragon is prowling around outside, very stressed. Could you put him at ease? He's frightening my cow and she's not going to produce milk. We were just getting enough for butter."

Groggily, Sanna reached out to Luteis. *Luteis?*

The shaking earth calmed.

Little one?

Yes, I'm awake. I'm all right.

Relief stained his voice. *I have been concerned. Jesse took you away. Elis guided me here.*

I'm sorry. I just woke up.

You are well, that's all that matters. Speak with your healer. I wait outside, with Cara and Junis and Elis and Sellis.

Emotions swelled higher. That's right. The forest dragons had come to defend her. Tears clouded her eyes, stinging with heat.

"Here." Lucey set something in her left palm. "It's water. Have a drink."

Her throat ached with thirst, so Sanna obeyed. When finished, she handed it back. "Thank you, Lucey. Can I go outside now and see my dragons? I'm all right. I swear. I just want to see them."

"Oh, Sanna. How little you have changed. You're not all right," Lucey said with mild amusement, "but you aren't the first witch who has attempted to convince me otherwise. You've been through something very traumatic, and I'm not just talking about giant spiders. It's fine to not be fine. Oh, and you're not going anywhere for a day or two, so don't ask me again."

Sanna opened her mouth to reply, but stopped. Unsure of what to say, she lay back down. Weariness swept through her, anyway. She didn't have the strength to fight or stumble around outside.

Maybe Lucey was correct.

An hour later, Lucey's heavy blanket, a hot cup of tea, and a warm chair near the fire restored balance to her wild thoughts. Lucey gently probed her wrists. Sanna sucked in a breath through her teeth, wincing. Electric pain spiraled up her arms, through the skin.

"Ouch."

"Ouch is right," Lucey said. "These are some interesting lacerations you have. They'll heal well enough, but you'll be smarting for a few days. My brother described a terrifying scene from last night."

"Very," she whispered.

Lucey squeezed her arm, above the injuries.

"Have some more tea, the herbs in it will help with these smaller, superficial cuts along the back of your arm. The salve for your wrists and ankles needs a few more minutes to set and then we'll get you bandaged up. They've aired enough to please me, for now. After we have bandages on the wounds, you can go outside, speak to your Luteis."

"Thank you."

"While that's settling," Lucey continued, and the low drawl in her tone told Sanna *exactly* what she'd want to say. "Let's talk about your eyes."

She opened her mouth to say, *I'd rather not*, but stopped. Not again. She'd spent the last month and a half running from it. She could have died because of her denial. Worse, any of the dragons might have died.

Time to face the literal darkness.

"I don't want to talk about it," she admitted quietly, "but I will."

"I know you don't. Who would?"

"It's hard."

Lucey settled next to her, a hand on Sanna's forearm. "I know that too, Sanna. But you can do hard things. I think you've made that abundantly clear. Whether or not those hard things are wise is another question."

Sanna swallowed the rising emotion, thick as a ball in her

throat. She tried to clear it, but it stuck anyway. Minutes passed before she could speak.

"I want to be *that* Sanna from before, not *this* Sanna. I didn't ask for this. I want to see the trees, not just smell them. I want to be able to walk through them, not just grope and stumble. I want . . ."

"You want your old life back," Lucey whispered.

Sanna nodded. Tears dropped down her cheeks, cutting a cool path against her flushed skin.

"I want to be *me* again."

"Do you think that's what happened?" The higher pitch of Lucey's tone indicated surprise. "That losing your sight took who you are away from you?"

"Yes! How can I be Sanna of the forest if I'll never set foot on another branch again? Can't run through the canopy, swing on the vines. I can't . . . I can't be *me* when I'm stuck on the ground, dependent on other witches and dragons and . . . it's not fair."

"You're right."

Sanna's heaving chest rose to a crescendo. Giant sobs flowed free in waves. Lucey held onto her, pulling her close. She ran a hand down Sanna's back and spoke a soothing melody. In her safety, Sanna released the building pain.

The rising muck she fought for weeks spilled free, like viscous oil. The sticky burst of it through her heart left her wide open, ragged, drowning. There was no stopping the pain. No holding back the tide.

She didn't want this ache.

The desperation.

The flailing tendrils of helplessness that consumed her in anxiety and fear. Swells of despair and regret and longing.

"It's not fair," Lucey said after a long pause, when Sanna's cries dwindled to hiccups. "So much of this situation isn't fair, Sanna, and I'm sorry. I wish life had never asked it of you."

Finally, the caged emotions expended. In their wake, she felt brittle and hollow. A shaky leaf, trembling in the wind.

Lucey leaned a little closer. "But you have one thing wrong, *amo*."

The tender Dragonmaster nickname, *amo*, my love, softened Sanna's puckered and weary heart.

"What is that?"

"Nothing is stronger than you are. Not even these fears, nor these emotions. Yes, life dealt you an unfair hand. You miss, and will miss, a lot of things. You didn't ask for this. Yet, you survive. You persist. You just need to do so a bit more *wisely*," she added wryly. "I don't know anything more *Sanna of the forest* than taking on the *Reine dux arachnae* by yourself, blind, in the middle of the night, to save others. Or trying to leave your sick bed to check on dragons? You are still Sanna Spence."

Sanna chuckled weakly. She used the back of her wrist to wipe the tears off her cheeks. The words she'd hesitated to say for so long came easily now.

"Lucey, I need help."

"You do."

"I want to live on my own, but I don't know how. It's not fair of me to ask so much of Luteis. I see what Mam meant now. He isn't enough, and he was never supposed to be. He's my friend, my heart, not my affliction."

"He's not *you*."

"No."

"But what a beloved witch you are for him to be so willing to give all that he could, and then some."

Sanna reached her free hand over, and put it on top of Lucey's. There, it trembled.

"Can you help?"

"Yes, we can."

Sanna tilted her head back, chin high. "Then I would be

most grateful if you could help me find a way to navigate this blindness. I want . . . I want to be myself again."

Lucey chuckled, wiped a tear from Sanna's cheek. Her delicate touch felt like the caress of a butterfly wing.

"You never lost yourself, Sanna. We always look forward, never back. You are simply learning the newer, stronger, better version of yourself. You can honor that part of your life, even as you look forward to a different one."

Her words swelled through Sanna's mind. *You can honor that part of your life.*

"I didn't think of it that way."

"You have a most epic challenge ahead of you. A challenge that few witches accept. A path that no one enters willingly. You trod a path that few have ever taken, one that will require tenacity, courage, bravery, and a great deal of help. You, Sanna of the forest, are a witch without measure."

Sanna squeezed Lucey's fingers. Hope inflated within. "You're right. This is my new life. Looking forward."

Lucey's smile was present in her voice. "Always forward, *amo.*"

The tears began to dry. Her trembling ceased, and the overwhelming swells of anxiety and grief ebbed into a less torrential sensation. The pain simmered in the background, not yet ready to be forgotten, but it didn't cling.

In acceptance, there was greater peace.

"Thank you for your help, Lucey. Thank you for . . . being a friend I didn't know I had. I need more of them."

"And you shall have them. Now, let's finish bandaging these wounds? Sonja has gone to tell your Mam where you are, just in case she's worried. Your dragon needs a little love, too, I think. I'd rather not deal with an irate, giant lizard near my cottage, thank you very much."

———

Sanna stepped onto Lucey's porch with a lightheaded feeling. No sooner had her foot landed than she felt the gentle tug of a serpentine tail around her ankle.

Little one?

She reached out a hand. "Luteis?"

The tail tightened. A wing scooped her up, depositing her gently on his back. She put her arms at the juncture of body and neck with a sigh of relief. His heat smoldered against her skin. She leaned into it.

Home really wasn't a place, like Mam had said. Home was the back of her dragon, where she belonged.

You're well?

"Well enough, considering."

He keened low in his throat, a painful sound.

I'm sorry, little one. I failed you. I could not protect you when it most mattered and—

"Luteis, no." She reached out a hand. Moments later, he touched it with his snout and a low moan. "It wasn't your fault. I should never have asked so much of you in the first place. Without you, I would have died."

But—

"No, let me finish. I love you, Luteis. You are my best friend. But that doesn't mean you should have to take care of me. I should be able to take care of myself. The depth of your love isn't measured by what you do for me, but how you accept me. Grow with me. If we are truly to survive out here, I can't do it alone."

He quieted for so long she thought she might have spoken only to herself. Finally, he replied.

I see that this is true. In protecting you too much, I actually harmed you.

"I needed to accept that I won't see again, and that's hard." Tears welled up in her eyes, thickening her voice. "I want to see again *so much,* but I can't. Which means I need to learn how to deal with this new reality. I didn't ask for this change, but it's upon me."

And this is why you are so strong.

Another tear dribbled down her cheek, just when she didn't think there could be more. This tear left behind not caverns, but sinews.

Power.

Veracity.

"Lucey knows someone that can teach me how to use a cane to walk around and spells that will make things like cutting easier. There are bumps that I can feel with my fingertips to read."

These are all positive things, little one.

"I know."

When do we start?

She swallowed hard. "I need to meet him first. Lucey says I can come here to her house."

You will still build a witch-place?

"Yes." She laughed. "One that you can sleep next to every night. Eventually, anyway. When we're more ready for it."

I find this plan acceptable. I will be here to protect you as much as possible.

"What we have is special, but if we lean on it too much, it's not safe. You understand, right?" She pressed the flat of her palm against her breastbone. "I'm not moving you out of your place in my heart."

Yes, I see this.

Tears bubbled up. "So you aren't angry?"

His snout cradled closer. *Never angry. I see what we didn't understand before. That this could not be. The new path is the best as you learn and accept.*

Sanna sobbed. His understanding set free the fears that

had bubbled up in her darkest depths. In the places she had avoided, because it all felt too overwhelming and frightening.

"I love you, Luteis."

As I love you, little one.

THIRTY-SIX

MAXIMILLION

Wildrose steeped in snowy quiet when they returned. A cool darkness swamped the house. Facets of the chandelier glimmered in the low light from the moon. The tacked carpet and vase of dried flowers seemed to hold their breath in anticipation.

Steady, unlike his thready heart.

They transported into the main foyer, downstairs. Caterina had left at intermission, Ronald shortly after. Griffin and Zander, emotional from the opera that Maximillion couldn't recall a single moment of, promised to plan a follow-up meeting later.

"We're friends, Max," Zander had said with an arm clasp. "Friends watch out for each other. Don't let Ronald bully you. We're here, and we know the Advocacy is, too. We'll talk about things for Griffin's hope of being a Council Member later."

In the halcyon of Wildrose, Isadora peered up at him. Her chin tipped back, inquisitive eyes sparkled in the dim light. Max reached up, touched her face. His hand shook. Over and over, her whisper swirled through his thoughts.

I love you. And I know that you love me. I'm sorry it took me so long to see it, Max. Burn my list. I am satisfied. I want to be with you forever.

"How?" he whispered.

She smiled. "You show me your love every day, Max. I just didn't understand it until now. You could say the words, but they wouldn't mean as much as what you do for me."

With a growl, he pulled her into his arms. Their lips crashed, colliding with the force of all his pent up pain. He growled, unable to bear the force of emotion that crashed through him. Grief threatened, ready to explode and consume. Adolescent terrors whispered promises of departure, of unworthiness.

She will not stay.

They didn't love you either.

You are unlovable.

Those voices were the reason he couldn't say the words.

The reason he tried so valiantly to push her away. Isadora deserved a better future than an unlovable lech of a husband, a murderer.

She eased back with a hitched breath. Her hands gripped his face.

"Max, do you know it? Do you know that you're lovable, despite what all of them did to you? I'm not them. I'm here now, and I choose to be, because you are the most lovable man I've ever known."

She'd said those words before, in the Southern Network. He hadn't been ready to receive them then—they frightened him wholly. If he didn't heed them, he stood to lose everything.

Above all, he adored Isadora. He respected her intelligence, her wittiness. She was a witch above repute, steeped in goodness. A witch that wouldn't lie, nor give away her love to those unworthy.

Which meant he was worthy.

He brushed a lock of hair out of her eyes and swallowed a budding pressure in his throat.

"Isa . . . no. I don't know it."

Her questioning face softened. Her fingers slackened against his cheek. She let them drop to his shoulder, trailing down his arms. Lines of fire illuminated in their path as she gripped his fingers.

"Tell me."

"It's ugly."

"I'm not scared."

"You might think differently of me. You might understand that there's something unlovable inside that will frighten you away." His voice turned husky. The vision of her, an angel before him, blurred. "You may never see me the same way when you see the dark night of my soul and I couldn't bear that."

She smiled, pressed her lips to his ice cold hands.

"My love," she murmured, "you are correct, but so wrong at the same time. I will never see you the same again, but only to love you more. *Tell me*."

———

He sat on a blanket in front of the fire, his back propped against an ottoman. Firelight bathed her in an amber glow. She'd taken down her hair, set aside earrings. Instead of an elegant gown that highlighted her perfect figure in the right places, she'd changed into her simple nightgown.

The weight of a million words lay heavy in his throat. The uneasiness of what he was about to reveal left him hollowed out. Here was the ultimate requirement. The culminating gift.

He offered up the sordid truth, as Charlie suggested.

Her hand found his. "I'm ready, Max."

You're not, he thought.

Throwing caution to the wind, he began.

"My mere handfasted Antonio out of spite for her sister, Serafina. Antonio and my mere secretly hated each other, but loved the turbulence of emotion their relationship inspired. Unfortunately, I was caught in the middle."

Isadora pulled her knees to her chest, cradled her head on top. He had her rapt attention. Wide-eyed curiosity, lined with love, that gave him the grace and strength to continue.

All issued forth.

The secrets. The darkness. The nights of hunger gnawing in his stomach. The days of empty longing. The hours he curled on the floor, trying not to cry from pain lest he draw Antonio's attention again. He stepped into the cesspool of memories with her at his side.

At some point, she curled up next to him. His arm anchored around her steadfast shoulder. He squeezed her hard —too hard. She didn't protest. The words came at a steady cadence, like a narrator detailing a story not his own.

His childhood, linear and fraught, laid out.

Voice hoarse, he finished two hours later. "I'm sorry, Isa. I'm sorry I didn't say the words, I just . . . I didn't know how to grapple with the fear of losing you because of something flawed within me. Now that I admit it, it seems . . . ridiculous and unfair to you."

Isadora peeled away from his shoulder. Her bloodshot eyes, filled with the stains of tears, captured him. His stomach caught.

How could he ever deserve her?

She squeezed his hands. "No apologies, Max. You can take all the time you need to heal. I'm here. I'm always here, through all of it."

He ran a hand down the side of her face. She closed her eyes, leaned into the touch. He swept the pad of his thumb over her cheekbone. His whisper drove from the deepest corners of his soul.

"I love you."

Her eyes burst open.

"I love you, Isadora Sinclair, and I loved you before I met you."

A breathless sound exhaled from her.

"You . . ."

His lips twitched in a smile.

"I've loved you since I first saw you, which is probably why I acted like I hated you. I'm sorry. I should never have put you through that. I . . . that is . . . love is power and . . . nothing in Alkarra frightens me like you do. Nothing reduces me to a pile of fear and rubble like my concerns for you, your safety, your heart. I would do anything for you."

He stopped, growled.

"You turn me into a right disaster. This isn't romantic at all."

She giggled, then climbed onto his lap and straddled his legs. Both her hands went to his neck, forcing him to stare at her. A stormy swirl of curiosity, hope, and—dare he say it?—adoration swirled there.

"I've loved you since then too, Max."

He shook his head. "No, Isa," he whispered, leaning closer. Their foreheads pressed together. "It's been much longer than that. I've known you years before the fateful day in the forest when we stumbled on each other."

Confusion clouded her features.

"What?"

"Years ago, I was in the paths. A wisp appeared. It was out of context and without a trail. In it, there was a child."

He recalled the day with a distorted sense of nostalgia. The first time she'd appeared to him, he'd been younger, filled with Advocacy business, a burgeoning career, and vinegar. The young girl in the wisp hadn't made sense. He'd dismissed it as a strange quirk of the magic.

Now he understood.

"A young girl, more child than not. Probably eight? I can't remember. I didn't think much of it, the wisps come and go. A while later, not sure how long passed, the same girl appeared. Again. And again. Over time, I came to expect her. Started to recognize the growing face, crinkled smile, and brilliant eyes. Sometimes, she was the only thing that I saw. Indeed, there wasn't even a path. Just . . . *her*."

By degrees, the emotions in Isadora quieted. Her shoulders rolled back, fingers opened at her side. Her fastidious attention reminded him of a held breath.

"She appeared on her own, through the years. I saw her at different times. She aged as time marched on. I started to look forward to seeing her. Her progress and smiles. One day, a trail led to her for the first time. She stood in a forest, surrounded by trees. Letum Wood, obviously, but I had no idea where. I also understood a silent command. I was to find her."

Her hand covered her mouth. Tears swam in a sparkling display of emotion. He could barely swallow past his own affection to speak.

"So I searched," he rasped. "I found her after several attempts at transporting around. The magic seemed to . . . step in and take me there."

"Me?"

"You."

She sucked in a breath, blinking fast. "What does it mean?"

He snorted. "At the time, I certainly didn't understand. You were infuriating and bull headed stubborn and . . ." He clenched his fists. "The most incredible witch I had ever met. I couldn't help or stop my fascination with you, though the good gods know that I tried. Isadora, I loved you before I even met you."

Her eyes swam with tears. A shaky breath followed. She studied him with a mixture of desperation and rapture.

"The South," she whispered. "You said—"

"I know what I said."

"Why?"

He kissed her softly and she melted in his arms. Reluctantly, he pulled away.

"Don't you see, Isa? You deserve better than me. You deserve a witch who won't be afraid of sucking you into his darkness, his quiet. I'm terrified that . . . if you spend too much time with me . . . I'll . . ."

Her hand pressed to his cheek. The magic of her touch infused him, spreading from head to soul. Max drew in a breath, inhaled the light scent of lavender. It infected him, filling his head with an effervescent sensation.

"What?" she whispered.

He leaned into her, nuzzling her wrist. "I don't want to change you, Isa. You are goodness and light and I crave you like a dying man. There is much solitude and silence and coldness in my life. If I were to have you, then lose you, I could not bear it. Yet, if it's love you seek, there is nowhere you will find it in greater abundance than my arms. Than Wildrose. I daresay the magic meant to make it clear that you were always supposed to be mine, if you'd have me."

He pulled her closer, felt her body pressed to his. Her stirring heat, the undeniable warmth that no fire could ever touch, saturated him. He wanted all of her.

The tips of her fingers sank into his hair, running along his scalp. Tears sparkled on her lashes, ready to fall.

"Max, I love you. I want to be with you and only you. Imperfections, lacking motivations, whatever we must endure. We can vow, tonight, under no duress or responsibilities, to do it together. We might have been handfasted by a High Witch months ago, but it's tonight that we are truly together."

"I will always love you, Isa."

He devoured her with a kiss.

Passion spiked through her body as his warm lips covered hers. She clawed him closer, banishing space, as an end to his final surrender. *I love you* slipped through his bloodstream like smoke.

He pulled away, arms tight around her waist. Isadora smiled adoringly at him

"Max?"

"Anything."

"Take me to bed?"

He paused, registering what she said with a blink. Shock appeared, then a silent question. She pressed a kiss to the tip of his nose.

"My love."

With a growl, he swept her into his arms. She laughed, arms around his neck, as he carried her to their new world.

Together.

THIRTY-SEVEN

ISADORA

One week later

A hand clamped around Isadora's wrist, tugging her back to bed with a flick. She giggled, dropped to the mattress, and spun back into Max's waiting arms. He captured her in a tangled embrace, legs wrapped in the sheets.

"Where," he murmured against her neck, "do you think you're going?"

"Well, I thought about breakfast. I also considered perusing the *Chatterer* to see if there are any job postings I could start to apply for. I suppose, now that we know we're going to remain handfasted, and Sanna is safe in Lucey's care, I might as well figure out what I want to do with the rest of my life."

He nuzzled her ear with a growl. "Breakfast is a good preparation for all of that, but I have different ideas for where we should start."

She laughed, shoving him away to stare him in the eyes. Undeniable affection burned there.

How hadn't she seen it before?

"Max, a request?"

"Anything, my heart." He reached up, brushing a lock of hair aside. The term of endearment rocketed around her chest like a wild thing.

My heart.

Those words might be careless for anyone else, but from Max?

They were everything.

"Tour Wildrose with me today? After breakfast, of course. Every bit of this house. We've already gone through headquarters and the basement, but I want to see the rest with you."

The simple request created an astonished expression. He pulled away to study her better.

"I'm sorry?"

She smiled. "I've been walking through Wildrose all by myself. It's lovely, and curious, and impressive. But there are stories hidden in it and I can't figure them out alone. It means so much to you. I want you to show me Wildrose."

He sucked in a breath through his nose, opened his mouth to speak again, and closed it.

"Wildrose?"

She nodded, smiling.

The corner of his lips pulled up in a smile. He trailed a fingertip over her eyebrows, down the side of her face. A lopsided grin crossed his mouth, making him look for all the world like a little boy.

"You really—"

"Yes. It's all I've wanted this whole time."

"I see."

"It was Charlie's, right?"

"Yes. Ranulf's before he died. He toured me through it

several times. Told me everything. I couldn't get enough. Read all the ledgers, the books."

His fingers flittered around the vast estate. Early morning light hinted on the far horizon, barely lightening the sky.

"I couldn't get enough of Wildrose, ever since I first laid eyes on it. It's the only home to which I've ever truly belonged."

"It's a very special place."

He quirked an eyebrow. "I thought you didn't like it?"

She frowned. "I never said that. I just didn't understand it. Now that I know, it makes sense." With a whisper, she leaned closer. Their foreheads touched, eyes didn't deviate. "It's all I've ever wanted, Max. The pieces of you that you don't give to anyone else. What do you think makes us so special?"

An undeniable surge of pleasure—of hunger—rushed through him. It darkened his eyes, sent a thrill all the way to her toes. Isadora grinned.

"Then, Mrs. Sinclair, I shall give you Wildrose. First? Breakfast."

He rolled her over, pinned her to the mattress. She dissolved into his loving touch, his gentle kiss, like a woman lost in the trails of love.

THIRTY-EIGHT

SANNA

The side of Sanna's face still ached. The depth of heat and irritation testified to a walloping bruise. Oh, she'd gotten herself into a mess, all right. Next? The careful steps of pulling herself out of it.

Lucey lived as quietly as Sanna had assumed. Sonja livened the cottage up in a brilliant way, with her frequent laughs and witty quips. Every now and then, the house rang with quiet until someone moved. Each step across a groaning floorboard or whisper of a cupboard door betrayed life.

A sound that Sanna rather appreciated.

The ease with which she tracked Lucey and Sonja in the home added yet another requirement to her list.

Noisy house, she thought to herself. *A must.*

A knock on the door sent a tremble of nerves through Sanna. "I'll get it," Sonja called.

Sanna set aside a teacup, not releasing it until she felt the firmness of the table beneath. Luteis prowled around outside . . . somewhere. He sent her errant thoughts randomly, revealing the depths of his unease.

Has he come? he asked, as if he heard the knock on the door.

Only just.

Well?

She fought back a smile. *I haven't met him yet. Sonja hasn't even opened the door.*

If she stood next to him, he would have been *harrumphing* in a very pouting way. The giant lizard had a streak of stubbornness fathoms wide. Not that she had so much room to make accusations.

"Sanna," Sonja said with a bright voice. "Our friend, Gilbert, has come to meet you. Put out your right arm, if you'd like to clasp arms."

Totally lost—Isadora had mentioned something about clasping arms, hadn't she?—Sanna lifted her right arm. A soft hand found hers, holding it tightly near the elbow. She returned the same, heart in her throat.

A kind voice followed.

"Sanna, it's lovely to meet you."

"You as well," she squeaked, barely audible.

"Have a seat," Lucey said. "The chair is just to your right, Gilbert. The table is at your eleven o'clock."

Gilbert's hand dropped away. Sanna retreated to her own chair, grateful to have somewhere else to go. A light thrum of excitement buzzed through her. She felt as if her new life had just begun.

Now? Luteis asked.

She scowled. *Just barely! Leave me alone.*

A growl followed, but Luteis silenced.

"Lucey, how are you?" Gilbert asked. His chipper voice rolled out with deep tones. A sturdy baritone against Lucey's gentle cadence.

"Much less busy these days," Lucey said with a laugh. "The need for the Advocacy is lessening . . . we hope. There are a few residual issues that require me to maintain a handful of volunteers and safe houses, just in case. For the most part, however, Sonja and I have been able to settle into our cottage and find a new normal."

Pleasure flushed his voice. "Wonderful. I'm so pleased to hear it. And Sonja? How do you enjoy the forest?"

"Very much. Oh, very much. It gets a bit dark so early, but we just light a few more candles."

The three of them laughed, and Sanna relaxed into the sound. She gripped the arm rests of her chair, fingers tight. A momentary lull in the conversation followed, and she panicked.

Was she supposed to speak?

Explain herself?

Her mouth opened, but Gilbert spoke before she had to.

"Miss Sanna, would you mind telling me about yourself? I'm always eager to meet another witch that has had sight, then lost it. So few can understand what we've really gone through, and I'm grateful that you're willing to meet with me."

Despite herself, she couldn't help but relax. Lucey put a comforting hand on Sanna's shoulder and a long sigh rippled through her body, removing the anxiety that had bunched her muscles.

She leaned a little closer to the table.

"You want to know about . . . *me*?"

He laughed genially. "Yes, I'm very curious. If you're willing to share?"

"Um . . . sure. I . . . I guess there's not much?"

"Oh," he said quietly, "I'd bet there's more than you think."

The clink of a glass followed. Bustling skirts preceded Lucey saying, "Sonja, perhaps you and I can sip our tea on the porch while Gilbert and Sanna get to know each other?"

"Oh," Sonja cooed, "A lovely idea. Call if you need anything. Teapot is at your ten o'clock Gilbert, and a cup at two, should you like a bit of black tea. Cream and sugar at twelve. It's already steeping. The bergamot isn't all that strong, as Lucey is quite finicky."

Lucey chuckled as she strolled past.

"Thank you, ladies," he called.

"I'm not used to this," Sanna blurted out as the door closed. "I'm sorry, I just . . ."

Gilbert chuckled. "Forgive me for some amusement," he said, not unkindly, "but no one is used to losing their sight once it happens. It takes some grieving and adjusting. Sonja and Lucey are the best of witches to help with such a transitory time."

She wrung her hands together. "Oh, I wasn't talking about that, but that too."

"No?"

"I mean meeting new witches. Talking with them. I don't . . . introduce myself to other witches. Honestly? I talk to dragons all day. They used to talk back but then I broke the magic and now only Luteis . . . agh. You see? I haven't . . . done this much. I don't know how!"

An astonished silence followed, far more laden than anything she'd experienced in the past. By Drago, but she'd rather the violent hush of the forest.

"You . . . that is . . ."

"I live in the forest," she continued, unable to stop. "Isadora, my twin sister, she says that witches in the Network would consider us foresters. I don't . . . maybe that's true. I don't know. I don't really know what that means. I . . . I have a dragon. His name is Luteis. I live with him and it's not working and you can't see it but there's a bruise. I almost died! And—"

"Miss Sanna, please." He chuckled. "Take a breath. I'm here all day, dear girl."

Gasping, she obeyed. His soothing tone pacified the panic. Until she heard the voice of a potential friend that understood the sightless netherworld, she hadn't realized how much she needed him.

Gilbert set his teacup down.

"Please allow me to say that I'm in no hurry," he said easily. "I've quite looked forward to our conversation the past several weeks, and have no obligations for the rest of the day. We can speak into the night, if you like. It certainly doesn't matter to either of us, does it?" He laughed. "I do tend to get tired around midnight."

She chuckled weakly.

"True."

In his voice, she thought she heard a smile. "I'm here as a friend, Sanna. If you need it, as a guide. There are more resources available to the blind than you might think. Spells, reading aids, canes. Things that would make your life easier, and I'm happy to tell you about them."

"Magic, you mean."

His voice piqued with renewed interest. "Well yes, of course. You don't do magic?"

"I haven't in the past, but I look forward to learning it."

"Not once?"

She swallowed hard. "Well . . . there's a story behind all of this. A big one with dragons and magic and distant places."

"Indeed." A thrill radiated through his voice. "So fascinating! I can hardly wait. Well, I believe we should start at the beginning. First, though, would it help if I told you a little more about myself?"

"Yes, please," she said eagerly. "I would like that. I can't promise anything, Gilbert. I know that I want and need help, but I don't know how to do magic. Life in the Network is a mystery to me. A-and I'm scared. Terrified."

Her voice trembled, but saying the words to a total stranger wasn't as frightening as she expected.

Gravity filled his tone.

"I expect you are. There are reasons to mourn, and even greater reasons you should allow yourself to do so. All while remembering that there is a great and beautiful life that awaits you on the other side of grief. This set back of blindness is by no means the end of your path. One day, you'll find yourself all the stronger and more powerful for it."

Sanna's throat thickened. She released the tears, allowing their healing balm, like a cool mist, to steal over her.

"Thank you."

The chair where he sat creaked as he made himself more comfortable. A sigh preceded a clink of teacup on plate.

"Well," he said in a musing tone. Sanna propped her chin on her hands and prepared for a new story and adventure not unlike her own.

From her very first friend.

"I began to lose my vision around twelve years old. I was young at the time and . . ."

———

The smell of cinnamon thickened the air.

Sanna perched at the edge of a chair, near a small table in Isadora's kitchen. The crack of an egg breaking, and a mumble from Max, broke the air. Sanna felt along the edges of a heart-shaped cookie cutter, then the soft dough beneath it.

A heart?

Really?

Just because Isadora was *so* in love didn't mean it needed

to permeate everything. She set it aside, searched for another one. A star.

Better.

A giggle from the other side of the room made Sanna roll her eyes. If they kissed one more time . . .

Isadora's bright voice sounded flushed with embarrassment when she cleared her throat and said, "Max is just finishing up the dough, then you can roll out the next batch, Sanna. The rolling pin is on your left."

Sanna reached for it, gratified when her hand landed right on the roller. Silently, she attempted a spell Gilbert had given her. Just one. She was too overwhelmed by more. A summoning spell.

The easiest, he had assured her. *I know of nothing so simple as this.*

The rolling pin leaped to her hand. She exulted.

It worked! Without wild dragons or gods descending from the sky in wrathful judgment. Jesse had been right.

"The dough is done," Max declared. "That's it. I need to go to my meeting, but I'll look forward to a batch of cookies to welcome me back. Sanna, always good to have you."

"Thanks, Max."

"Best of luck!" Isadora said, then ended with another giggle. Another smack on the lips preceded the crisp staccato of Max retreating into the hallway. Sanna reached for another cookie cutter, grateful for a few moments alone with her sister. The *thunk* of Isadora setting a bowl on the table rattled her cutters.

"So?" Isa drawled.

Sanna reached for the bowl, found it at first attempt, and put her hand inside. Silky cookie dough awaited. The smell of sugar and butter twirled through her nose. Her stomach rumbled, so she snatched a pinch and popped it in her mouth.

Delicious.

"So . . ." Sanna drawled, splatting the dough on the cutting board. "I met with Gilbert for the first time three days ago."

"Lucey said it went very well, from what she could tell."

"Yes, it did."

Isadora paused. Sanna struggled to know what to say. *Gilbert is very nice* fell flat. *I'm excited to learn more from him* didn't quite cover it. Neither did *I'm still terrified because eventually I'll have to go into the Network to learn things there.*

"It'll be good."

The lame finish made Isadora giggle.

"Grief, Sanna. You don't have to handfast him. He's just going to teach you how to manage without sight. You'll get to learn a whole new world!"

"Yes, there's that."

"And magical spells to help you navigate on your own."

"That, too."

"How will all of this start?"

"He's going to meet me at Lucey's every day to learn for an hour. We started with an easy spell. He's going to teach me how to walk around an unknown witch village, too."

"Impressive!" she cried. "Can you transport if you're blind?"

Sanna shrugged. "Apparently? Harder to do at first, I guess, but then you can go to places you've physically been before. Not quite sure how it works."

"Very interesting." Isadora paused. "Are you excited? It seems as if it might be sort of . . . overwhelming."

Sanna breathed through the returning tightness. "Of course I'm overwhelmed. Yes. I mean, after what happened in the forest, I want to be safe. But I'm a little scared. It's new."

"Very new. Is Luteis taking it well?"

"Yes. He understands. He's happy for me to be independent, and I won't have to leave much yet."

"Mam is ecstatic to have you next door."

Sanna managed a breathy laugh. Living next door to Mam and Elliot hadn't been all that bad. In fact, she'd rather enjoyed the company, and Luteis had easy access. Junis and Cara had visited as well. She couldn't speak to or ride them, but their presence delighted her all the same.

"I'm proud of you, Sanna. This is a lot of change. This is a lot of . . . a lot!"

Resolute, Sanna pulled in a deep breath. "Yes, it is. But that's okay. Gilbert reminds me that I only have to think about today, and that helps. Like Lucey said, it's still *me* going through this. I'm still courageous, brave Sanna, just in a different way."

"Yes!"

"And then I can actually do things again. One day, I'll have a house and I'll invite you over and fix dinner for you and Max."

"We would love that."

"Me too," Sanna said quietly. All the pervasive terror of these changes ebbed in knowing she had a path.

Luteis's voice filtered into her head.

What are cookies?

She stifled a smile. He waited for her in the forest that skirted Wildrose, seething hot amongst the trees while she sat inside. His abundant curiosity about the inside of such a large witch structure knew no bounds. His questions had been relentless.

Cookies are pieces of food that taste sweet.

Might I try one?

She laughed to herself. *Sure.* She'd have to make one in the image of a flame.

Is this what you will be doing with the Gilbert witch?

Sort of.

Hmph. And has your sister taken you to the curious room she spoke of?

The room of curiosity is next on our list, after cookies.

His protectiveness since the arachnid incident had been intense—something she appreciated, but had to assuage.

"What about you?" Sanna tossed a piece of dough between her two hands, enjoying the squishy feel of it in her bent knuckles. "Have things smoothed out between you and Max?"

"Yes, very much so." Isadora sighed. Sanna could easily picture her faraway look. She'd always been more romantic. "Max and I had several good talks. Marriage is hard, but . . . I love it. I wouldn't want to do it with anyone but him. He loves me."

Sanna gaped. "He told you that? Max?"

"Yes. In words. It meant so much."

"I'm glad! He's an idiot if he doesn't."

"I tend to agree," Isadora said lightly, then both of them burst into laughter. Sanna plucked a heartier piece of dough from the bowl and squished it onto the flat surface. The rolling pin sank. She pressed her fingers along the edges, feeling her way while Isadora bustled at her side, stirring something.

"Now," Isadora said with a sigh. "The challenge is figuring out what I'm going to do with my life."

"What do you mean?"

"Wildrose is lovely, but I'm about to go out of my mind with boredom. You're settled, Mam is handfasted to Elliot so the Dragonmasters are all cared for, and things are so lovely between me and Max. In just a few weeks, I'll have everything all fixed in the house the way we want it, so . . . I need something. Max says we'll become very busy with social events through the summer, which would be nice."

Sanna's head tilted to the side. She hadn't thought of what

Isadora would do next. Isadora had been so wrapped up in working for the Advocacy, going all kinds of places in Alkarra for and with Max, that Sanna hadn't given much thought to what awaited her sister on the other side.

"Babies?" she asked.

Isadora scoffed. "Not yet. Max might faint if he had to deal with a squalling newborn. Besides, I haven't quite decided on that."

"Good."

"We'll figure it out later. We just decided we can live together without killing each other," she said with a laugh that told Sanna she didn't really mean it that way. "Max needs to meet Mam and Elliot, too."

"Elliot will love Max. Daid would have approved."

"You think so?"

"Definitely."

A comfortable quiet stretched between them as Sanna finished rolling out the cookies. She pressed the cutter into the soft dough, using her fingertips to find where the previous one existed, and where to put the cutter next. The quiet movement of the kitchen, the snap of the fire, the smell of dessert in her nose, and contentment rolled through her.

Life wasn't what she'd expected.

And that was just fine.

Also by Katie Cross

All books are available in ebook, paperback, and audiobook at www. katiecrossbooks.com and on all online ebook, audiobook, and paperback retailers.

The Dragonmaster Trilogy

FLAME

Chronicles of the Dragonmasters (short story collection)

FLIGHT

The Ronan Scrolls (novella)

FREEDOM

The Dragonmaster Trilogy Collection

The Sisterwitches Series

The Sisterwitches Book 1

The Sisterwitches Book 2

The Network Series

Mildred's Resistance (prequel)

Miss Mabel's School for Girls

Alkarra Awakening

The High Priest's Daughter

War of the Networks

The Network Series Complete Collection

The Isadora Interviews (novella)

Short Stories from Miss Mabel's

Short Stories from the Network Series

Hazel (short story)

Alkarra (short story collection)

The Network Saga Suggested Reading Order

1. The Parting (novella #1)

2. The Lost Magic (full-length novel)

3. The Lamplighter's Daughter (novella #2)

4. Merrick (novella #3)

5. The Rise of the Demigods (full-length novel)

6. Priscilla (novella #4)

7. Viveet (novella #5)

8. Prana (novella #6)

9. Derek (novella #7)

10. The Forgotten Gods (full-length novel)

11. The Returning (novella #8)

12. Regina (novella #9)

13. Leda (novella #10)

14. The Sister (prequel to WOTG #1)

15. The School (prequel to WOTG #2)

16. The Council (prequel to WOTG #3)

17. The Goddess (prequel to WOTG #4)

18. War of the Gods (full-length novel)

19. The Finales (a collection of novellas)

20. Marten (novella #11)

The Historical Collection

The High Priestess

The Swordmaker

The Advocate

The Reader Request Series

The Gods

The Plummet

The North

The Wander

The Return

Viveet Forged

ABOUT THE AUTHOR

Katie Cross is ALL ABOUT writing epic magic and wild places. Creating new fantasy worlds is her jam.

When she's not hiking or chasing her two littles through the Montana mountains, you can find her curled up reading a book or arguing with her husband over the best kind of sushi.

Visit her at www.katiecrossbooks.com for free short stories, extra savings on all her books (and some you can't buy on the retailers), and so much more.